AF226207

Haven Island PD
Protecting Paradise
DETECTIVE
Lucian
Neri Lopez

Detective Lucian
Haven Island PD: Protecting Paradise

Neri Lopez

Siren Book & Craft LLC

Copyright © 2026 by Neri Lopez
Publisher: Siren Book & Craft LLC
Editor: Michelle Zammataro
Cover Designer: Neri Lopez
Cover Model: Joel Ros
Cover Model Photographer: J. Ashley Converse Photography
Cover background image: Neri's beach photo and Vecteezy.
Maps are fictional and designed by Neri Lopez with images from Vecteezy

This work includes themes of sexual assault and kidnapping. Some readers may find it disturbing or triggering. Reader discretion is advised. If you or someone you know has been sexually assaulted, please know that you are not alone and that there are resources that can help you through this difficult time. If you are or have been a victim of sexual assault, please contact your local police department and call the National Sexual Assault Hotline at 800-656-467. Or you chat online at http://www.rainn.org

Haven Island

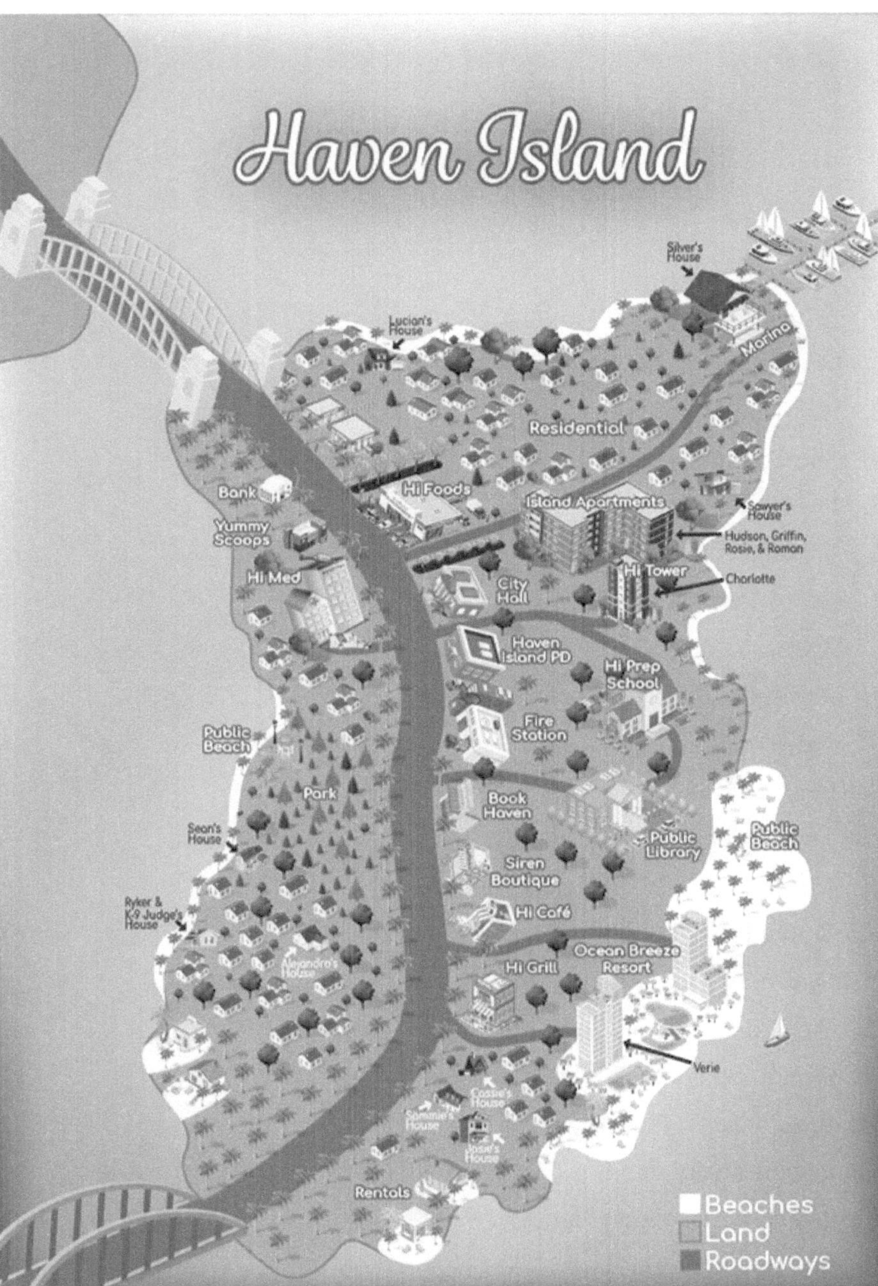

Contents

Chapter 1

Intruder

Lucian

"Josie!" I hollered as soon as I opened the door.

I drew my gun and scanned the front hallway, my heart pounding in my chest. The piercing sound of sirens blared behind me, growing louder with each second. I requested backup but rushed to the location as soon as dispatch reported the caller as being Josie Hale.

"Dammit, Josie! Where the hell are you?" I entered the living room and listened for any noise. *Where was she?* Her car was out front. She had to be here somewhere. If anyone hurt her, there would be hell to pay.

Officers Sean O'Reilly, Charlotte Spencer, and Hudson Shaw burst through the front door behind me.

"Charlotte, Hud, finish checking the downstairs." I motioned my gun toward the stairs. "Sean and I will check upstairs. When Ryker gets here with Judge, have him sniff every fucking thing in this house."

"Got it," Hud mumbled and motioned for Charlotte to follow him.

Sean followed me up the stairs. The first bedroom we cleared was empty. We slithered along the wall into the next one. They were all empty. At the end of the hallway, I spotted a narrow room. Must be a bathroom.

"Josie!" I banged on the door. "Open the door. It's Detective Lucian. Are you alone?"

I heard crying behind the door and motioned to Sean to kick it down. I braced my gun, ready to shoot if anyone other than Josie was behind the door. Sean kicked it open, and I stepped in. Josie was alone, sitting with her knees up to her chin, arms wrapped around her. I put my gun away and crouched down in front of her.

"Josie, it's me. You're okay now." I ran my hands over her arms, but she cringed at my touch. Had they hurt her? "Josie, I need you to look at me," I whispered.

"Lucian!" Several boots stomped in the hallway, making their way toward me. "We're clear."

Josie was shaking so hard her body looked ready to crack.

"Stay out there. Close the door. I'll be out with Josie in a second."

The sound of the door clicking shut raised Josie's tear-stained face toward me. Her mascara ran down her face.

"Is...I...Is he gone?"

"Yes, who was here, Josie? Let me help you." I murmured.

She looked at me. The hurt in her eyes was a piercing plea.

"He called and set up an appointment." She swallowed, taking a second to continue. Her eyes glued to the wall—avoiding eye contact.

"I met him here. I wasn't worried because I've never encountered issues with potential homebuyers, but my alarm bells went off when his hand touched my backside on our way up the stairs. I wrote it off as an accident, but when we entered the main bedroom, he shoved me on the bed. I lost my balance and bounced on the bed. When he leaned over me, I kicked him several times. He screamed out and doubled over when one of my strikes hit his crotch. He grabbed himself and dropped onto the bed beside me. I pushed him over the side and ran out. He was cussing, and I heard him limping behind me, so I ran in here, shut myself in, and called 911. I would've run downstairs, but he was so close to me, I thought the bathroom was better. He pounded on the door until you guys arrived."

"What's his name?"

"He said Thomas Kincaid."

"Like the painter?"

"It's a fake name, isn't it?" Josie gazed into my eyes. Tears streaked down her face, and her lip wobbled.

"Yeah, probably so. Let's get you out of here." I helped her up.

"Are you sure he's gone?" Josie grabbed my arm like a lifeline.

"They wouldn't give us the all-clear if anyone was still around." I said slowly and wrapped my arms around her. "I'm sure they checked every nook and cranny."

Josie didn't sweat the small stuff. She preferred to give me shit over my not solving jobs quickly enough for her liking. Especially when her friends were involved. Like the time the shattered storefront window of Sammie's shop revealed an empty cash register. In that moment, her verbal assault was fierce, and she didn't mince words. But this Josie, standing in front of me trembling and scared, was a new side I'd never seen before. I wasn't sure how to comfort her.

"We're coming out!" I opened the door. Sean and Charlotte stood in the hallway waiting for us.

I went out first while Josie's fingers clung to the back of my dress pants. Being a detective, I rarely wore a uniform. My uniform was a suit with the badge on my belt.

"Are Ryker and Judge here?" I asked Sean.

"They're downstairs."

"Charlotte." I motioned to her.

Charlotte was an officer with Jones County until she transferred to Haven Island two years ago. She and Hudson were the same age and joined around the same time, but she had three years of experience, making her the perfect patrol partner for Hudson.

"Stay with Josie. I need to go talk to Ryker." I pulled Josie's hands off my pants, my fingers brushing against hers, before I faced her. "It's gonna be okay."

Josie nodded and hugged Charlotte. This was a small town where all the locals knew the officers. Josie and Charlotte must be friends. Or at least close enough to warrant a hug. Charlotte would take care of Josie while I followed the leads. I wasn't used to crying females. In my job, I gathered the pieces of the puzzle and figured it out. No emotions, just evidence. I went downstairs to see if they had uncovered any clues.

"Ryker," I called out. "Find anything?"

"The back door was open," Ryker shouted. "Forensics is on its way to dust for prints."

"Have them check the main bedroom and the bathroom at the end of the hall. He attacked Josie in the bedroom, and she locked herself up in the bathroom."

"How is she?" Ryker stopped in front of me.

"Shaken up."

"You got a name?" Ryker gritted out.

Ryker and Josie had been friends since high school, but from the look on his face, I wondered if they'd been more. Not that I cared. Just an observation.

"He called himself Thomas Kincaid," I looked at Ryker wryly.

"Douchebag."

"Yep."

"I'm gonna have Charlotte follow Josie home so I can wait for forensics."

"Josie shouldn't be driving. I can take her home."

I'm not sure why it bothered me to have Ryker drive Josie home—but it did.

"No, stay here with Judge. I want him to sniff every fucking inch of this house."

"You got it." Ryker nodded and pulled Judge along.

"What the hell happened?" Chief came storming through the front door.

I retold him the entire story.

"Well, we know it wasn't Lincoln since his ass is in jail." Chief snorted. "Are you taking Josie home?"

For the past several months, the island had been hit with a string of break-ins. Siren Boutique—owned by Sammie, the Chief's wife—and the local bank were clearly tied to her ex-husband, Lincoln. But the other incidents didn't fit his usual pattern. Those burglars were still out there, and we hadn't gotten close to identifying them yet.

"No, we've never had a case like this before, and I need to figure out if he was targeting Josie or realtors. Either way, I'm gonna catch the son of a bitch." Walking into a house with strangers was difficult enough. Realtors shouldn't have to worry about being attacked while doing their jobs.

"I can stay and finish up. You take Josie home. I'm sure she's shaken up." Chief looked around. "Where is she?"

"Upstairs with Sean and Charlotte."

"Josie!" Chief walked to the bottom of the stairs. "It's Alex. Come on down."

No one ever called Chief Alejandro by his first name. It was always Chief—or sometimes Alex, if you were a close friend. Chief had a soft spot for Josie because she was close to Sammie. Sammie had been Josie's parents' preferred babysitter when they were kids.

"Alex!" Josie ran down the steps and flew into his arms.

Why did I feel a pang in my heart when she ran into the chief's arms? She didn't run into my arms when I saved her. Josie buried her face in the chief's chest and unleashed a whole new set of tears on his shirt.

"It's gonna be okay. We'll figure this out." Chief ran his hands over her back. "Lucian is gonna take you home." He pulled her back and leaned down to look at her. "Go wait in his car. We'll be out in a minute."

"Okay. But I don't know which car is his." Josie nodded and wiped her tears. "What about my car?"

"I'll ask an officer to drive it to your house. Don't worry about that."

"I'll walk her to Lucian's car and wait with her." Charlotte put her arm around Josie and led her outside.

"Are you sure you're okay staying here and finishing up for me?" I frowned and watched Charlotte lead Josie out of the house.

I'd never left a crime scene to take a victim home—not once. Duty pulled one way, Josie pulled the other, and for the first time in a long while, I didn't know which part of me was supposed to win. But this was Josie, and something in me refused to let her walk away alone. Her tears gutted me, tearing at places I didn't even realize were still vulnerable. I hadn't dated in years; work made sure of that. Yet for her... I'd do anything to see her smile again.

Wait, why was I thinking about dating Josie when I should be her bodyguard, not her boyfriend? Pull it together, Loverboy. I closed my eyes. *Chief,* my mind begged him, *save me from myself.*

"Absolutely, go. I'll talk to you later." Chief nodded.

So much for that. "I'll take her to the station for her statement while it's fresh in her mind. Then I'll take her home."

"You're all heart, Detective," Chief mumbled.

I turned and glared at Chief. "What's that supposed to mean?"

"As Chief, I know she needs to give a statement now. But as her friend, I can see she's barely holding it together," he said, his voice gentling. "Take her statement at the station tomorrow. Go easy on her."

Chief rested a hand on my shoulder. "I've seen you two go head-to-head before, and that's the last thing she needs tonight."

"I promise to be on my best behavior." I crossed my heart.

Chief wasn't wrong. Every time Josie confronted me about how poorly I did my job, my gut reaction was to be rude right back. I figured if she could dish it out, she could take it. Today was different.

"We'll see." Chief snorted.

"If I'm not, I'm sure your wife will tell you." I grinned.

"Yep, so don't fuck it up for me." Chief pointed at me. "I'm not a fan of the doghouse."

"Gotcha."

"I'm counting on you."

"I won't let you down, Chief."

Chapter 2

I See You

Vincent

Three seconds. It took me three seconds with my black gloves to pick the lock on the back door and enter the house. *Who's the best lock picker on this fucking island now?* I hurried inside and relocked the door. *People were so stupid.* They should have a security system to keep people like me out of their homes. *And they talk about stupid criminals, ha. What about stupid homeowners?*

I walked past the kitchen and living room into the bedroom. The puffy comforter lay perfectly on the bed with a shit ton of pillows. *Who fucking made their bed anymore?* Several perfume bottles sat on top of the dresser. I grabbed one and sprayed the air. A strong, sexy scent filled the air. I thought about taking it, but that's not what I was here for.

My eyes swept the room, searching for a hiding spot. Then I spotted it—the floral painting. *Hell yes.* One bloom had a black center with enough color for the camera to blend right in. I tossed my bag onto the bed and pulled the canvas down. It was featherlight, no glass, only a thin layer of fabric between me and a damn perfect idea.

I cut the black center of the flower out and hung it back up. With a pencil, I placed a dot on the wall. The camera had to be mounted on the wall behind the hole—that part proved tricky. I attached the sticky strips to the back of my camera. Technology—you had to love it when they developed these small, lightweight cameras. *A special thank you to all those parents who couldn't stop themselves from watching their babies and pets when they were away.*

I held the painting in one hand, the camera in the other. When I had it lined up where I needed it, I pressed the camera against the wall and waited for the adhesive to catch. Slowly, I peeled my hand away. *Perfect.* I eased the painting back into place—flush and steady. The hole aligned where it should, the canvas resting seamlessly over the lens. *Damn, I was good.*

I stepped toward the side to make sure the canvas wasn't sticking out. *Nope.* Perfect fit—thank you very much. I pulled my phone out and connected to the camera. I could see myself on the screen. Most cameras had a small light that came on when activated, but lucky for me, the flowers from the canvas covered it up. *I was a fucking genius.*

My partner and I discussed messing up the place, but he disagreed with me. But shit, I wanted to do something else to disrupt her life. She was too fucking perfect, and I didn't like the way she spoke to me.

Fuck it, I wanted to play with her a little bit. I opened all her drawers until I found her underwear drawer. *Jackpot!* I arranged them on the bed and tossed the drawer onto the floor. I stared at my work, but it didn't look scary enough. It needed something else. I rummaged through my bag of tricks and found a pad of sticky notes.

I wrote filthy thoughts and things I'd like to do to her and laid them on her lingerie. Fuck that red one with the garter belt was hot as fuck. I bet her nipples would look perky behind all that lace. Between my thoughts and all my notes, I was getting worked up.

I unzipped my pants and shoved my hand in my underwear.

"Ow! Fuck me!"

Note to self: don't grab your dick while wearing gloves. I pulled the glove off and dropped my pants and underwear to the ground. I maneuvered my dick around to make sure I hadn't done any permanent damage. Nope, it was perfect and hard as a fucking rock.

I rubbed one out while I licked her red negligee. Thank fuck, I had enough sense to put the negligee against my dick to catch my climax. *Fuck, my hands were wet.* My come dripped from my hands, the negligee, and my dick. I guess lace was not the best substitute for a towel. Stepping out of my pants, I grabbed my underwear and dried myself off.

Damn, I needed that release. To hell with Thomas. He didn't need to know what I did. His phone didn't have the app for the camera. *What he didn't know couldn't hurt him.* I tossed my black underwear into my bag and rechecked my camera. *Perfect.* Double-checked the lingerie laid out on the bed. *Also, perfect.* Well, my work was done. I grabbed my bag and left the same way I had come.

Chapter 3

Why Now? Why Me?

Josie

I stood beside Lucian's car with Charlotte, waiting for him to come out. I couldn't face the house, so I turned my back to it and stared at the street lined with cop cars.

"Josie."

I jumped when Lucian touched my lower back and spun around to glare at him.

"Sorry." He raised his hands like a hold-up. "I didn't mean to startle you. Let's get you home."

"Okay. Let me grab my keys." My unsteady fingers rifled through my purse. "I can't find my keys," I cried out before I turned my purse upside down and dumped out all the contents, scattering them on the driveway. I dropped to the ground, sitting crisscross applesauce, and held my face in my hands while I broke down.

"Hey, hey," Lucian squatted next to me. "It's going to be okay."

"How!" I cried. "How am I ever going to feel safe again?"

"Leave that to me." Lucian removed my hands from my face and wiped my tears. "I'll figure out who did this and arrest his ass."

"Promise," I whispered.

"Promise." Lucian gazed at me, concern filling up his eyes. "But first, I need you to do something for me."

"What?"

"I need you to go down to the station with me and give me your statement. The quicker you do that, the quicker we can start looking for the guy."

Really? I was falling apart, and all he wanted was my statement? *Unbelievable.* Lucian lived up to the rumors about him. He was a machine with no emotions.

"Okay." I nodded. "Let's get this over with."

"Attagirl."

Lucian snatched up my keys and helped me up. "Don't worry about your car."

Charlotte gathered my things, put them in my purse, and handed it to me. "Here, Josie."

"Thanks, Charlotte."

Lucian gave my keys to Charlotte. "Chief went upstairs. Can you give these to him? He said he'd ask someone to drive Josie's car back to her house. I'm gonna take her to the station for her statement and then drive her home."

"Sure." Charlotte palmed the keys and left.

"Come on." He opened the door for me. Well, at least he had manners. "Let's get out of here," he said before he shut the door.

On the drive to the station, I couldn't stop thinking about why this was happening to me. My real estate business was finally getting off the ground. In a couple of months, I could stop working as a guest services agent at Ocean Breeze Resort and apply all my focus to selling houses. I'd put away a nice nest egg, and word of mouth had increased my clientele.

I knew where to find houses on Haven Island, and if nothing was available there, I kept up with the mainland house and rental market too, but I preferred to help buyers or sellers on the island.

As a member of the Realtors Association, I'd heard the horror stories—agents cornered, stalked, or worse. But those were mainland problems. Haven Island was different. Safe. Peaceful. Or so I thought.

None of the island agents had ever mentioned anything like that—at least not at our meetings or on our private page. Sure, a few had posted reminders: park near the exit, keep your phone in hand, double-check IDs. I'd scrolled past every one of them. Because I *knew* this island. I grew up here. It was supposed to be safe—until today.

I should've let Thomas enter the room first. *Why didn't I do that?* I'd learned about it in one of our safety seminars. If I had done that, he never would've had the chance to throw me on the bed. Thank goodness my survival instinct kicked in, and I got away. Otherwise, he might've trapped me in that bedroom.

He had seemed so nice on the phone and was well-dressed when we met at the house. Never in a million years would I have believed he was there to hurt me. A shiver ran up my spine at the thought of what might've happened to me.

"Hey." Lucian reached out and placed his hand on my shoulder. "It's okay now."

"Sure." I stared out the window and remained silent until we reached the station.

Lucian came around and escorted me through the station to his desk. I sat in the chair facing him.

"Can I get you some coffee?"

"No, I'm fine." I mumbled, placing the purse on my lap. I fidgeted with the zipper. "I want this to be over." I wanted to go home, take a shower, curl up in my bed, and pretend this day never happened.

"Okay." Lucian sat behind his desk and clicked away on his keyboard. The screen faced him, so I couldn't see what he was doing.

"Can you describe the man?"

"Yes, he was white, about your height, and professionally dressed in a suit."

"Hair color? Eye color?" Lucian typed as I spoke.

"Brown hair, brown eyes."

"Any tattoos or markings that stood out?"

"No." I looked down. "His suit covered his body from the neck down." Lucian nodded. "What color was the suit?"

"Black," I scrunched up my nose. "No, a dark blue because I remember it looking nice with the red tie. Very patriotic."

"Was the tie patriotic?" Lucian squinted at me.

"No, sorry, it was the blue suit, red tie, and white shirt."

"Got it." Lucian's fingers continued to click away. "Tell me how you met him and what happened from the moment you got there."

"He called my cell number. He said he got my card from Ocean Breeze." I glanced at Lucian. "They allow me to put my business cards in the lobby."

"That's nice of them. Go on."

"He said he'd seen a house that was for sale on Leonard Street, and he wanted me to show it to him."

"Is that one of your listings?"

"No, but he wanted to hire me as his buyer's agent."

"Why didn't he call the number on the for-sale sign?"

"I don't know. I didn't ask." *How the hell should I know why he didn't call the number on the for-sale sign?*

"Why not?" Lucian intertwined his hands on his desk and leaned toward me.

"I don't know." I threw my hands up.

Why was he interrogating me when he should be out there finding the criminal? Did he forget I was the victim?

"I wanted the business. Is that okay with you, Detective?"

"Okay, but why didn't you check the name he gave you? Thomas Kincaid? Didn't it strike you as odd—the same name as the painter?" Lucian's glare burned into me, his voice low but sharp. "You'd risk your life for that?"

"Are you done berating me? I know you must think I'm an idiot. We can't all be as perfect as you, Detective." I snarled at him before I stood and shoved my purse onto my shoulder. "Can I go now?"

"Josie." Lucian pushed back from his chair and stood, regret written all over his face. "I'm sorry." He came around the desk toward me. "Please—sit. I wasn't trying to accuse you of anything. You're not stupid. I'm pissed at him, and I took it out on you. That's on me."

He eased me back into the chair. "Let me get you some water."

Lucian leaned into the doorway and barked for someone to bring a bottle, the edge still in his voice, though no longer aimed at me. A deputy came in and placed the water on his desk. Lucian opened it for me and slid it toward me.

"Let's continue from when you met him at the house."

"The house was for sale by owner," I glared at him.

"Was the owner there when you arrived?"

"No, he said he was unavailable and left a key under the mat."

"Ooookay," Lucian frowned but didn't say another word.

What was that look for? It wasn't unusual for a seller to be out when I arrived—life happened—but something in the air warned me this time. I should've listened to my gut. The missing lockbox on the door was unusual, but at least they'd left the key under the mat, which was better than me crawling around the yard hunting for one of those fake rocks with a keyhole underneath. Besides, the house had just been listed. Everything should have been routine.

"I walked in, and he followed. I gave him a tour of the downstairs. Everything seemed fine. He said his wife would want pictures, so he took out his camera and took photos of the rooms."

"Were you in the photos?"

"Maybe," I shrugged. "I'm not sure. I tried to leave the room when he raised his phone, but I'm sure he caught me in some of them."

"You didn't think that was strange?" Lucian interrupted.

"No." I rolled my eyes at him. *Had he never bought a house or watched those shows on TV?* "Some buyers take photos and others take videos to show their spouses or kids when they can't come. I'm sure I've been in lots of photos throughout the years."

"Then what happened?"

"We went upstairs, and his hand ran up my backside."

"Your back." Lucian squinted. "Like your spine?"

"No." I crossed my arms. Heat crept up my neck, burning my cheeks before I could stop it. "His fingers slid from front to back between my legs, a place he had no business touching unless we were lovers. Is that vivid enough for you?"

"Yeah," he growled. "I got it. What I don't understand is why the hell you kept going with the tour?"

"Because I needed to sell the house," I glared at his holiness. "I'd like to work only one job instead of two, and I'm so close. Haven't you ever been close to reaching a goal that you could taste it?" God, he was so infuriating.

"Yeah." He cleared his throat. "Sorry. Go on."

"I hurried up the stairs and showed him the main bedroom. He followed me inside and made a lewd comment about how I would look naked spread out on the bed seconds before he shoved me onto it. I bounced up, kicked him, and pushed him over, like I told you. Then, I ran out the door, slamming it shut, and bolted to the last door at the end of the hallway. I didn't know it was a bathroom until I locked myself in. There was a small window, but I was afraid that if I jumped from the second floor, I might break something. So, I opted to call 911. Hoping you guys would get there before he broke in." I took a sip of water.

"I'm glad you called. Did anyone know you were there?"

"No, it was my lunch break at Ocean Breeze. I thought I'd make it back before anyone noticed." The regret hit hard. I should've let someone know where I was going. I should've shared the client's name. I should've done so many things differently.

"How long was he banging?"

"I don't know. It seemed like forever, but then he stopped. He must've heard the sirens and left."

"I'm going to show you some mug shots. Let me know if you recognize him."

Lucian pulled an iPad out of his desk and clicked several buttons before he handed it to me. I swiped through multiple pages, but his picture wasn't there.

"No, sorry." I handed it back to him.

"Don't be sorry. I'll ask the Jones County Sheriff's Department, JCSD, to send me some of their mug shots and have you look at those within the next few days. Is there anything else you remember?"

"Yes. I think there was someone else downstairs. When I ran to the bathroom..." I rubbed my forehead. "I thought I heard footsteps by the stairs while Thomas was in the bedroom. But I might be mixing things up. It all happened so fast."

"You look beat. Let me take you home."

"I have to go back to work at the resort." I stood.

"Uh no. Not a good idea. Chief wants me to take you home, and that's where I'm taking you. Wouldn't you rather go home?"

"No, drop me off at the resort. I'm already late and have a lot of explaining to do."

"Fine. But only if you promise to call me when you are done, and I'll drive you home."

"I can get a ride." I put my purse over my shoulder and grabbed the water bottle.

"Josie," Lucian snapped. "I will take you home. You don't even have your car." He sounded frustrated with me. "Call me. I'm texting you my number now."

"How do you have my number?"

"I just looked you up on my computer to write your report. I have your number and address."

"Oh, right." My phone dinged. I didn't look at it.

"That wasn't me." Lucian turned his phone around. His message hadn't been sent.

I pulled out my phone, read the message, screamed, and dropped my phone like a hot potato.

Chapter 4

The Green-Eyed Monster Makes an Appearance

Lucian

What the hell? Josie's face went pale. Her body teetering ready to fall. I grabbed her and sat her back down.

"Take a sip." I handed her the water bottle.

Leaning over, I picked up her phone.

"What's your password?"

"Huh?" Josie looked like a deer caught in headlights.

"Never mind," I mumbled and put the phone up to her face.

It opened, and I clicked her messages app.

> Thomas Kincaid Buyer: I don't know why you ran from me, but I love a good chase.

Fucking hell! The asshole was after her, not a random realtor. No way in hell she was going back to work tonight. I was taking her ass home, and I wasn't leaving her side until I arrested the douchebag.

"Josie, I need to give your phone to our Criminal Investigative Division team, and then I'm driving you home."

Taking deep controlled breaths, she murmured, "What about work?"

I pointed to my desk phone. "Call them. As of right now, you are on vacation."

"I can't do that." Her vacant eyes stared at the phone on my desk. "I have bills to pay."

"Fine. Tell them you need a couple of days off while we come up with a game plan."

Nodding, she moved her hand toward it with the slow care of someone approaching a coiled snake.

"I'll be right back. Do not leave this office." I pointed at her.

With trembling hands, Josie dialed. I walked her phone to CID and handed it over to Corey.

"I need you to find out who this caller is. His IP address and any information you can locate."

"Absolutely." Corey took the phone, plugged it into his computer.

"I'm gonna take Josie to get something to eat. Hopefully, at Hi Grill. Call me with any updates."

"I'll buzz you as soon as I have anything."

"Thanks.

I returned to my office. Josie was ending her call.

"Thank you for being so understanding. Yes, sir."

"Everything okay?" I stood next to her.

"Yeah, Mr. Sanders said to take as much time as I needed. Summer's over, and he has enough staff to cover my shifts."

Josie was calmer now that I was taking her home, the tension draining from her shoulders in a way that made my chest loosen, too. She mentioned showing the house during her lunch break. She must have rushed out the door without eating. The least I could do was feed her before she passed out on me.

"Are you hungry?" I walked to my door and held it open.

"A little."

"Perfect. Let's go to Hi Grill. I'll feed you before I drive you home."

"Okay." Josie stopped in front of me, meeting my eyes. "I'm not gonna lie, Lucian—I'm scared. But I don't want him running my life, whoever the hell he is."

Her voice was steadier this time, stronger than before.

"I understand." I nodded and placed my hand on her lower back. She scrambled away from my touch. *Fucking Asshole!*

"Let's talk about a game plan over an early dinner," I mumbled and motioned for her to walk ahead of me.

***

We drove to Hi Grill in silence—same as the ride to the station. I wanted to ask what was running through her head, to find some way to help, but she gave me nothing. Her expression was calm, almost too calm. Stoic. When we pulled up, Cassie greeted us at the door, her smile breaking the tension hanging between us.

"Oh, my God, Josie!" Cassie wrapped her up in her arms. "Sean called and told me what happened. Are you okay?"

I wasn't surprised her husband, and fellow officer, had called her. Cassie and Josie were childhood friends. *Why did everyone ask such a stupid question when something bad happened? Of course, Josie wasn't okay. That fucker tried to rape her.* I was in a grumpy-ass mood. I clamped my mouth shut and kept my stupid comments to myself.

"I'm shaken and scared, but I don't want to let him win." Josie's body stiffened, and I would've believed her if her voice hadn't wobbled.

"He won't." Cassie smiled at her. "You're made of stronger stuff. He picked the wrong girl to mess with."

"Thanks, Cass."

Coming from Cassie, who'd been drugged and kidnapped, that was saying a lot about Josie's character.

"Of course. Follow me. Whatever you want is on the house." Cassie grabbed a couple of menus. "Yours too, Detective."

"You don't have to do that. I can pay for Josie and me." I smiled at Cassie.

"Nonsense," Cassie huffed and led the way to a booth. "What do you want to drink?"

"I'll just have water," Josie answered and set her menu down.

"Water for me, too."

"Okay, I'll be right back to take your order." Cassie went over to the next table.

"Do you know what you want?" I murmured.

"What do you think?" Josie rolled her eyes.

If you were a local, you didn't need a menu at Hi Grill—you already knew it by heart. Carl and Judy, Cassie's parents and the proud owners of both Hi Grill and Hi Café, rarely changed a thing except for the holiday specials. Their Thanksgiving dinners in November were the stuff of island legend. But it was only September, which meant the regular menu would hold steady for another couple of months.

"Yeah, I always order the burger and fries. How about you?" I put my menu down.

"That or chicken tenders. I love the way Carl makes them extra crispy."

We placed our order when Cassie came back with our waters.

"Has what happened today happened before?" I intertwined my hands and placed them on the table in front of me.

"Not to me."

"It's happened to other realtors on the island?" I was stunned. I hadn't heard of anything happening like that before.

"Not on the island, but on the mainland." Josie took a sip of water. Her eyes darted around the room.

"I'm not gonna let anything happen to you." I reached out with my hand to grab hers and stared into her eyes.

Josie gave me a half-smile. "Sure."

"I mean it, Josie. You're safe with me." I squeezed her hand.

"There's Ry and Judge." Josie released my hand, like she'd touched fire and got burned. She beamed and popped up, hands waving above her head. Since when did she call him Ry?

"Hey." Ryker scooted in next to her and gave her a big hug. "I stopped by the station, and Corey said you were here with our esteemed detective." Ryker placed Josie's keys on the table in front of her. "I wanted to give you these, personally." Ryker winked at Josie.

"How'd you finish at the house so fast?" I frowned. Pissed off that he was winking at her.

"What are you talking about? It's been a couple of hours since you left the Leonard Street house."

Were we at the station that long?

"Charlotte drove Josie's car and said she'd call a rideshare home since she arrived at the Leonard Street house with Sean. Dude, we're HiPD. Efficient as fuck." Ryder turned to Josie. "How are you doing?"

Josie rested her head on Ryker's shoulder. "Better now. Hey, Judge."

Judge's head peeked out from under the table between her legs.

What the fuck? What the hell did she mean 'better now'. Better now that Ryker was here? Better now that Judge was with her? Better now that she wasn't alone with me?

"Did you guys find anything else?" I spoke through clenched teeth.

"No, but forensics was still dusting for prints when I left. Chief is still with them." Ryker held out his hand and waved Cassie over.

"Hey, boys," Cassie smiled and pet Judge, who crawled out from under the table toward Cassie. "What can I get you?"

"Can I have a burger, fries, and water?" Ryker smiled. "And a plain burger patty and water for Judge."

"Of course." Cassie nodded. "Coming right up."

"So why are you here?" I blurted out to Ryker.

"Why are you being such an asshole?" Josie stared at me, and Ryker smirked. "He said Corey told him we were here, and he wanted to give me my keys."

Wow, protective much?

"Wait." Josie's eyes got all squinty. "How did Corey know we were here? You spoke to him before I agreed to come eat."

Ryker coughed 'busted' into his hand. *Asshole.*

"I was already planning on asking you, and hoped you'd agree." I glared at Ryker. "I'm not being an asshole. I just want to know why he's not working."

"Chief said I was done. Judge and I were hungry. I knew you were here. This is the best burger place. Boom, we came here." Ryker beamed at me.

"Are you taking it to go?"

"Lucian! Why are you giving Ry such a hard time?" Josie scoffed.

"He's just busting my balls. Right, brother?" Ryker cocked his eyebrow.

"Right." I nodded and drank some water to stop my mouth from blurting out any more offensive remarks at Ryker.

Clearly, Josie didn't think three was a crowd—she looked perfectly content with Ryker. Maybe I should've taken the hint and left them alone. I hadn't realized there was something between them. All this time, I thought they were just friends. Watching them laugh and bump shoulders, though, made me feel like an idiot for ever thinking I had a chance. *Chance at what? Where did that thought come from?*

"Here you go, everyone." Cassie and her mom delivered all our plates. "Dig in."

"Thanks, Cassie," I grumbled.

I took a big bite of my burger to keep my mouth shut while watching Ryker and Josie. Normally, Hi Grill's burgers were heaven, but this one turned dry and lifeless, like sawdust. I should've set it down and walked out, but I'd be damned if I let Ryker take her home. She was my responsibility—not his. So I stayed put, chewing in silence while they laughed and leaned toward each other. *Fuck me.*

Thirty minutes later, my stomach ached from inhaling my burger and fries while Josie took her time finishing hers. When the bill came, I grabbed it before Ryker could. Cassie had only charged him for his meal—and at half price. Because I'd already taken the bill, I handed Cassie my credit card and paid for Ryker's meal. The quicker she rang it up, the faster we could leave.

Hi Grill, like most places on the island, gave law enforcement a fifty percent discount. We appreciated the gesture and returned the favor—shopping local, eating local, and always tipping well.

"Thanks, Detective." Ryker smiled at me.

"You're welcome," I grunted.

"I could've paid for my food," Josie smirked.

"Yours was free, remember," I mentioned.

"Are you gonna tip her?" Josie crossed her arms and glared at me.

"Of course, I will." I looked at her as if she'd grown three heads. My momma raised me right—I always tipped. Josie had been so relaxed and cheerful with Ryker; why was she busting my balls now? "Can't you just say thank you like Ryker?"

Cassie dropped off our copy of the bill for my signature on her way to another table.

"Fine." She pasted a half-assed fake smile on her face. "Thank you so much, Detective Lucian. You are the best."

Well, that was a crappy thank you. I frowned.

"Can we go now?" Josie pushed Ryker so she could scoot out of the booth.

"Absolutely." I signed it, stood, and waved to Cassie on our way out.

"I can take Josie home." Ryker winked at me.

"Not in your K9 patrol vehicle, you can't." I pointed to his car. "You don't have a backseat." K9 patrol vehicles left the back space for their dogs.

"I wouldn't put her in the backseat like a perp even if I had one. She's small. She'll fit in the front. I don't have a lot of crap on my passenger front seat today."

"Yeah, I can fit." Josie wound her arms around Ryker's arm and gazed up at him.

"Not a chance." I reached out and grabbed her arm like a perp whom I was escorting to my car. "You're coming with me."

"Hey, take your paws off me." Josie scolded and pulled her arm out of my hold.

Judge made a low growl. *Really? Judge growled at me? What the hell?*

"She's okay, boy." Ryker stooped and pet Judge. "Our detective is just grouchy. I'll call you later, Jo." Ryker straightened, and Josie hugged him.

"Bye, Ry."

Not one to ignore Judge, Josie stooped and hugged him, too. It was a fucking hug fest for everyone except me. Which sucked because I was the one who barged into the house to save her ass. The least she could've done was save a hug for me. *But why should she hug me? Why did I crave her hug?* I'd never wanted a hug from a victim before. *Why now? Why Josie?*

"Good boy." Josie grabbed his muzzle and gave him lots of kisses. She giggled when he licked her face. "See you later, Judge."

"Bye, Jo." Ryker chuckled. "Call us if you need anything."

"Thanks, Ry."

"See you at work tomorrow, Detective." Ryker smiled and tugged Judge's leash.

"Yup." I nodded and followed Josie to my car. I wanted to put my hand on her lower back, but that didn't go so well for me last time.

I didn't drive a patrol vehicle—my job was investigations and recon. As a detective, I didn't transport perps, which meant I got the unmarked car with regular back seats. Not that it mattered. I wanted her up front, beside me. I opened the passenger door for Josie before sliding behind the wheel.

"So, you and Ryker, huh?"

"What are you talking about?" Josie buckled in.

"Are you guys dating?"

"None of your business." Josie stared out the side window.

"Oh... kay. I was just making small talk."

"I'd rather ride in silence," Josie mumbled.

"Noted."

I shut my trap and drove her home. *How could she be so fucking nice to Ryker and then treat me like shit? What was up with that?*

Chapter 5

The Notes

Josie

Thank goodness Lucian stopped talking. The man drew attention without trying—his eyes, like stormy seas, could disarm anyone, and his skin radiated warmth like a sun-drenched sculpture. Damn, but he was moody. One minute he was full of sweet tenderness, and the next he barked orders like the world might crumble if he didn't take charge. The shift hit like whiplash, but deep down, I had to admit it turned me on.

Today had been stressful enough without having to make small talk with him, especially after he was so rude to Ry. I loved Ry. He was my grade school champion and best guy friend. I knew all the officers teased each other with sarcasm, but Lucian seemed offended by Ry. *Was he jealous? Why else would he ask me if I was dating Ry? Like I would date someone I thought of as my brother. Eww.*

Lucian's intensity was nerve-wracking. Every time his eyes met mine, my resolve slipped a little more. *Could he read the thoughts spinning through my head?* If he could, he'd be shocked to know how many of them involved doing wicked things to that hard, disciplined body of his. He was the cool drink of water I'd been craving, and I lived for the moment his iron control snapped.

What can I say? Everyone needs a hobby—mine just happened to be more fun than enduring a psychopath's mind games.

"Josie."

His voice startled me out of my thoughts. I looked up and realized we were sitting in my driveway with the engine idling. *How long had we been sitting there with me lost in my lustful thoughts?*

"Uh, thanks." I unbuckled, and he shut off the engine. "You don't need to come in." I stepped out of the car and shut the door.

"Yeah, I do." Lucian walked around the car toward me. "I want to check your locks and windows. Make sure no one came in while you were gone."

He had a valid point. *What if Thomas Kincaid was inside waiting for me?* That thought sobered me up and sent a shiver down my spine. I stayed beside his car and hugged myself.

"Hey." Lucian placed his hands on my shoulder. "It's gonna be okay. I'm not gonna let him hurt you."

"I know you will try, but you can't be with me 24-7."

He pulled me in for a hug—that was new. Lucian had never hugged me before. His musky, manly-smelling cologne tickled my nose. I returned the hug and burrowed into his neck, holding on for dear life. Remembering every single scent and feel of this moment. Lucian held me tight with one hand on the back of my head while the other massaged circles on my back. I could stay like this forever.

Wait—what was I doing? This was Lucian. Detective Robot, king of composure and zero emotional display. Although he hadn't acted robotic when he comforted me. *Did he even date? Or was he married to the job?* I pulled back and folded my arms, trying to rebuild the walls he'd taken down.

"Should I stay out here while you check my house, or follow you in?" I kept my eyes on the ground. I couldn't bear to see the distance in his gaze after feeling the warmth of his arms around me.

"I'd prefer you got back in the car." His voice sounded raspy.

Had that hug gotten to him, too? I glanced up, hoping to catch some sign that he'd sensed it—a wicked, sensual spark buzzed through me—but he was already opening the car door, all business again.

"Sure." I got in.

"Here." Lucian handed me his key fob. "Lock yourself in. If you hear any sounds that scare you, get in the driver's seat and go straight to the station. I'll be there as soon as I can. Okay."

I nodded.

"I mean it, Josie. Don't go in there." He pointed at my house. "If someone is in there, I don't want to have to worry about you. I can take care of myself. Promise me you'll do what I said."

"I promise." I met his eyes, letting him see how serious I looked. Relieved, he couldn't see my crossed fingers hidden behind my back. No way was I leaving him behind.

"Give me your keys." Lucian held out his hand and wiggled his fingers.

I rifled through my purse and placed the keys in his hand.

Lucian shut the door and tapped on the window. "Lock the doors."

I wanted to give him shit for ordering me around, but fear had a stronger grip on me than my pride. Someone might be inside my house. So, I nodded and hit the door-lock button.

Lucian gave me a small nod in return, then drew his gun. After a quick sweep of the yard, he moved toward the front door, checking every angle. The knob didn't budge. Locked. He slid the key into place, lifted his weapon, and swung the door open in one swift motion—ready for whatever waited inside.

I held my breath as Lucian stepped inside. *Please God, let no one be in there.* The thought of someone rifling through my things made my stomach twist. I loved this house. It wasn't just walls and a roof—it was my childhood home. A modest, three-bedroom ranch filled with memories that still lingered in the walls. The idea of an unknown person violating that space filled me with an unbearable sense of dread.

My dad had been one of the island's physicians, and small-town life meant he was always on call. Vacations were rare, and freedom was something they'd spent decades earning. Because they'd lived on Haven Island their entire lives, after my dad retired, they were eager to travel the world, starting with the States, followed by other countries.

They bought an RV, packed up their dreams, and drove off to chase them—leaving me with the house and the memories we built. With the mortgage paid off, all I had to carry were the monthly bills. The moment they pulled out of the driveway landed like both a gift and a goodbye.

I was glad my parents finally got to enjoy their golden years, but I missed them. Meanwhile, I still hustled—working two jobs. I worked twelve-hour shifts at the resort from six to six. But I had worked there for so long that if I had a house to show, they let me do it in the afternoons. My paycheck would reflect my lack of hours unless I went back to work after the showing and made them up.

They made for long days, but I loved the flexibility the resort offered. All I needed was one more sale before the end of the year, and I could finally cut my hours—or maybe even quit working at the resort altogether. Little by little, I'd built a decent nest egg. My future was looking like more than just a dream.

I heard sirens and glanced around, trying to place the direction. This was a quiet neighborhood, tucked near the Ocean Breeze Resort—sirens didn't usually echo here. Maybe they were headed to the resort. There'd been a recent string of thefts there.

The sirens got closer—too close. Then Ryker's K-9 patrol vehicle swung into my driveway, lights flashing. My pulse spiked. *What the hell was going on? Where was Lucian? Was he hurt?* Had I been so lost in my own head that I missed a gunshot—or someone slipping out of my house?

I stepped out of the car. "Ry, what's going on?"

"Stay in the car, Jo." Ry frowned and put his hand out to stop me. "Judge and I will be right back."

"What's happening?" I had to know what was going on in my house. Lucian stepped onto the front porch. I bolted out of the car and slammed the door, ready to follow Ry and Judge.

"Josie," Lucian shouted and stepped aside, allowing Ry and Judge into my house. "Get back in the car!"

"No, what's going on?" I stepped in front of him and crossed my arms. "I have a right to know what you found in my house."

"Fine." Lucian threw up his arms in exasperation. "Follow me."

"How does Ry know what's going on, and I don't?" I glared at him.

"Because I called him."

"Oh." It must be bad if Lucian called for backup. "Tell me what you found."

"Someone was in your bedroom and went through your drawers."

"What? Wh... which drawers?"

A knot tightened in my stomach, and dread spread through my body like ice water. My breath caught, the hairs on my neck prickling in warning. Blood hammered in my ears, each beat sharper than the last as nausea surged up my throat. I had to steady myself.

"Your underwear drawer."

I swayed, but Lucian caught me, wrapping me up in his arms. Oh. My. God. Someone had touched my underwear? *Seriously?* There was no way I could wear them again—and my lingerie wasn't cheap. It was one of my guilty pleasures, ice cream being another. I wore my sexy undergarments for me—because those lacy sets made me stand taller, breathe deeper, feel powerful... untouchable. And now? I'd have to toss them. Fantastic. Nothing like losing my confidence and half a paycheck in one day.

"Are you sure you're ready to go in there?"

That psycho was not getting into my head. I refused to hand him that kind of power. Dammit, I was Josie Hale—queen of customer service, kick-ass realtor, loyal daughter, and ride-or-die friend. I had survived worse days than this, and I would survive this too.

"Yes," I straightened and stared Lucian in the eyes.

"That's my girl." Lucian held my hand and led the way.

What did he mean by 'That's my girl?' Since when was I his girl? So many thoughts raced in my head, but all I wanted to do was bury it in the sand, hoping everything went away. Today had to be a dream or, more like, a nightmare.

I froze in the doorway to my bedroom. Every dresser drawer was open except one, clothes spilling over the edges like the aftermath of a storm. The missing drawer lay upside down on the floor beside the bed—my underwear drawer.

My lingerie lay across the bed, each bra placed above its matching panties. Between every set, a small, ripped-up note. My hand flew to my mouth. Heart hammering, I stepped closer, reaching out—hesitating—before my fingers brushed the edge of the first note.

"No!" Ry and Lucian screamed simultaneously.

I jolted and stepped back into Lucian, who wrapped his arms around me. "That's evidence. We need to check for fingerprints."

"B... but it's my lingerie. My prints are already on it." I turned to Ry.

"Yes, but we need to photograph them where they lie on the bed." Ry motioned toward the bed.

"Exactly where he left them," Lucian said from behind me. "Besides, there might be prints on the notes that aren't yours."

I glanced down and read the notes closest to me. The handwriting was jagged, heavy, pressed hard into the post-it note. The one between the purple lace bra and panties said.

I can't wait to bite your nipples through this.

My stomach dropped. I read the one on top of the see-through light pink one-piece.

Shave for me before you wear this.

An icy chill slid down my spine. Each piece on the bed had a message. Each message was worse than the last.

By the time I reached the last note, my vision blurred.

You're mine now, Josie. Evade the cops. I'm all you need. I'm coming for you soon.

My hand flew to my mouth as the room tilted. He'd been here—close enough to touch everything I owned. Close enough to stalk me.

"I'm gonna be sick."

Chapter 6

The Red Set

Josie

I tore out of Lucian's arms and bolted for the bathroom. The second I lifted the toilet seat, my stomach gave out, and everything I'd eaten at Hi Grill came up in a violent rush.

A warm hand swept my hair away from my face. He didn't say a word, just stayed close, steady. When the heaving stopped, a towel appeared in front of me, his hand still hovering—ready, waiting. Judge sat beside him, mewling. Lucian flushed the toilet.

"Judge, go to Ryker," Lucian mumbled.

Judge nudged my leg and scampered off.

"Hey," Lucian said softly, his voice rough around the edges. "Breathe, Josie. You're okay."

I wiped my mouth with the towel he'd handed me, avoiding his eyes. "I'm fine." My voice cracked on the lie.

He crouched beside me, close enough that I could feel his body heat. "No, you're not," he whispered. "And that's okay. You don't have to be."

For a long moment, the only sounds in the room were the hum of the overhead fan and the pounding of my heart. He reached up and tucked a strand of hair behind my ear, his touch gentle—too gentle for a man who usually barked orders and carried a gun.

"I won't let him hurt you again," he said.

Something in his tone—steady, lethal, and sincere—made me believe him.

"What can I get you?" Lucian whispered.

"A new day filled with love and laughter instead of fright and despair," I mumbled.

"I'll see what I can do." He ran his hands over my face, tucking more hair behind my ears. "For now, let me help you off this floor and into the living room. Your couch has got to be more comfortable than this tile." Lucian helped me up.

"I need to brush my teeth first." I grabbed my toothbrush and froze. "You don't think he did anything to my toothbrush, do you?"

"Like what? Rub it up against his crotch?"

"Ewww. No!" I threw the toothbrush in the sink. "I was thinking more of cleaning my toilet with it. But what you said is disgusting."

"More disgusting than cleaning your toilet?" He quirked his eyebrow, and I heard Ry chuckle behind him.

"Well, no, but how did you come up with a toothbrush in the crotch?"

"You'd be surprised by what we see and hear?" Lucian smirked.

"Amen, brother," Ry confirmed.

"You guys are grossing me out more than before I hurled." I squeezed toothpaste onto my finger and ran it over my teeth and around my tongue. I spat it out, and then I used mouthwash, savoring the cool, minty freshness.

Lucian led me out of my bedroom and into the living room while Ry blocked my view of the bed. I sat on my couch with my head in my hands. *Life sucked.*

"Here, drink this." Lucian handed me a glass of water.

"Thank you." I took a sip and stared at the glass.

A commotion at the front door pulled me from my thoughts. I looked up to see two men step inside, both wearing jackets that read HiPD CSI Unit across the back. One carried a camera; the other held a black evidence bag.

"Hey, Jamie, Kyle." Lucian pointed to the bedroom. "In there. Ryker and Judge are already in there."

"Will do, boss." They nodded to Lucian and left us alone.

Lucian sat beside me, elbows resting on his knees, hands clasped loosely in his lap. His voice was calm but careful. "Can you tell me if anything's missing, Josie?"

I glared at him. "How should I know? I was too busy reading those gross messages to look around before I barfed."

"Can we call a cease-fire, please? I'm only trying to help you." Lucian's voice was low, the edge gone. His eyes said the rest—*please let me in.*

I wanted to fire off a comeback, to insist I didn't need rescuing—but something in his eyes caught me mid-breath. The fight slipped away, replaced by bone-deep exhaustion and a strange, growing trust. I exhaled. "Sorry...I'm out of sorts. Truce."

"I understand." He ran his hand up and down my back. "I hate to ask you this, but can you please go back in there with me and tell me if anything is missing?"

So much for the nice guy routine. "Are you fucking serious?" I stared at him.

"Unfortunately, yes." Lucian sighed. "I'm sorry, but the quicker we know what's missing, the faster we can figure out what the hell is going on and catch the bastard."

"Give me a minute." I took another sip, closed my eyes, and sank back into the couch. *Happy thoughts,* I told myself. I needed to find one happy memory to hold on to.

Cooking with Mom in the kitchen—her humming to old songs while I stirred the sauce. Or sitting on the counter in her bathroom as she brushed makeup over my cheeks, making me face away until she was done. She'd spin me around, waiting for that little gasp, that *aha moment* when I saw myself through her eyes.

The memory warmed something deep inside me. I smiled. I could do this. I was ready to face that bedroom. No man was going to take my beautiful memories in this house and twist them into nightmares. Sure, I'd have to install security cameras, buy new clothes, and definitely replace my bed—but *fuck him.* This was my home. He wasn't going to scare me out of it. I opened my eyes and met Lucian's gaze head-on.

"I'm ready." I stood and ran my hands down my thighs. I could do this. I'll read the notes later—not right now. Although maybe it was better to read them on an empty stomach.

Lucian didn't say anything right away. His jaw flexed, that muscle in his cheek tightened like he was fighting to keep his expression neutral. But his eyes—those storm-gray eyes—softened.

"Good," he said finally, his voice low and steady. "That's the fire I need you to hold on to. You don't give him an inch, Josie. Not one."

For a heartbeat, neither of us looked away. Then he exhaled, his mouth curving upward at the corners. "You're tougher than half the people I've served with," he added, and something in his tone made my chest ache in the best way.

I huffed out a laugh, even though my throat tightened. "Guess that's one way to say I'm stubborn."

Lucian's mouth twitched. "Stubborn works."

"Good," I said, forcing a smirk I didn't quite feel. "Because it's the only thing keeping me from falling apart right now."

The words slipped out before I could stop them from exposing my vulnerability. He stayed beside me, gazing into my eyes before he shifted closer, his knee brushing mine. The contact was small, but deliberate—grounding.

"I got you," he whispered. "You don't have to hold it together every second."

The words hit harder than I expected. I stared at his hand resting between us, steady and strong, and before I could talk myself out of it, I slid my fingers over his.

He didn't move, didn't speak. Just tightened his grip—solid, reassuring, like a silent promise that I wasn't facing this alone.

For the first time since walking into that nightmare of a bedroom, I believed him.

Lucian stood and pulled me up with him, his fingers intertwined with mine as he guided me back toward the bedroom. My gaze landed on the bed, and my stomach twisted—the notes, the clothes, the violation of it all. Then I noticed it.

The red one-piece set. Gone.

Of course he'd take that one—the lacy one-piece had a matching garter belt. The sexiest thing I owned. *Damn pervert.*

Chapter 7

Temptation is a Slippery Fucker

Lucian

I stayed close to Josie, watching every slight tremor in her hands, every flicker of panic that crossed her eyes as she stared at her lingerie and those terror-filled notes scattered across the bed. The sight hollowed me out. The emptiness in her expression hit harder than any punch I'd ever taken. I missed her laugh—the spark that made her who she was. I'd give anything to see that light in her eyes again.

I took a slow breath, forcing my voice to stay level. "Josie," I said in hushed tones, "look at me."

Her gaze lifted, unfocused at first, then locked on mine. I could still see the tremor running through her.

"Let's take this one step at a time," I said. "You're safe right now. I've got you."

She swallowed hard, nodding, but her eyes darted back toward the bed. "My red set is missing," she whispered.

"Was it a top and bottom like those?" I pointed to the bed.

"No." She cleared her throat. "It was a one-piece with a garter belt."

"Can you describe it for me?" I winced but had to ask.

"Do I have to?" She looked at me with pleading eyes.

"Uh, you can describe it to Ryker...if you feel more comfortable talking to him." I rubbed the back of my neck and prayed she'd prefer to talk to me and not Ryker. I know they're close, but dammit, I wanted her to put her trust in me. To want to talk to me.

Josie looked away and stared at the floor. "The bodice looked like a bathing suit but lacy with a plunging neckline, high-cut sides, and a low back dipping into a thong."

Fuck me. The way she described her lingerie—the softness in her voice, the hint of vulnerability under it—hit harder than I wanted to admit. My pulse spiked. I shifted my weight, fighting to focus on the pain in her eyes instead of the pull in my gut and the hardness growing in my pants. This was not the time—I was a professional.

Maybe Ryker should've been the one to hear it. Because right now, I wasn't thinking like a detective. I was thinking like a man who wanted to take her up against the wall and claim her. Show everyone, including that asshole, who she really belonged to. I wanted to protect her from everything and everyone. *But did she even like me?*

My hands needed something to do, so I pulled out my notebook and wrote every detail she said, attempting to be an attentive detective instead of a drooling pervert. I dragged in a slow breath and forced my shoulders to relax. Getting lost in how she made me feel would not help her—it never would.

I turned toward the evidence on the bed, every detail sharpened in my mind. The scattered notes, the missing lingerie, the violation. That was where my focus needed to stay.

Anger simmered beneath my calm exterior, cold and controlled. Whoever had done this had crossed a line, and I wasn't just going to find him—I was going to make sure the bastard never came near her again.

"Is that all that's missing?" The words came out rougher than I intended—too low, too intimate. I cleared my throat, trying to pull the professionalism back into my voice.

"Yes." Josie pivoted and hurried out of the room.

I pulled out my phone and snapped a couple of photos of the bed and dresser, my voice low and steady when I spoke to Ryker, Jamie, and Kyle.

"I want every fingerprint, every fiber, every damn trace this guy left behind. He's not getting away with this." I glanced at Ryker. "Does Judge have her scent so we can eliminate it from whatever he finds?"

"She's known him since he was a puppy." Ryker grinned at me. "He's always had her scent."

Fucker. Did he have to say that while he handled her undergarments? Fuck, I hope they are just friends. I'd hate to beat the shit out of one of my brothers. Of course, Judge had her scent. That was a stupid question. I'd better control my body and put my head in the game before I make a fool of myself—not that I hadn't already.

"Can you tell if Judge scented the same guy that was in the Leonard Street house with Josie?"

"He growled when he sniffed her undergarments and the notes. I'm hoping the perp left prints on them, but I'm not sure it's the same guy." Ryker held up the pink lacy undies.

"Will you bag those already?" I snapped at Ryker.

"Sure thing, brother." Ryker smiled and made it a point to put them in a baggie and zip it up. Shaking the baggie in front of me. "You wanna help?"

"No," I glared at him. "I'm gonna go talk to Josie."

"I can go comfort Jo if you want to bag her undies." Ryker wiggled his eyebrows.

At a crime scene, civilians never understood why we joked. They'd look at us as if we were heartless bastards. Maybe they thought we enjoyed the chaos, or that the blood and the bodies didn't get to us anymore. But that couldn't be further from the truth.

What they didn't see was the part where the silence presses in until your ears ring... the part where the smell sticks to your clothes long after you've showered... the part where some victims start to look like people you love.

You stare at enough horror, you either laugh a little or you break. Those were the only two options.

So yeah, we cracked jokes. Threw sarcasm like life preservers. Shoved each other's shoulders just to remind ourselves we were still human. It wasn't disrespect. It was survival. A pressure valve before everything in our heads exploded.

And the guys who joked the loudest? They were usually the ones who cared the most.

"Shut the fuck up." I turned to Kyle. "Anything yet?"

"Sorry, no prints so far," Kyle tried to hide his fucking smile. *Fucker.*

"But we'll bag all these items after Jamie's done with the photos and take them down to the station. Maybe we'll get lucky, and he rubbed them on his face or something," Kyle said as he continued to dust the furniture.

A screech sounded behind me, and I spun around. Josie stood with her hands covering her mouth. Her eyes scanned all of us. Then she took off at a dead run.

"Nice going," I blurted to Kyle and darted after her.

I caught her at the front door. She pressed herself against the door, digging her fingers into her face as she cried—the wood muffled the sound.

"Shh, it's going to be okay," I whispered in her ear. "I got you."

She spun around in my arms and wrapped her arms around my waist, crying into my chest. Thomas Kincaid, or whatever the fuck his name was, was going to pay for putting Josie through this. Psychopathic piece of shit.

"Who is this guy?" Josie mumbled into my chest.

"I don't know, but I will find him."

"What am I supposed to do now?" She lifted her face and looked at me. Tears streaked down her cheeks.

"You can't stay here." I ran my thumb across her cheek, wiping them.

"I can't stay with Cassie or Sammie. I'd feel like a third wheel. They're both recently married, and Sammie already has four kids at home to take care of."

"Where are your parents?"

Josie stepped away from my embrace and wiped her face with her hands. "They're traveling around the U.S. in an RV. I think they're in Montana right now. I don't want to upset them. Ugh, why is this happening!" She strode into the kitchen and grabbed some tissues.

I followed her and stood by the doorway. "I don't know yet."

Taking several deep breaths, she sat on a stool by the kitchen counter. "I can talk to Mr. Sanders and see if I can rent a room at the resort."

"You can stay with me." I cleared my throat and crossed my arms, braced for a no.

"I don't think that's a good idea." She sighed.

"Why not?"

"I...I'd rather stay with a friend."

"We're not friends?" I frowned.

"Not really." She played with her tissue instead of looking at me.

"She can stay with me," Ryker stated as he came out of the bedroom with Judge.

Shut the fuck up, brother. Did I not make it clear enough that I wanted to be the one to protect Josie? I should've spelled it out for him when I was in the bedroom.

"Can I?" Josie perked up and smiled at Ryker. My stomach dropped. She looked at him as if he were her hero. *Why couldn't she look at me like that, dammit? Then again, why did I want her to?*

"Sure, Judge and I would love to have you over. We haven't had a sleepover since high school."

What did he mean by a sleepover? Did they sleep in the same bed? Wear matching pajamas? Have pillow fights? My mind was spiralling out of control.

"You promise to make me hot chocolate and popcorn?" Josie slid off her stool.

"And find the perfect scary movie. Absolutely." Ryker put out his hand to seal the deal, but Josie ran into his arms and hugged him.

"Thanks, Ry."

And that's my cue to drag my ass out of that fucking kitchen.

"Now that it's settled. Ryker, take her to your place, and I'll finish here with Kyle and Jamie."

"Sounds good. Pack a bag, Jo, and let's blow this popsicle stand. Kyle said it's okay to get clothes out of your closet because it doesn't seem like the scumbag went in there, but you can't take any undergarments."

"That's okay. I'll go commando—" she said over her shoulder on her way to her closet, "—until I can buy more."

Fuck me. Not the image I needed—her heading home with another man to snuggle through movies and spend the night half naked. *Shit. My life sucked.*

Chapter 8

Gotta Go

Josie

I stepped into my bedroom and kept my eyes fixed on the closet, refusing to glance at the bed in case anything still lay there. My stomach dipped, but I pushed through it. I opened the closet, grabbed a few dresses and work outfits, and thew them into a suitcase. It didn't matter if they wrinkled—Ry's place was only a short drive away, and right now, getting out of this house mattered far more than perfect clothes.

I zipped the suitcase and took a slow breath, steadying myself. My hands were shaking, but I curled them into fists until they stopped. This wasn't just a room. This was my bedroom with lots of wonderful childhood memories. Thomas Kincaid would not taint my memories and take that away from me. I would clean everything up when the police finished and move back in.

I lifted my chin, stepped out of the closet, and ran smack into Lucian's chest.

He gripped my arms, holding me steady. "Are you going to be okay?" he frowned.

"Yep, I'm good with Ry and Judge. I'll be fine." I nodded.

He didn't look happy. He hesitated and said, "Call me if you need anything."

"I'll be fine." I gave him my best fake smile. I knew Ry, Judge, and I would have a great time at his house, like always. Still, a tiny part of my mind drifted to the rigid—but ridiculously sexy—detective I could've been staying with.

The second I crossed the doorway, a wave of nausea rolled through me—too many flashes of yesterday, too many what-ifs—but I forced my feet forward. One step. Then another. At the threshold of my bedroom, I paused long enough to whisper, *You're okay.* Then I grabbed the handle of my suitcase, walked down the hall, and didn't look back.

"Ryker!" Lucian screamed and stepped into the living room. "You and Judge stay with her at all times until I figure this out."

"You got it, bro." Ry took my suitcase out of my hand. Judge nudged my leg with his muzzle.

"Thanks, Judge." I pet the top of his head.

I looked over my shoulder to thank Lucian, but he'd left the room. *Was he mad at me for going with Ry?* Ry was the best kind of guy friend—the dependable one. Since high school, I'd always been able to count on him. He somehow always knew what I needed and how to make me feel better.

I followed Ry to his truck, shocked that Lucian wasn't saying anything to me about riding in the front passenger seat like last time. He must've gotten over it. Ry put my suitcase in the trunk.

"So," I buckled in and glanced at Ry. "Do you have all my food requests at home, or do we have to stop off at the grocery store?"

"I got everything we need at home for tonight." He headed to his house. "Are you hungry? I mean, you hurled your lunch." I smacked his shoulder.

"Jerk."

Ry grinned, "How about some steaks for dinner?"

Judge howled in the back.

"I think Judge and I would love steaks." I laughed. "On the grill?"

"Is there any other way?" Ry smirked.

On the way to his house, we argued about what movie to put on, just like old times. Ry lobbied for the last Nightmare on Elm Street, but I wanted the new one about hauntings. And just like back then, I won.

Once inside, I hollered, "I'll let Judge out!"

Ry's place was a modest, one-story beach cottage, the kind that looked sun-kissed and lived-in from years of salt and weather. Wide windows caught the afternoon light and spilled it across the floors in warm, golden streaks.

I strode through the house and out the sliding glass doors. Out back, Ry's porch opened to a private stretch of sand and sea—quiet, steady, peaceful. The waves rolled in with a soft, rhythmic crash that loosened something tight in my chest. The breeze carried salt, sunscreen, and that familiar driftwood warmth I'd grown up with.

Judge bolted out after me. He did his business on a patch of grass and spent the rest of the time running around in the sand.

For the first time all day, my shoulders eased. The view reminded me why I loved Haven Island. The ocean waves crashing on the shore, familiar and serene, unchanged by time. Here, the world seemed a little safer, like the ocean itself stood guard. I was glad I'd come home with him.

Ry came out a few minutes later and joined me. "I put your suitcase in my bedroom. I'll take the couch."

"I feel terrible taking your bed."

"Since when?" He arched his eyebrow at me.

"Guilty." I smiled.

Ry shook his head and smiled. "I'm fine on the couch. Can you prep the veggies and toss the salad while I start the grill?"

"Yep, on it." I pivoted and headed toward the kitchen.

I opened the fridge and couldn't help but smile. Just as I expected, it was packed with salad greens, chopped veggies, and neatly labeled containers. Ry had always been the picture of clean eating—unless he stopped by Hi Grill, which wasn't often. He enjoyed cooking his own meals, heavy on the protein and light on the carbs.

It's a shame I wasn't into him—because, honestly, that body was proof his discipline worked. Cassie, Silver, and I always teased him about it, but none of us ever crossed that line. To us, Ry was the little brother we never knew we wanted. Since all our birthdays came before his, it gave us automatic seniority—and we took full advantage of it. We vetted every girl he showed an interest in, just like big sisters should. He looked out for us, and we did the same for him.

I pulled out zucchini, cherry tomatoes, bell peppers, and onions. A grilled veggie kabob sounded delicious. With all the fixings on the counter, I chopped and skewered the veggies. Then placed them in aluminum foil, brushed them with olive oil, and sprinkled rosemary, oregano, thyme, salt, and pepper.

Perfect. I put the foil on a plate and walked it out to Ry. "Here are the veggie kabobs."

"Yum, thanks." Ry grabbed the foil and placed it on the grill. "Sit out here and talk to me."

"I was gonna make the salad."

"Make it later. Let's catch up."

"Okay." I pulled out a chair from his outdoor table and sat. Judge came over and sat at my feet.

"How are you really doing, Jo?"

I knew that was coming. Ry always knew when I was upset.

"Not good," I mumbled, my gaze fixed on the horizon. I loved watching the waves breaking against the shore with a rhythm that sounded older than time. Each crash stole a little of my fear; each retreat carried it back out to sea.

The breeze shifted, salty and soft, wrapping around me like the island itself was trying to calm me down. The ocean had always been my sanctuary—wild, untamed, honest. Maybe that's why I could never imagine leaving Haven Island. It's home—my personal paradise.

"I'm scared. Mad at him. Hell, I'm mad at myself for letting him get to me." My leg bounced so fast, Judge groaned and laid his head on my lap, causing me to stop. I rubbed his head and sank into my chair. "Thanks, Judge."

"I'm so sorry this is happening to you." Ry flipped the steaks. "But I can promise we'll keep you safe. Especially Lucian." Ry threw a smile my way.

"What do you mean?" I tilted my head and stared at him. *What was that look for? What did he know that I didn't?*

"Duh." Ry winked and pointed the spatula in my direction. "He's into you."

"You mean he likes me?" I scrunched up my nose.

"Uh, yeah." Ry rolled his eyes and turned back to the grill. "That's what into you means. I know you're not that dense not to notice it."

"I mean, we're friends... or maybe frenemies." I shrugged. "We argue all the time."

"I think that's passion boiling over."

"What the hell are you talking about?" I straightened in my seat.

"I think... that you guys are so into each other that you argue as a form of foreplay." Ry shrugged and checked the veggies.

"Really? Have you lost your mind? The only reason he's being nice to me is because of what that asshole is putting me through. I'm a job."

"I don't think you are just a 'job'." Ry used air quotes around the word job. "Go get me a clean plate for the steaks and another for the veggies." Ry waved the spatula toward the kitchen. "The veggies are done."

Perfect timing because I wanted to stop talking about Lucian. *Thank you, veggies.* I returned with the plates and handed one to him. Ry placed the aluminum foil with the veggies on the plate, and I set it on the table. He kept the other one by the grill.

"These steaks are perfect." Ry did a chef's kiss. "Yours is definitely not mooing."

Ry liked his medium rare, and I hated seeing any pink. Over the years, we had agreed to disagree on our taste preferences.

"Ha ha. What do you want to drink?"

"For you, there's a bottle of Sauvignon Blanc in the fridge. I'll just have water."
Ry always kept a bottle of my favorite wine chilled in the fridge.

"You are the bomb. I love you." I hugged Ry but jumped back when I heard Judge bark.

In a swift move, Ry pushed me behind him and drew his gun. Lucian came out from the side of the house with Judge next to him. Tail high, nose locked in Ry's direction, proud of his discovery.

Chapter 9

Surprise!

Josie

"Lucian?" The name tore out of me the second he rounded the corner of the house, shock slamming into me.

"Hey bro, what are you doing back there?" Ry asked before he put his gun back in his waistband. The question wasn't suspicious, just curious.

Lucian held up his hands. "I didn't mean to interrupt. I wanted to check on Josie."

Judge spun around and planted his paws on Lucian's shoulders, licking his face with all the enthusiasm in the world.

"Hey, Judge." Lucian rubbed his back and gave him lots of kisses on his muzzle. "Good boy."

"I was fine until you scared the shit out of me." I glared at him. *What the hell?* "You could've knocked on the front door."

"I heard your voices. Besides, this is where Ryker and Judge hang out most of the time." Lucian rubbed Judge's face. "Right, buddy."

"I didn't know you were coming. I cooked only two steaks." Ry pulled the steaks off the grill. "But I can defrost another one quickly if you're hungry."

"Nah, I'm good." Judge lowered himself to the ground, and Lucian's eyes lifted to meet mine. "I wanted to make sure you were okay. You were pretty upset when you left."

"I'm okay." I looked past him to the ocean waves.

"You sure you don't want to stay and eat with us?" Ryker placed the plates on the table.

"No," Lucian replied with a small grin. "Thanks, though. I need to get back to the station—Kyle and Jamie are uploading their reports, and I want to review them as soon as they're in."

Ry turned and winked at me. "I'm gonna get us some wine."

My eyes widened. *Why was he leaving me out there with Lucian?* I'd told him everything that had happened. *What else could the detective want from me?*

"How are you really doing?" Lucian walked up to me.

"Freaked out, I guess." I shrugged. "Nothing like this has ever happened to me. I mean, I've had persistent guys hit on me, but eventually they walk away."

Lucian reached out and grabbed my hand. "I'm gonna find out who Thomas Kincaid is and nail his ass to the wall. I promise."

I released his hand. "Lucian, you haven't even been able to find the kids who are breaking into the rental homes. How can you make me that promise?" I stepped around him to watch the waves.

It was the same argument we'd had a dozen times. Our real estate company managed several of those homes, and our clients were furious—scared, even. The break-ins never left behind actual damage to the homes, just a deliberate mess of cigarette butts and empty beer bottles.

Nothing was stollen. But that didn't matter, as the rental company still seethed with anger and frustration over the lack of arrests. The trespassers always left a heavy scent of smoke, weed, and stale alcohol that clung to the furniture in every room like it belonged there. The message was obvious enough. Someone had been in every one of those rentals, and they wanted us to know it.

"Dammit, Josie, I'm trying. I have a plan to catch those little shits."

I spun around. "What do you mean, little shits? Do you know who's breaking in? Is it kids?"

"I can't tell you who our suspects are." Lucian rubbed the back of his neck.

"What are you going to do?" I crossed my arms.

"I can't tell you that either." He looked at the floor and shook his head.

"Well, isn't that convenient?" I grumbled. "Is there anything you can tell me?"

"Dammit, Josie. This is what I do—dig through the details until I have enough to make an arrest." He snarled, frustration tightening his jaw. "I can't give you information that could jeopardize my case. Ryker keeps things from you too, I'm sure."

"Maybe he does." I let the words drip with attitude. "Maybe he doesn't." I lifted a shoulder in a careless shrug and gave him a look that kept him wondering how much Ry tells me.

"Ryker's smarter than that. He wouldn't throw his career away. So if you're going to lie to me, try harder." He growled the last words, frustration simmering under the surface.

"I don't answer to you." I planted my hands on my hips and shifted my weight to one side.

Lucian's arms shot up in frustration. "I never asked you to." He paced a few steps, then whirled back toward me. "Is it too much to ask for you to be honest with me?" He placed his hand over his heart. "To trust me?"

"Hey, guys." Ry stepped out and looked at both of us. "Is everything okay out here?"

"It's fine," I said through gritted teeth.

"Yeah, fine." Lucian's jaw ticked as he glared at me.

Lucian kept opening and closing his mouth like a frustrated fish, clearly dying to say something but swallowing it back. He probably didn't want to start a fight in front of Ry. I stared him down anyway, daring him to make another snide comment—I was more than ready to fire back. Ryker's little grin flickered in my peripheral vision. The air between us was so thick you could cut it with a knife.

"Ryker," Lucian broke our staring contest. "You and Judge stay with Josie tomorrow. Keep your radio on. If we need you, we'll call."

"You got it." Ry nodded and set the wine-filled glasses on the table by our plates.

I sat down, cut up my food, and ignored Lucian. Anything I said right now would come out mean, and my parents always taught me that if I didn't have something nice to say, I should keep my mouth shut. Not that I usually followed that rule with Lucian—but I wasn't dragging Ry into our squabbles.

"Call me if you need anything, Josie." Lucian's husky voice reached my ears. I could feel his eyes on me. "I'm fine." I looked at Ry and smiled. "I have Ry."

Lucian left, and Ry sat down.

"That wasn't very nice, Jo."

"He'll get over it."

Chapter 10

Artists... NOT

Thomas

"**H**ey, Jackass," I hollered as I slammed the front door. "Why weren't you at the Leonard Street house? If you'd been there, we could've grabbed her. Where the hell were you?"

"I got stuck in traffic. When I got there, I heard you scream and caught a blur of her running away from the stairs." Vincent said from the couch, where he was drinking a beer, watching a show about creating the perfect cons.

I stormed in front of him, blocking his view of the TV. "Why didn't you come upstairs and help me? I could've used your muscles to bust down the bathroom door."

"I thought if I stayed downstairs, I could catch her if she tried to get away." Vincent shrugged.

"You don't do the thinking around here." I pointed to my chest. "I do."

"Sorry, man."

Something wasn't adding up. "If you were downstairs, why the hell didn't I see you when I ran out?"

"When I heard the sirens," Vincent shrugged. "I took off. What took you so long?"

"I was dodging cops through backyards all the way to the resort so I could blend in with the fucking tourists." I crossed my arms over my chest. "I didn't have a car, remember. You dropped me off and were supposed to pick me up." I arched my eyebrow at him.

"So how'd you get here?" Vincent took another drink.

Why the hell did I saddle myself with a partner who could rewire a security grid blindfolded but didn't possess the basic street smarts of a concussed pigeon? The genius behind a keyboard, sure—but drop him into the real world and he's glitching like a cheap knockoff robot. I planned everything. I ran the operation. He was supposed to be the muscle—the tech-savvy enforcer—yet somehow he managed to be both brilliant and brain-dead at the same time.

Honestly, if that man had two brain cells left, they weren't speaking. They're not even on the same continent. Was it really too much to hope he'd use one of them once when shit went south?

"I had to call a car service, genius." I grumbled.

"Sorry. I ran late with the camera installation, and I didn't want to get arrested."

Fucking asshole. I glared at Vincent. He'd installed those fucking cameras a million times. *Why was today any different?*

"We're supposed to be a team. What part of that do you not understand?"

"I don't know what else to say. I messed up." Vincent leaned around me, his eyes going back to the television. "Get a beer and chill the hell out."

"How am I supposed to chill out?" I stepped back and swung his legs off the couch just as he was taking a drink. It spilled all over his shirt.

"What the hell, man!" Vincent stood brushing the beer off his shirt with his hand." I said I was sorry."

The damn idiot was spreading the beer all over the rest of his shirt.

"Well, don't fucking strand me next time." I dropped onto the couch. "How the hell am I supposed to get her now? She saw my face!"

"She doesn't know your name. I mean...," —Vincent chuckled and took a gulp of his beer— "she thinks your name is Thomas Kincaid." He slapped his leg and laughed, almost spilling the rest of his beer.

"Jackass," I mumbled. She didn't know my real name, but if she saw me, I'm sure she'd recognize me."You're gonna have to meet with her next time."

"What! No! You're the one that does all the talking. We could dye your hair blonde, and you could grow a beard." Vincent grinned.

"And I could cut off your fucking ear like your namesake, motherfucker." I bolted off the couch and went to get my own damn beer. "I knew I should've sent you to that fucking house, but you're much better at installing cameras."

"Hey, if you're going into the kitchen, get me another one." Vincent lifted his arm in the air, waving his beer bottle.

"Do I look like your fucking maid?" First, he left me flapping in the wind, and now he wants me to serve him. Hell no.

"You are the painter of light. So, get me a beer and lighten my mood." Vincent guffawed.

"Fucking idiot," I sneered and muttered under my breath but still went to grab us beers. We'd been partners for over two years now—long enough to perfect our games with the women we kidnapped. Our women's fate depended on them and how they reacted to our enjoyment. Fear was a bitch! And we loved taming that bitch. The louder the women yelled, the more turned on we got.

Sharing a cell turned into our training ground. Every day locked up, we honed our ideas, sharpened our plans, carved out a blueprint for chaos. Walking out of jail gave us the fresh start we needed to the game we'd been dying to play.

Sometimes we let the women walk away. But, we preferred... drawing things out. Breaking them down piece by piece, watching their hope flicker out before we sent them off to whatever god they begged for. We were generous like that.

And this island? Our newest playground. The women seemed too trusting. Too soft. Too easy.

Perfect.

Game on, Josie Hale. Game on.

*** Vincent ***

Thomas and I were halfway through our beers, hooting and hollering for our favorite football team to win the game, when my phone buzzed. That sound cut through everything—the crowd noise on TV, Thomas's running commentary, even my heartbeat.

I recognized the alert at once. I'd programmed it for her. It told me my pretty little realtor had finally walked into her bedroom.

Thomas leaned forward, eyes gleaming. "That it?"

I tilted the phone just enough for him to see the notification. His grin spread slow and mean. We'd been waiting for this moment all night.

"It's time," I said.

I grabbed my phone and opened the app.

"The fucking cops?" Thomas blurted, then grabbed my phone. "Wait, why the fuck is all that lingerie on her bed? What the fuck did you do?"

While he stared at me with his eyes bulging out like a cartoon character, I took my phone back. I still hadn't told Thomas about the lingerie on the bed episode, and since the app was only on my phone, he didn't have a front-row seat to it—until now.

"I told you to only install the damn camera and get the hell out," Thomas snarled and waved the phone in my face. "So explain to me why you deviated from our plan?"

Thomas's face turned red. Had he been a cartoon character, steam would have been coming out of his ears along with a loud whistle sound. I kept my mouth shut. Then, his gaze sharpened, and his mouth dropped open.

"That's why you were late picking me up. It wasn't the installation that took too long." He jabbed his finger at the screen. "You were late because you did that shit."

I grabbed my phone out of his hand. I'd had enough of his temper tantrums.

"I couldn't just leave the camera," I scoffed. "I figured throwing the clothes on her bed would be a distraction."

"Well, you figured wrong. That distraction can be disastrous. Please tell me you didn't leave any prints?" Thomas glared at me.

"I'm not an idiot. I wore gloves." I looked at him like he had three heads and prayed he didn't ask me if I did anything else in her bedroom.

I mean, I wore gloves until I pleasured myself. But Thomas didn't need to know that. That was my secret, and I would take it to the grave. We continued watching the cops collecting all the evidence on the bed. Josie showed up only once to go to the closet and pack some clothes.

"You didn't fuck with her closet too, did you?"

"No," I grunted. "I only messed with the lingerie in her dresser drawer and set up the camera."

"Let's hope they don't find the fucking camera." Thomas grumbled. "Do you think she'll go back home? I mean, she packed a fucking suitcase."

"I don't know. Let's leave it for a few days." I whispered.

We watched the feed until the cops finally cleared out. The detective was the last to leave—of course he was. He moved around the room like a caged lion, pacing, searching, listening for something only he could hear—always hunting.

My pulse stayed tight the whole time he prowled along the wall facing the bed. If he had leaned closer to the flower bouquet painting, he might've seen the cut in the canvas and found the camera staring him in the face.

But luck was on our side today.

When he finally flipped off the lights and walked out, we both exhaled in relief. Close call. Too close. And it meant one thing. Next time, we'd have to be smarter than a lion that didn't give up the hunt.

Chapter 11

Boiling Mad

Lucian

Motherfucker! Why the hell did I think stopping by was a good idea? As I reached the back of the house, her voice carried through the yard—telling Ryker she loved him. The words stopped me cold. My chest tightened, my pulse spiked, and for a second I couldn't breathe.

Then Judge barked, sharp and sudden. Should've known the damn dog would scent me before I even stepped close and blow my cover. I should've walked away the moment I heard her voice. But I couldn't. Not when every part of me was burning with the thought that maybe she'd already chosen someone else.

Coming around that corner, I was grateful for Judge's greeting because the way Ryker stood in front of Josie, so protective, caused my gut to clench. *How the hell had I missed their chemistry?* I'd seen them together a hundred times over the years, but one of them was always dating someone else. I guess that kept me from noticing the way they looked at each other when they thought no one was watching.

Now it was obvious—painfully obvious. They loved each other. From ten feet away, the truth hit me like a sucker punch. *Shit.* I needed to back off before I ended up booking a one-way ticket to Hurt Island.

My mouth watered at the sight of the two juicy steaks on the grill. But I was not about to stick around while they eye-fucked each other. Hell no. I hightailed it out of there, drove through a drive-thru, and went to my office to review all the evidence.

Bless Kyle and Jamie—they were nothing if not thorough. They'd already uploaded all the photos for the report, every angle covered. I printed the files and spread the copies across my desk, letting the scene take shape in front of me.

Looking at all that lingerie, I couldn't help but picture Josie wearing it. I'd never seen her naked, but my imagination was fan-fucking-tastic. Her rosy nipples and soft breasts trapped behind all that lace, ready to be set free into my hand or mouth.

Did she shave her nether region or go au naturel? Not that I cared either way. Her body in clothes was beautiful to me, so I'm sure I would love her naked. I would make sure to worship every inch of her delectable skin from the top of her head to the tips of her toes.

My body hardened, and I needed to think about the case, not a naked Josie wearing any of those items—time to call Kyle and see if he had any other info. I'd try his desk phone first. He was a workaholic, like me.

"Hey, Detective," Kyle answered on the first ring.

"I figured you'd be here."

"Just like you," Kyle chuckled. "I figured you'd want an updated report. The items with potential fingerprints have already been sent for processing."

"You figured right." I smiled, not that Kyle could see me.

"I'm uploading the last of the information now. I told Jamie to go home—I'd finish it up. I'll let you know as soon as they identify Thomas Kincaid."

"So it was an alias?" I rubbed the stubble on my chin.

"Yep. But JCSD and the feds are working on it."

"Sounds good. Don't go home too late. I'm sure your wife and kids would love to see you before they go to bed."

"I won't. But Julie understands. She knows I can't leave work until I've processed all the information. Otherwise, I'll toss and turn all night. And she hates that."

"Yeah," I chuckled. "That would suck if you kept her up."

"Yup, no doghouse for me. I learned after fifteen years—happy wife, happy life."

"I get that. Have a good night."

"Will do, Detective. Don't stay here all night."

"Yeah, we'll see. I don't have such a wonderful woman waiting for me at home warming my bed."

"You could. The ladies love you." Kyle laughed.

"Yeah, yeah, yeah. See you tomorrow."

The guys always gave me a hard time. My longest relationship was two months. After that, the ladies tired of my long hours and distracted attention.

I tried, but I couldn't help it if every case was a puzzle I had to solve. I was married to my job, and they hated it. Kyle was lucky Julie was so understanding.

"Night, Detective."

I hung up the phone and opened the rest of the files Kyle sent over. After printing everything, I gathered the photos and pinned them to the corkboard in my office. The lingerie shots and the enlarged copies of the notes went on the left side—together they painted the clearest picture of the stalker's escalation. On the right, I grouped every detail related to Josie's break in—front doors, bathroom doors, bedroom doors—anything the intruder had touched or manipulated.

Along the bottom, I laid out the evidence from the other house break-ins: timestamps, entry points, all the disturbed items, and what wasn't. *How were they all connected?* Stepping back, the board finally gave me a broader view of the pattern forming. Or maybe the pattern I *didn't* want to admit was there.

On another corkboard, I grabbed a stack of index cards and began outlining each incident using Josie's statements. One by one, I pinned them in the order as they occurred, starting with the incident at the house on Leonard Street—clean, organized, impossible to ignore.

For the unidentified suspect, we used generic silhouettes until we had a confirmed ID. I printed out a blacked-out head-and-shoulders profile and wrote **THOMAS KINCAID** across the top in bold letters, then pinned it dead center on the first board.

Next, I printed a photo of Josie and placed it on the second board—close enough to show the connection, far enough to keep my hands from shaking.

The moment I stepped back to look at the big picture, something hot and ugly twisted in my chest. Seeing them both on my wall together—her bright, defiant smile near a faceless predator—made my pulse thrum with a low, simmering anger.

She didn't belong anywhere near him. Not on paper. Not in a file. Not in his goddamn sights.

Studying the board again. The notes. The lingerie. The attempts to grab her. It was all too calculated, too rehearsed. Kincaid wasn't just intruding—he was mapping her life, inch by inch. Testing boundaries. Building up to something bigger.

My jaw clenched. I braced my hands on my hips, forcing a slow breath.

"Not happening," I muttered under my breath. "You are not getting to her. Not on my watch."

The words swirled around my mouth like a promise. No, more like a vow.

*** .

I spent the entire night in my office, combing through every detail and pinning everything related to the case on the board. I didn't care how small the detail—minor details were often the ones that cracked a case wide open.

By the time the first streaks of sunlight cut across my desk, my eyes burned and my coffee cup was empty. I pushed back from the board, sighed, and reached for my office door. I needed a fresh pot if I was going to make any sense of this today.

Someone beat me to the coffeepot. The bittersweet scent of fresh coffee drew me toward the lounge. I poured my cup and headed back to my office.

My mind was spinning. I had so many questions for Josie and her co-workers. Opening up a new document, I typed them up so I wouldn't forget them.

Knock, knock.

Chief peeked into my office.

"I was afraid you'd be here. Did you spend the night?" Chief walked in and sat in the chair opposite my desk with his cup of coffee.

"I did. I'm missing something, and it's driving me fucking crazy." I rubbed my eyes.

"You should go home. Maybe it will come to you after a few hours of sleep."

"Nah, that never happens." I drank some coffee.

"Anything I can help you with?"

I motioned with my coffee toward my side wall.

"Holy shit," Chief stood and walked over to it. "You've been busy."

"Yep." I followed him.

"Why is one of your shirts hanging over the left side?" Chief grabbed the bottom corner and lifted it before I could tell him. He let out a low whistle. "Wow, now I see what you were covering."

"I didn't want every person who walked in here to see Josie's underwear posted on my wall. It's on a need-to-know basis."

"Gotcha." Chief let go of my shirt, and it covered the images. "Any prints?"

"Kyle sent everything to Jones County and the feds. They'll get back to him the moment something lines up. They understand the stakes—and they know this one isn't like the others. A woman's life is at stake."

"Let me know if we need to ask them for any other help. I know when you focus on a case, you really delve in and don't stop."

"Thanks," I mumbled while I looked over all the evidence. "Look at all this. Does anything look out-of-place other than the drawer that's upside down on the floor? I've been staring at it all night, and I feel like I'm missing something."

Something wasn't right, but I couldn't quite put my finger on it. All the other drawers were untouched. The clothes in the closet also hung untouched, and nothing was out of place in the bathroom.

"What's that black thing sticking out from under the bed?" Chief pointed to the black object partially covered by the bedspread.

"Is that a man's underwear?" I leaned into the photo.

Holy shit. It blended into the bedspread. *Was it a man's underwear or another one of Josie's panties?* I ran to my desk and called Jamie since Kyle had probably slept in.

"Hey, Detective. What's up?"

"Pull up photo evidence number eight and stay on the line with me."

"Okay. Got it." Keys clicked away as Jamie opened the file. "Go."

"In the bottom right corner, do you see that black thing?"

"Yep."

"Is that part of a man's underwear?"

"Not sure, but I know we didn't bag it. Dammit. I'm sorry, Detective."

"No problem. I'm gonna drive over there now and recheck the scene. I'll bring back anything else I find."

"I can't believe I missed that. Kyle is gonna kill me," Jamie groaned.

"Nah, he'll just fuck with you for a long-ass time." I chuckled because Jamie was in for some serious ribbing—not only from Kyle. Everyone in the department would get in on that one. "I'll let you know if I find anything else. Don't beat yourself up. See you later."

"Later." Jamie hung up.

"We are so gonna give him so much shit." Chief shook his head and set his cup of coffee on my desk. "I'm coming with you. Another set of eyes won't hurt."

"Thanks, Chief. I appreciate the help." I grabbed my keys, and we jogged to my car, praying that no one had crossed the police line and that fucking underwear was still there.

Chapter 12

You've Got a Friend

Josie

L ast night had been what I needed. Ry fed me—like he always did when life got rough—and we made it through part of a scary movie while Judge sprawled across my lap like a four-legged security blanket.

At first, I wasn't sure I could handle anything frightening after everything that happened, but I refused to let Thomas Kincaid take that from me too. I didn't want him to win even the smallest battle.

Ry humored me and put the movie on, but after I jumped one too many times—and Judge almost climbed into my shirt trying to "protect" me—Ry switched it to an old rom-com. He didn't tease me or make a big deal out of it. He changed the channel to make me feel better, the way he always does. Leave it to Ry to always know exactly what I need.

I stepped into the kitchen, trying to shake off the last shadows of the night. Cooking always settled me, gave my hands something to do when my mind wouldn't stop spinning. Ry's fridge contained everything I expected—eggs, chopped veggies, everything neat and healthy and so him. I cracked the eggs and whisked them. The familiar motion eased the tightness in my chest. As the pan warmed, I sliced a few tomatoes and let myself breathe for the first time that morning.

Ry had taken care of me without making me feel broken. Now I wanted to return even a small piece of that kindness. Wiping my hands on a towel, I went to find him.

I knocked on Ry's bedroom door and waited. No answer. The silence hung heavier in the air than it should've. I twisted the knob and pushed the door open. He had already made his bed—tight, neat, military-level precise. Judge sat in his doggie bed, tail thumping once in greeting but otherwise keeping still, waiting for directions.

"Hey, Judge." I walked over to him for some loving. Judge rolled onto his back, giving me his belly. "You're such a good boy."

"You wanna rub my belly? I'm a good boy, too." Ry said from the bathroom door.

I glanced up—and almost forgot to breathe. Ry had always been in excellent shape, but damn... he'd taken it to another level. Lean muscle, defined abs, a physique that came from discipline, not vanity. Too bad I'd spent my whole life thinking of him as a brother. Made appreciating the view feel both wrong and... well, a little unfair.

Ry glanced over, catching me mid-stare. One brow lifted—slow, amused, way too knowing.

"Jo," he said, tugging a T-shirt over his head, "if you're gonna gawk, at least hand me my coffee first."

Heat shot up my neck. "I was not gawking."

"Sure," he said, grin widening. "And Judge doesn't shed."

Judge barked once, like he agreed.

I huffed and crossed my arms. "I was just making sure you're alive. When I knocked on your door, you didn't answer. I got worried."

"I didn't mean to worry you, Jo." His frown turned into a smirk. "But feel free to run your hands over my chest and feel my hard abs since you already eye-fucked me." Ry lifted his arms in a bodybuilder pose. "Or would you rather feel my guns?" He wiggled his eyebrows.

"You're such a jerk." I stood and shoved him. He burst out laughing. And just like that, the ridiculous moment passed—back to us being us. "I am not rubbing your belly, your abs, or your guns. But I made you breakfast, so finish up and meet me in the kitchen."

"I could get used to this. I don't have to go into the station, and you're cooking me breakfast. I'll babysit you any day."

I chuckled on my way out.

"Hey, Jo!" Ry shouted. "Can you let Judge out?"

"Yep, come on, Judge. Let's go potty."

Judge followed me, and I opened the sliding door. He ran out, did his business, and came right back.

Ry always had a way of lightening my mood. I plated our breakfast and set the dishes on the table, moving around his kitchen like I'd done it a hundred times—which, honestly, I had. His fridge was predictable, and his drink options even more so. The only things he ever kept on hand were milk and coffee—his one true vice.

Right on cue, his coffee pot began its ritual. Grinding the beans, dropping them in, and filling the kitchen with that rich, comforting morning aroma. I'd grab a cup later. For now, water would do just fine.

I dropped a scoopful of doggie kibble for Judge and waited for Ry.

"Thanks, Jo." Ry came into the kitchen and kissed the top of my head. "I appreciate you."

"I poured you a cup of coffee, but I didn't know if you also wanted water or milk."

"No worries. I'll get some milk." Ry opened the refrigerator. "Do you need anything else?"

"Nope, I'm good. Just waiting for you."

"Don't wait for me. Eat your eggs before they turn cold."

I scooped up a spoonful and took a bite. I wasn't a talented chef, but I could hold my own in the kitchen. Cooking was more of a necessity than a passion—I did it because I had to eat, not because I loved it.

When I was younger, Mom handled all the cooking, and I was the designated dishwasher. As I got older, she taught me a few of her favorite recipes, but she enjoyed the process so much that I sat back and watched, soaking in the warmth of those moments rather than the skills themselves.

"Mm," Ry said with a mouthful. "These eggs are super fluffy, Jo. You put milk in them?"

"I did because I know that's how you like them."

"You can cook for me any day." Ry smiled after he swallowed.

"You're funny." I pointed my fork at him. "You are a better cook than I am."

"Not with eggs." Ry winked at me and then got serious. "How are you feeling today?"

"I'm scared to show a house by myself." The words slipped out before I could swallow them, and my voice cracked. "Which sucks because I'm a fucking realtor and that's... literally my job." I stared down at my eggs, pushing them around the plate like they might give me answers.

Ry's voice softened. "What were you supposed to do today?"

"I have to work at the hotel in the morning until noon," I mumbled. "Then I have another showing at two."

His brow arched. "With Thomas Kincaid?"

"No!" I jerked upright. "God, no. I'm never showing him another house after yesterday." My pulse kicked hard just saying his name. "It's a married couple from the mainland."

Ry nodded once. "Judge and I will go with you."

"All day?"

"Well, yeah." He scoffed. "You heard Detective Lucian. He told me to stick with you. And that's what I plan on doing."

I frowned. "But you'll be bored when I'm at the hotel."

"Nah," Ry stood and rinsed his plate. "Judge and I will recon the place. Check all the entrances, walk the perimeter. We don't mind."

He opened the dishwasher and slid his plate inside before he held out his hand for mine. "You done?"

"Yeah." I handed it over, throat tight. "Thanks."

He washed it without a word, then glanced at me over his shoulder. "Go get dressed, Jo. We'll head out when you're ready."

I nodded, swallowed hard, and headed to the bedroom. When I closed the door behind me, the soft click echoed like a shout. I'd held back everything I didn't have the courage to say. The thought of leaving Ry's house made my palms sweat and my chest tighten, but I couldn't hide here forever.

I had to move forward. I had to stop letting Thomas Kincaid steal space in my mind, my job, my life. Pressing my back to the door, I took a shaky breath, and whispered to myself, *You can do this.*

And for the first time since yesterday with Ry and Judge by my side... I almost believed it.

Chapter 13

Check Mate

Lucian

Chief Alejandro and I ducked under the police tape as we reached Josie's house. Nothing looked different from when I left, which somehow made my skin crawl even more. We headed straight to the bedroom.

That's when we noticed it—a dark shape half-hidden beneath the bed frame. I pulled on gloves and took a small evidence bag from my back pocket. A slow exhale left my chest as I crouched down. Sure enough, I stared at a pair of men's boxer briefs. Stiff in one section. The kind of detail that made my jaw clench.

I lifted the evidence bag and showed it to the chief. "Looks like we've got another calling card."

Chief's mouth tightened as he studied the evidence bag. "Son of a bitch," he muttered, rubbing a hand over his jaw. "He's escalating. Take this to the lab and see if Jones County or the feds can fast-track it."

I swept the room again, muscles tight and ready. The air hung stale, off—like the bastard had forced the walls to keep his secrets. "He's bold," I whispered. "Leaving this evidence behind."

Chief gave a grim nod. "Bold or stupid."

"True," I said, meeting his eyes. "I'm not sure, but I will find out."

Chief studied me for a moment longer. "Does Josie know you're back here this morning?"

"No." My jaw flexed. "And I'd like to keep it that way until we have answers."

Chief sighed, but he didn't argue. He knew me well enough to read the meaning behind my tone.

"Lucian," Chief said quietly, "you think this is personal?"

My stomach went cold. "Yeah," I said. "I do. And I can't wait to get my hands on him," I growled. "How the hell am I going to tell Josie I found this under her bed?"

"I don't know, but it would be best if she heard it from you."

"I'm not so sure about that." I shook my head. "She seems to like Ryker more than me. Maybe he should tell her."

Why was I saying any of this to Chief? Simple. He was the only person I trusted enough to see them. We'd served together in the 75th Ranger Regiment under U.S. Army Special Operations Command. I filled the specialist slot in our nine-man squad, while he led us as staff sergeant. When he left, I followed him to Haven Island PD. We weren't just brothers in blue—we were men who'd bled and fought in the same dirt.

"Don't be a pussy. Man up and claim your girl." Chief snorted.

"What the hell are you talking about?"

"You know you like her. Hell, you've been flirting with her for years. We've all seen it, which is why no one at the station will ask her out. Ryker loves to fuck with you—you're easy prey when it comes to Josie."

"How can you be so sure Ryker doesn't want her?" I braced my hands on my hips.

"Because he's fucking known her since grade school and they've never dated. They think of each other as siblings."

"How the fuck do you know that?" I stopped and glared at him.

"My fucking wife." He crossed his arms and stared at me. "Don't be an idiot. You know she babysat them when they were kids—they've been close for years. Amazing how the guy who notices everything manages to go blind the second Josie's involved."

"Whatever," I grumbled, bagged the underwear, and closed the baggie. "Let's see if we missed anything else."

Chief and I searched under the bed and between the mattresses. We even stripped the sheets and pillowcases off the bed and bagged them. Leaving other evidence behind was not an option. We were taking anything else that looked suspicious. I crouched again, this time running my gloved hand along the underside of the bed frame. Nothing. I checked the vents next—clean. Then the closet, moving aside boxes one by one. Still nothing.

"I'll take these out to the car." Chief grabbed the bags. "Are you coming?"

"Give me another minute."

Something wasn't right. I crossed my arms and looked at the dresser. My eyes did a thorough pass of the top, drawers, and around it. Perfume bottles seemed to be in place. I ran my finger over the top and didn't feel any dust. This was one time I wished Josie had forgotten to dust so I could see if anything was out of place.

I stepped into the bathroom. Everything seemed in order. The shower floor and the sink were dry. I bagged the toothbrush Josie refused to use yesterday, just in case. The way the pervert left those sticky notes, I would've thought he might leave a note on the bathroom mirror, but nope, it remained clean and note-free.

I glanced around at all the pictures hanging on the wall. *Who knew she liked flowers so much?* I wondered if she had a garden out back. Chief stepped into the bedroom.

"Anything?"

"No, but I bagged her toothbrush." I held it up. "Josie was afraid he did something to it. May as well check it out."

Chief stood next to me, no doubt scanning the room like me.

"I just feel like I'm missing something."

My gut clenched, urging me to scan my surroundings rather than retreat. Something was off. Something I'd missed. *But what the hell was it?*

"Did you check all the drawers again?"

"Yep."

"The closet."

"Yep."

"I know you checked the bathroom since I found you in there, and you gave me her toothbrush."

"Yep."

My gaze swept the four corners of her room, clearing each one by habit. I wasn't stepping out until the tension in my gut eased and I'd confirmed I hadn't overlooked a damn thing. My sixth sense never lied—never—and right now it hammered a steady 'Warning, Will Robinson' through my head.

I moved in a controlled pattern, slow and deliberate, circling the space the way I'd been trained. Back and forth, changing angles, checking shadows, assessing entry points and blind spots. Chief held position behind me, staying still but alert, eyes tracking where mine went as he conducted his own silent sweep.

Chief tapped my shoulder. He pulled out his pad and wrote: Listening devices?

I shrugged.

He wrote: I'll go get my bug detector.

I continued to pace and stare at everything. Chief came back and ran it over every surface and object in the room.

"We're clear."

I grabbed his pad, and I wrote: cameras?

We lifted several pictures off the wall, but didn't find anything. A painting of a bouquet of flowers hung facing her bed. A faint glint caught my eye. I removed the canvas. A lens.

Anger surged through me as my fingers closed around the micro-camera mounted behind the canvas, aligned with a hole cut into the center of a flower. A direct line to the bed. To Josie.

"Motherfucker," I muttered under my breath.

Chief heard me and spun around. "What now?"

I pointed.

His eyes widened. "Tell me that's not what I think it is."

"It is," I said, voice tight, fists clenched. "He had eyes in here."

Chief blew out a breath. "He's been watching her. But for how long?"

"Hopefully since yesterday," I grunted, placed my hand over the lens, ripped it off the wall, and turned that shit off. His peeping-Tom days were over. "We'll have to see if Kyle can check the footage."

I took a slow, steadying breath, though it did nothing to calm the heat burning in my chest.

"Now I'm glad he left such a fucking sick display on the bed. Otherwise, Josie would've come home and changed her clothes in front of that fucking pervert." I placed the camera into an evidence bag.

Chief shook his head. "Let's get this to Kyle. He should be able to trace the model, and where they bought it. Maybe he can find the buyer or an IP address."

"We've got to move fast," I growled, my eyes glued to the tiny lens. "Thomas Kincaid, or whatever the fuck he's calling himself, isn't stopping just because we found his toy. He's escalating too fast for my liking."

"Agreed." Chief swallowed. "Lucian...she's in deep trouble."

"Yeah." I nodded once. "But so is he."

"Lights and sirens, Detective!" Chief hollered and ran out of the room. "If he saw you rip it off the wall, they're already covering their tracks."

"You read my mind, Chief." I took off after him.

Stupid Plan

Vincent

I slept hard, only to jolt awake when my phone buzzed—sharp enough to cut through the silence in my bedroom. My eyes snapped open. *Had Josie come back? Why did she pack a bag if she planned on returning the next day as if nothing had happened?*

I snatched my phone from the nightstand, pushed out of bed, and cleared the hall in three long strides before pounding on Thomas's door. After my lingerie debacle, he demanded to be told everything—especially when it came to her.

He didn't respond, firing up my irritation. I didn't have the patience for his lazy mornings. I twisted the knob hard and shoved the door open.

"Thomas," I barked, kicking the side of his mattress. "Wake up. We've got movement."

Thomas groaned and yanked the pillow over his head. "What the hell, Vincent? It's barely morning."

I ripped the pillow away. "Get up."

He blinked through the dim light, hair sticking up in every direction, eyes narrowing as the fog cleared. "This better be about her."

"It is." I shoved my phone in his face. "My alert went off."

That woke him faster than a fresh cup of coffee. He shot upright, snatching the phone out of my hand.

"She's back home?"

"I don't know yet," I said, taking my phone back. "But something triggered the feed."

Thomas swung his legs over the mattress, rubbing his face. "About damn time," he muttered, a grin forming. "I knew she wouldn't stay away."

I sat next to him, but didn't answer. A knot in my gut told me this wasn't good news—this was movement we didn't expect. And unexpected was dangerous.

"Oh, no!" I hollered. "The lion's back."

"What the fuck are they doing?" Thomas murmured.

Bent over my phone, we watched the detective and the Chief tear the bed apart. The Chief took the bedding and walked out, but the detective kept pacing that fucking room—again and again and again.

"You're not gonna fucking find it," I laughed. "Stupid cop. Let's grab a beer and watch this cop make a fool out of himself."

"It's too fucking early for a beer." Thomas groaned but stood.

"It's never too early for a beer and a show," I said, already grinning like an idiot. We moved in sync toward the kitchen, shoulder to shoulder, neither of us willing to take our eyes off the live feed on the screen. The chief returned, and now they both continued to scan Josie's bedroom again, and every second they lingered made my jaw tighten.

Thomas yanked open the fridge, grabbed two beers, and shoved one into my hand without looking away. I twisted the cap off mine, never breaking focus. If they found the mini camera—we were fucked.

"So far, so good." I muttered.

We sat on the couch, eyes locked on my phone.

I smiled. "He's not gonna find it. I'm that good."

"Make it louder." Thomas pointed to the side of my phone. "I can't hear what they're saying. Is the volume not working?"

I raised the volume all the way, but the only sound we heard was a faint, crackling hiss.

"Oh, wait. They're checking for a listening device. Stupid fucks." I slapped my thigh. "I outsmarted you assholes!" I screamed at my phone.

"We're clear." The Chief said.

"What the hell is he writing now?" I hissed.

If Thomas got any closer to my phone, he'd end up leaving grease marks on it with his fucking nose.

"Hey." I shoved him away from my phone. "Back off, you're blocking my view." Thomas shot me a nasty glare before we both refocused on the screen.

"Oh, shit. No, no, no, no, no!" My hands shot to my head, gripping hard as disbelief crashed into panic when the detective lifted the canvas off the wall. "No fucking way!"

"I guess they're not so stupid after all." Thomas jabbed a finger in my face, fury sharpening every word. "You fucking idiot."

My stomach plummeted because instead of Josie's bedroom, we got a clear shot of that fucking detective's smug face staring straight into the camera—letting us know he'd already won. His gloved hand covered the lens, and the camera feed died. A chill crawled up my spine. Not fear—rage. Pure, burning rage. Thomas glared at me, waiting for me to explode. But I didn't. Not yet.

My mind spun with different ways to outmaneuver that arrogant asshole. Who the hell did he think he was, staring us down like he had us figured out—like he didn't fear us for a single damn minute? He didn't know it yet, but he upped the ante.

"I can't believe he fucking found it," I murmured.

"If you'd done what I told you to do—" Thomas pointed his finger in my face "—the police wouldn't be there again, and we would've gotten a nice peep show. Now they have the camera. You fucked up."

"Fuck!" A scream tore out of me, and I hurled my phone across the room with everything I had—like a pitcher firing a fastball straight down the line, praying for a strike.

"Nice." Thomas slammed his beer down, foam spilling over the rim. "Now we have to purchase a new fucking camera and a phone, dumbass. Can they find our location?"

"First, I need to wipe everything from that camera so nothing can get traced back to us."

"Us?" Thomas shot up from the couch, snatched my phone off the floor, and threw it at me. "Fucking fix this. I told you not to do anything except install the camera. You fucked this up. You unfuck it up or I'm gonna fuck you up."

Shit! My cracked screen refused to recognize my face. Wait—maybe the screen protector took the hit instead of the actual screen. I peeled it off, but nope—the real screen stared back at me, shattered.

Dammit. I had to enter my password several times before it finally opened.

At least the phone still worked. I deleted the app and my account, but a sick thought hit me—*what if it still routed back to me?* I sprinted to my bedroom and backed up the phone to my computer. I couldn't risk losing everything. The second the backup finished, I ran a factory reset, wiping the phone clean. The screen went black.

Good.

I dropped it to the floor and stomped on it, crushing my phone until it splintered into pieces. Tomorrow I'd buy a new one. With every shard scooped into my cupped hands, I went to find Thomas.

"It's done." I thrust the broken pieces toward him.

"Isn't everything backed up somewhere out there?" Thomas waved his arms around in the air.

Information never disappears, even when you can't see it—but Thomas didn't need to know that. I didn't need his condescension stacked on top of everything else. All I wanted now was to find Josie and make her pay. No one had ever found my cameras before. Those things cost a damn fortune.

"No," I grunted. "We're good, but we need to adjust our plan. We've gotta stay several steps ahead of that detective because if he's on to us..."

Thomas finished the sentence for me. His gaze was calm, cold, and deliberate. "...then this game just got a hell of a lot more dangerous."

He glared at me and left the room.

Chapter 15

Ocean Breeze Resort

Josie

I needed to work. If I stayed in Ry's house all day, I'd go insane—my thoughts spiraling. I wasn't built to sit still or hide from my life. I moved, I pushed, I handled things. Right now, I needed to get to the resort and lose myself in my shift. Work was the only thing that still felt normal.

"Thanks for coming, Ry and Judge," I got out of the car.

"Hey, Jo." Ry caught my arm and gently pulled me to a stop. His voice was calm, steady—the kind that settled nerves without trying. "If you recognize anyone, or if anything even feels off, text me. We'll be close."

He clipped Judge's leash, giving me one more reassuring look before heading toward the side of the hotel to start his perimeter check. Judge trotted beside him, already in work mode.

I entered the lobby and went straight to the guest services desk. The resort manager, Mr. Gene Sanders, was behind the counter.

"I thought you were taking a few days off?" He frowned.

"I need to work. It helps to keep my mind off what happened." I went around the desk and stored my purse under the counter. "Sorry, I'm not in uniform."

"I'm just glad you're here and you're okay." Gene gave me a side hug.

I loved Gene. He'd been one of my dad's best friends for as long as I could remember—the kind of man who slipped into the background of my childhood like a favorite uncle. He was also my first employer, giving me a job the moment I turned sixteen. I started as a maid, cleaning rooms after school, then worked my way into the restaurant, and eventually up to the front desk.

The front desk became my favorite job at the entire resort. I loved watching the doors open, catching that first spark in a guest's eyes when they stepped into the lobby and absorbed the charm of Haven Island for the first time. Welcoming people to the place I grew up—the place that shaped me—was like sharing a piece of home with every single one of them.

"Thanks, Gene."

"I'm gonna go back to my desk. Call me if you need me." Gene motioned to the phone on the desk.

"I will," I smiled and logged into the computer.

"I mean it, Josie. If you feel you can't finish your shift. I'll finish it for you." Gene waited by the doorway, waiting for me to look him in the eye.

I glanced up. "Thank you. I promise I'll buzz you, but I'm okay."

Gene nodded and slipped through the door behind the guest services desk—straight into his office. He preferred being within arm's reach of a problem, ready to step in before it ever became one, yet far enough to finish his work without constant interruption.

Everyone kept giving me the same mantra—*call me if you need me.* And while I appreciated it, part of me grew tired of feeling like I needed a babysitter to walk through my own life. I didn't want anyone treating me like a fragile flower. Kincaid might have shaken me, but he wouldn't make me run scared forever. I refused to hand him that kind of power.

Besides, now I had Ry and Judge by my side. With those two around, the odds of Kincaid trying anything again were slim to none. He'd be stupid even to attempt it. My first guest came through the automatic front doors, snapping my mind into work mode.

"Good morning," I smiled. "Are you checking in?"

The rest of the morning went well. I never had to text Ry. Every once in a while, Ry and Judge strolled through the lobby. Ry would make eye contact, I would nod, and he would continue on his way. At noon, Tiffany came in to replace me.

"Josie!" Tiffany ran behind the counter and strangled me with her bear hug. "I heard what happened. Are you okay?"

"How did you hear?" I tilted my head and frowned.

Tiffany's mouth tightened, one eyebrow rising in a silent challenge.

"Never mind," I sighed, holding up a hand. "It's fine. I'm good."

News traveled faster than the tide in a small beach town. Of course, she'd heard. She'd bet money the locals talked about it this morning over coffee at the Hi Café.

"Do you need a place to crash?" she asked.

"No, I'm staying with Ryker and Judge."

"Ooo, I'd love to stay with that hunka man and his gorgeous dog." Tiffany winked at me.

Yeah, Ry always got the ladies' attention, though he didn't date a lot. And if Judge didn't like the girl, she was last night's news.

"Are you sharing his bed?" Tiffany wiggled her eyebrows.

"No," I laughed at her antics. "We're just friends. He's like a brother to me, so get your mind out of the gutter."

"How can I when he is yummy enough to eat?" Tiffany licked her lips.

"Speaking of his yumminess, I need to text him so I can eat lunch before my next showing." I pulled out my phone and texted Ry.

"Josie," Tiffany stated in a firm voice. "Are you seriously gonna show a house after what happened?"

"Uh, yeah. It's my job, and I'm so close to not having to work two jobs." I grabbed my purse. "Besides, your hunka man is coming with me, so I'll be safe." I winked at her.

She was so lost in her fantasy that she didn't notice Ryker walking up to the desk.

"Tiffany's coming with us?" Ry asked, one eyebrow arched.

Tiffany jolted upright and spun to face him. "Hi, Ryker! Hi, Judge! How are my favorite guys?"

Ry gave her a polite nod. "We're good. Jo, you ready?"

"Yep." I hugged Tiffany and stepped out from behind the desk. "I'll talk to you later."

"Okay!" Tiffany waved enthusiastically. "Call me if you need me."

Ugh, I needed to learn to live with those six words because everyone and their mother kept saying them to me constantly. I shouldn't complain, though. Having caring friends and being loved gave me a warm and fuzzy feeling inside.

Ry and I headed toward the door, and I couldn't stop smiling to myself. Tiffany had a huge crush on him, but he was oblivious. Judge picked up on it more than he did, and he was a dog.

Tiffany didn't do subtle. The girl honed in on Ryker the minute he walked into a room. And that dreamy look she gave him before we left? Classic Tiffany.

Part of me hoped she'd eventually fall for someone who noticed her—because she'd make a killer girlfriend. The other part? Well... Ry's utter lack of awareness oddly soothed me because he was the same sweet, steady guy I grew up with. For all his muscles and Delta Force training, he still moved through life like an adorable golden retriever who had no idea every woman within fifty feet wanted to pet him.

As we stepped outside, Ry shook his head, a faint grin tugging at the corner of his mouth. Judge trotted between us, nose to the ground like he already had a mission.

"She's got it bad," Ryker murmured.

I blinked. "Wait—you actually noticed?"

He snorted. "Jo, I'm not blind. Just... selective." He held the door open for me. "Besides, Tiffany gets that look in her eye every time I walk by. Judge thinks she's going to feed him a whole steak if he stares cute enough."

Judge barked as if in agreement.

Ryker shot the dog a look. "See? Even he knows."

I laughed under my breath; the tension easing just a little.

Ry glanced at me, softer this time. "Don't worry. I know she's just being sweet. I'm not looking to break any hearts. Besides, she's too young for me."

"Oh, my God. We're only thirty. You act like she's twenty years younger than you."

"She's ten years younger than us, and you very well know there is a huge difference between twenty and thirty as opposed to thirty and forty."

"Whatever." I rolled my eyes.

"Where do you want to eat?"

"Now I know you're an old thirty if you have to ask me that question. No wonder you think she's too young. You're old enough to lose your memory."

"Ha ha. Hi Grill it is."

***

We teased each other the whole drive, slipping back into our usual rhythm. Judy seated us in a booth, and we both ordered our regulars without even looking at the menu. If I didn't eat at home, Hi Grill ranked a close second. It always tasted better than my cooking, and I didn't have to wash dishes when I finished.

We talked while we waited for our food—Ry told me about his rounds at the hotel, how uneventful everything had been, how nothing and no one suspicious had shown up on the property. I heard his reassurance loud and clear. *You're safe.*

"Do you have any updates on my case?"

"Nothing yet." Ry shook his head.

When our meals arrived, we dug in and kept talking about anything other than the case. The conversation flowed as easily as it always did.

Ry wiped his mouth when he finished his meal. "Let's go to the grocery store after your showing. I want to buy some lunchmeat and chicken to cook on the grill."

"Sounds good. I don't want to keep eating out." I was on a budget, and buying lunch or dinner several times a week was going to delay my plans.

"Me neither." Ry patted his stomach. "Gotta stay in tip-top shape to keep up with Judge."

"I'm pretty sure your six-pack abs aren't going away anytime soon." I shot him a sideways grin, eyebrows raised as if challenging him to deny it.

Ry had been a workout fanatic ever since he took a weightlifting class in high school. He loved the discipline, the routine—and yeah, he loved the attention his physique got him back then. Girls lined up for a chance with him. He had an extremely active social life.

But lately? He'd quieted down. Pulled back. He didn't date as much as he used to. Something must've happened, something he wasn't ready to share with me. And Ry only kept things to himself when they messed with his heart. Sometimes I could get him to talk to me about it, but more often than not, he shut down.

I glanced up at the clock on the wall inside Hi Grill. I had a twenty-minute window to pay my bill and then go to the house to meet with my clients. Time to switch gears.

"We've gotta go." I caught Judy's eye and waved her over.

She bustled to our table with a smile. "Do you guys need anything else?"

"Just the check," I said. "I have a house to show in twenty minutes."

Judy turned her attention to Ryker, giving him that classic *you'd better say yes to my question* mother stare. "Are you going with her?"

"Yes, ma'am." Ry put a hand over his heart like he was taking an oath. "Judge and I are sticking to her like glue today."

"Don't you dare let her out of your sight," Judy warned, pointing a finger right in his face.

"Yes, ma'am." Ry's grin widened as she walked away. "She is such a mother hen to you girls."

"Yeah," I said tenderly. "Judy's always been there for me. Especially now that my mom's hardly ever home."

"I bet you miss your mom." Ry's expression softened.

"Every day." I took a sip of water, wiped my mouth with a napkin, and dropped the napkin on my empty plate. "But I'm glad my dad retired and they get to travel. She and Dad spent their whole lives taking care of everyone on this island... taking care of me. So when they finally hit the road, I wanted them to enjoy every minute."

Ry didn't push. He never did. He could always sense when I had more bottled up, even before I knew how to say it. And, like the best friend he'd always been, he waited—silent, patient, giving me space to breathe. He knew this part of me too well. The part that tried to act strong, but failed when the cracks showed.

"I'm happy for them," I continued. "I really am. They deserve to see the world." I swallowed. "But sometimes it feels like they're out there living big, exciting lives, and I'm just... here. Working. Managing everything alone. I could use one of my mom's hugs right now."

Ryker's hand brushed mine—a silent squeeze, nothing more. Strong. Steady.

"Have you told them what's going on?"

"No." I shrugged. "If I say anything, they'll ditch the RV wherever they are and be on the next flight home. Besides," I added with a grin, "I have you and Judge to protect me. What more could a girl want?"

"You are not buttering me up with that look." Ry squinted at me, trying to figure out what angle I was playing.

"What look?" I asked, all innocence.

"Never mind," he muttered with a sigh, shaking his head. "You always win anyway."

"You're such a sucker for a damsel in distress," I snickered.

"You're not alone, Jo," he said gently, fully aware I'd tried to shift the focus onto him instead of myself. "You've got people. You've got us."

Ry gave my hand a firm squeeze before letting go, then waved it in the air.

"That's the best part of living in a small town," he said with a laugh. "If your parents aren't around, just go to your neighbor—they'll parent you for free."

And in that moment—between the scent of Judy's coffee brewing, the warm hum of diners chatting, and Ry looking at me like he meant every word—I believed him.

"So true."

"Here you go." Judy placed the bill on the table and placed her hand on my shoulder. "Call me if you need anything."

Those damn six words. I reached for the bill, but Ry was quicker.

"I got it." He pulled out his wallet.

"I can leave the tip." I took out my wallet.

"Nope," he made a popping sound at the end of the word. "It's on me. Besides, you know Judy always gives the officers a discount.

When Ry laid the bill on the table with a few folded bills on top, I noticed the discount right away—but his tip was for the full price. The gesture made me smile. I always did the same whenever Judy slipped me a deal on a meal. It's our unspoken way of taking care of each other.

"Okay. But I'm paying for the groceries." I slid out of the booth.

"We'll see." Ry draped his arm over my shoulder and grabbed Judge's leash.

Chapter 16

Put a Rush on It

Lucian

Chief and I ran into the forensics lab. Chief dropped the garbage bag on the floor next to Kyle. I kept my baggie in hand. His desk already overflowed with evidence bags and papers.

Kyle whirled his chair around and stared at the bag next to his desk before he noticed the baggie in my hand. "I see you found lots of goodies for me. Damn, I can't believe I missed all that."

"We've kept you very busy between Lincoln and Elias. I think you need another helper." Chief crossed his arms and quirked his eyebrow.

"Yeah, yeah, yeah. I've heard that before." Kyle sighed.

"Look, I'll even do you a solid and let you choose your assistant. And—" Chief continued sweetening the deal "—I'll include you in the interview process."

"I think it's an excellent idea, Kyle," I blurted. "Why not train Jamie to handle more than photos and filing your reports? He's been with the department for a couple of years—he knows what you need."

"Yeah, I could use the help." Kyle nodded, eyes drifting to the pile of items on his desk. "Jamie's a good guy. We work well together."

"Perfect." Chief slapped him on the back. "I'll talk to him as soon as his shift starts today."

"What about the interview?" Kyle asked with a frown.

Chief lifted a brow. "Do you want to interview anyone else?"

"No."

"Then it's done." Chief gave a firm nod. "Jamie gets the job—if he wants it."

"Thanks, Chief." Kyle broke into a smile.

"Julie's gonna thank you for that decision." I spoke up. "I'm sure she'll enjoy having you home at a decent hour."

"I'm sure you're right." Kyle grinned and pointed at the baggie in my hand with the black underwear. "I take it this is the black item under the bed?"

"Yep," I agreed and handed it to him. "That lovely item has a dried substance on it. Chief and I think it might be semen, but we need you to verify it."

"Perfect. I love unknown dried substances," Kyle said wryly and tossed it onto his desk. "What's in the bag?"

"Because of the unknown dried substance...." I pointed to the evidence now on his desk. "We stripped the bed and brought all the sheets in, too. I'm hoping we can match his DNA to someone in the system."

Kyle nodded.

"The underwear should be enough for that, but more evidence never hurts." Chief nudged the bag with his shoe.

"And for our ultimate gift to you..." I pulled a baggie from my jacket pocket. "We found a camera aimed at the bed—set up to record Josie."

"Holy shit," Kyle muttered.

"Can you trace the IP address or something that links us to a suspect? In a perfect world, the IP holder and the DNA come back as the same person—fingers crossed."

Kyle grabbed the underwear baggie.

"Wait." I thrust the camera at him. "Do this first because our suspect might have seen us when we found it and is getting rid of evidence as we speak."

"Why the hell didn't you start with that, Chatty Cathy?" Kyle slipped on a pair of gloves, pulled the camera from the baggie, and hooked it up to his computer.

"Chatty Cathy, my ass. I'm not the one rambling about interviews," I shot back with a glare.

"Huhn." Kyle snorted. "Whatever."

"I'm gonna call Ryker and give him an update," I said over my shoulder as I headed out of the room.

Jamie walked down the hallway heading my way. "Hey, Jamie. Chief wants to talk to you." I motioned with my thumb behind me. "He's in there with Kyle."

"Uh, okay, thanks."

I headed to my office and shut the door. Time to call Ryker. He answered on the second ring.

"Hey, Detective. What's up?" he said a little too casually.

"We found more stuff in Josie's bedroom." I snapped. "Is she there with you?"

"Yes, and No."

I froze in my tracks. "What the hell does that mean, yes and no? I don't have time to screw around with you, Ryker. Are you with her or not?"

"Yes, I am with her while she shows a house, but no, I am not in the same room as her." A soft rustle followed—him shifting, going alert, glancing around until it finally hit him that this wasn't a joke. "Heading her way now."

My teeth clenched so hard my jaw hurt. "Why the fuck not! What if she gets attacked again?"

Ry let out a breath that told me he was seconds from rolling his eyes. "Pretty sure she can outrun the seventy-year-old couple looking for a beach house. But just to ease your mind—Judge is with them."

I pinched the bridge of my nose, trying to smother the spike of panic clawing its way up my throat. Judge was competent—hell, half the time I trusted the dog more than I trusted people. Still, it didn't stop the anger simmering just under my skin.

"You're such a dick."

"Yes, Detective, I do have a large one," Ryker chuckled. "But I'm more than just my penis."

"I'm gonna shove it down your mouth if you don't stop fucking with me."

"I'm not interested in fucking you," Ryker snorted. "I bat for the other team."

Fucker loved to rile me.

"Can you be serious for a minute?"

"Yep." Ryker's voice dropped an octave. "What did you find?"

"Ryker, listen to me," I said, each word measured. "I need eyes on her at all times. It's not a normal case anymore. We found evidence that he's been watching her. Recording her. And he's escalating."

I ran through everything with Ryker and asked him where they were. Ry went silent. I could feel the shift in his demeanor as the weight of my words settled on him.

"Got it," he said, voice low now. Serious. "I won't leave her side."

"You'd better not," I muttered. "Don't tell her what's going on. I'll update her when I have more evidence."

"I can tell her what you have so far."

"No, I'll do it." I preferred to be the one to tell Josie what I had found. That began another argument with Ryker until I heard her voice.

"Ry, we can go now. They left to think about the house. Who's on the phone?"

"Detective Lucian. Hang on, I'll put him on speakerphone."

"Why are you calling Ry?" Josie's accusatory voice came through loud and clear. "What's going on?"

"Josie, I need to talk to you. In person. Ryker's going to text me where you are." My phone dinged. I clicked on the address. "I'll be there in ten minutes. I need you guys to sit tight and wait for me."

"Okay. I'll start turning off the lights and closing up the house."

"Thanks. See you soon."

I slid my phone into my pocket, pulse still pounding, the air around me thick with the certainty that every second Josie was out of my sight was another second too close to danger. Because the police station was in the middle of the island, I wasn't far from their location.

***

I pulled into the driveway of the white bungalow and parked next to Ryker's K9 patrol vehicle. When I knocked on the door, Ryker opened it.

"Did you tell her?" I asked before I stepped inside.

"No." Ryker shook his head. "You told me not to."

"Thanks."

I wiped my feet on the welcome mat outside and followed Ryker inside. Judge sat like a perfect soldier in front of Josie—until he spotted me. Then he launched himself across the room, planting both front paws on my shoulders like he expected me to hold all eighty pounds of enthusiasm.

Even bracing for it didn't help. I still stumbled back a step. You try catching a Belgian Malinois launching himself at you at full speed. It's like being hugged by a missile.

"Hey, Judge." I rubbed both sides of his face and pressed a few quick kisses to the top of his head. He mewled and covered my cheek with a wet lick.

"Judge, come," Ryker ordered. Judge trotted to his side and dropped onto his haunches, all business again.

I stepped farther into the living room. "Josie," I said gently, "how are you?"

"Fine. What's going on?"

Fine. Right. Her leg bounced so hard the cushion vibrated. If that was fine, then I was the Queen of England. I sat across from her, leaning forward.

"We found some additional items in your bedroom. Our forensics team is going through them now."

Her eyes sharpened with fear. "What did you find?"

"A camera."

Josie drew in a shaky breath. Her hands lifted to her face, her head sinking into them as if the weight became too much. She broke my damn heart. My hands itched to reach for her, to offer something—anything—but would she let me?

"Oh, my God."

I hesitated, unsure whether to tell her the rest.

Ryker didn't give me the chance. "Tell her all of it," he said bluntly.

Josie's gaze snapped between the two of us. "What is Ry talking about?"

I swallowed and kept my voice steady. "We found a pair of men's underwear in your bedroom. There's... an unknown substance on it. We sent it to the lab."

Josie's head shot up, eyes wide. "You're saying he—" She choked on the words. "He pleasured himself in my room?"

"We believe so, yes," I breathed. "The lab will confirm it."

"Are you serious?" Her voice cracked into a sharp, horrified pitch as she lurched to her feet. "That pervert jerked himself off in my bedroom?"

"Yes." I stood too, wanting to steady her, but giving her space. "I'm afraid so. We'll know more after they test the substance."

Josie turned away from us, shoulders lifting as she tried to breathe through the shock. Ryker and I exchanged a helpless glance—neither of us sure what she needed, both of us desperate to give it to her.

Then the sound hit—soft at first, then breaking apart into muffled sobs that hollowed out something in my chest. I didn't hesitate. I crossed the space between us, wrapped my arms around her from behind, and pulled her against me. Her whole body trembled, shaking hard enough that each shiver moved through me.

"I'm so sorry, Josie," I whispered into her ear.

She turned to me and clutched the front of my shirt. The moment she let go—really let go—the dam broke. I held her through every shaking breath while her tears soaked my shirt.

"I've got you," I murmured, pulling her tighter against my chest. "You're safe. I promise you... you're safe."

I rubbed slow circles across her back until her sobs softened, then faded.

Josie straightened, swiping at her face with trembling hands. "Why is he doing this?"

"I don't know." I cupped her cheeks, lifting her gaze to mine. "But I promise you this—I'm going to find him and lock him up."

She swallowed hard. "Do you think both incidents were Thomas?"

"I think so," I admitted.

"But how did he do that to my house if he was with me at the showing?" Her brows pulled tight, confusion and fear swirling behind her eyes.

"Maybe he did it earlier," I said. "Weren't you at the resort before you met him at the showing?"

Josie pulled away from my hands and sank onto the couch, arms wrapping around herself as she rocked. "I was... but that would mean he's been stalking me."

"Yeah," I breathed, lowering myself into a crouch in front of her so we were eye level. "I know."

"I can't believe I have a stalker like Cassie did. What is going on in Haven? Where are these men coming from?" Josie's voice cracked.

"I'm not sure," I admitted, "but you know exactly what Thomas looks like. If you see him anywhere—anywhere at all—you call me." I closed my hands over hers.

Josie nodded, then glanced at Ryker. "Ry, I'm ready to go," she said, voice small but steady. "Can you leave me at your house with Judge? I don't feel like going to the grocery store. What if he's watching?"

"I'll go," I blurted out before Ryker could speak. The thought of the two of them having another cozy night without me twisted something sharp in my chest. "It's better for Ryker and Judge to stay with you. Just text me what you guys want and I'll pick it up."

"Sounds good. You can stay for dinner." Ryker grinned, as if he knew what I was doing.

I stood as Josie pushed up from the couch and walked straight into his arms. He murmured something low—soft enough that I couldn't catch the words—but the tension eased in her shoulders. She nodded and slid her hand into his as they headed for the door.

We stepped outside. Josie scanned the yard. Her hand shook so bad, she couldn't fit the key into the lock.

"I'm sorry about all this, Josie," I mumbled.

I took the key from her trembling fingers and locked the door for her. She stepped back into Ryker's arms, leaning into him like she needed the support, and together they walked toward his car. Ryker helped her inside, then opened the door for Judge. One bark, one leap, and they were gone.

I stood there like an idiot, watching the taillights disappear down the road. That's okay, I told myself. I'd see her after my quick grocery run.

After finding that camera—and seeing her fall apart in my arms—I realized something with absolute clarity. I wanted to be her protector. The one she turned to and trusted to keep her safe.

And maybe, once this nightmare was over, I'd finally tell her how I felt. But wanting something and deserving it were two different things. I wasn't sure which category I fell into yet.

All I knew was this—when Josie shook in my arms and buried her face in my chest like I was the only solid thing in her world, something inside me locked into place. A decision. A vow. The kind that didn't need words.

I'd spent years solving cases, tracking monsters, putting drug dealers, abusers, and cowards behind bars. But none of that compared to the fire burning in my soul until I found Thomas Kincaid. This wasn't duty. This wasn't a badge. This was personal. Too personal.

Ryker sensed my feelings for Josie ran deep. Hell, it seemed like he knew before I did. The way he wrapped his arms around her, the way she relaxed into him—yeah, that burned more than I wanted to admit.

But it didn't matter. Not right now. Right now, all that mattered was keeping her alive. I'd talk to Ryker about it later. When the dust settled. If it ever settled.

If I had to shove my feelings into a box and bury it under professionalism, I would. If I had to work these clues until my eyes bled, I'd do that too. If I had to drag this bastard out by his hair and cuff him myself—fine. I'd do anything for her.

Josie Hale wasn't just another victim. She wasn't another case file to pin to my board.

She was the first woman in years who made me feel something real. Something dangerous. Something I didn't want to lose.

And God help the man who thought he could touch her again because he would have to do it over my dead body.

Chapter 17

Plastic Bag Football Lessons

Josie

W e were on our way to Ry's house when my phone buzzed in my purse. Lucian was texting me.

"It's Lucian. What do we want from the grocery store?"

"Chicken that I can grill tonight." Ry glanced my way. "You looked in my fridge yesterday. Do I have enough veggies? Do I need any more?"

"I told Lucian about the chicken. I added fruit, broccoli, and lunch meat for sandwiches. Do you have bread?"

"Whole wheat."

"Peanut butter?"

"Extra crunchy."

"Now I know why we're friends," I grinned.

"Yep." Ry winked. "I got your back."

We pulled onto the driveway. I looked around, making sure I didn't see Thomas.

"Hey." Ry reached over and squeezed my thigh. "Relax. You go inside. I'll check the perimeter. Besides, you're safe here."

"Thanks, Ry."

Ry locked me inside the house with Judge while he did his perimeter sweep. I sank onto the couch, feeling the weight of everything settle over me. I didn't want to see anyone—not Ry, not guests, not even Lucian. Not right now.

I pulled a pillow under my head, tilted it just right, and closed my eyes. Maybe if I pretended hard enough, just for a minute, the world would stop spinning.

"All clear." Ry came over, lifted my feet, sat down, and put my feet in his lap. "What do you want to watch?"

"I don't care," I mumbled.

"Mindless TV it is."

I chuckled. Ry and I loved scary movies, but we were equally obsessed with those wild relationship shows—the ones where people flew to another country, lived together for ninety days, and got married. I could never do that, but hey, some of them found true love.

We always rooted for the couples who made it, but half the fun was watching the disagreements and shaking our heads at their terrible decisions. Sometimes we even argued with the TV. Though most of the time, we agreed on how ridiculous people could be.

A new episode had dropped into Ry's recorded list. He hit play. The first couple on the screen wanted to add a girlfriend to their relationship. Wow. Good for them if that worked, but I could never share my fiancé with another woman. The girlfriend was bisexual and wanted to explore her sexuality—which was her business. I couldn't imagine sharing my man with anyone.

Then came the cougar couple. I cheered for her because normally people cheered for the man when the woman was younger, but not the other way around—you go, girl—but next time, pick a better younger guy. Preferably, one who wouldn't cheat on you behind your back.

Knock, Knock

"That must be Lucian." I jumped off the couch.

"Yeah," Ry snorted. "You don't like him at all."

I pushed his feet off the coffee table on my way to the door.

"Smart ass." I mumbled.

"I call them as I see them."

What the hell was he talking about? Thank goodness Lucian bought our groceries, and I didn't have to walk around the grocery store scared to turn the corner into the next aisle, afraid to see Thomas lurking near me. I opened the door to a smiling Lucian. I knew I was gawking when he motioned toward me with the groceries.

"May I come in?"

"That's a lot of bags." My eyes bulged. He was carrying a lot more bags than I'd asked for unless he cleared the store of all its broccoli and chicken.

"I added a few extra things I thought you might like." Lucian shrugged. "May I?"

"Oh." I held the door open and stepped out of the way. "Yes, of course."

"Hey, Detective." Ry hollered from the couch. "What's up?"

Judge greeted Lucian—without jumping on him—and sniffed the bags before Lucian set them on the counter.

"Sorry, buddy," Lucian told Judge, scratching behind his ear. "I didn't buy you any treats. But your dad can grill you some chicken."

"He knows I will," Ry called as he stood. "I'll go start the grill!" He slid open the back door and disappeared outside.

I followed Lucian and Judge into the kitchen and helped put away the groceries. He'd stocked up—chicken, steaks, veggies, my favorite lunch meat. Of course, he paid attention.

"I hope you like ice cream," Lucian said, pulling out two containers. "I grabbed Rocky Road and Cookies and Cream."

"I'm not picky about my ice cream." I grinned." I love both."

"Perfect." He slid them into the freezer. "How are you holding up?"

"I'm good." I grabbed the chicken and added spices so it would be ready when Ry came to pick it up.

He searched my face as if he didn't quite believe me. "No problems since you got here with Ryker?"

"No."

"That's great." He nodded, though the tension in his jaw didn't ease. He looked away as if checking himself before asking, "What are your plans for tomorrow?"

Judge mewled by the sliding glass door. Lucian stepped away and opened it to let him out. Judge always stayed glued to Ry when he wasn't shadowing me.

"Same as today," I said. "Work until lunchtime. Then I'm showing that couple another house."

"How many have they seen so far?"

"Two. I'm hoping tomorrow's the charm. Third time's supposed to be lucky, right?" I left the chicken on the counter and grabbed the veggies, chopping as I talked.

"Or three strikes and you're out." Lucian smirked.

"You're such a pessimist."

"Can I help you?" Lucian stared at the veggies. "I can chop."

"Perfect." I handed him the zucchini. "Cut this up into slices."

Lucian did as asked, and in no time, we had a mound of veggies in foil ready for the grill. We were cleaning up when he grabbed all the plastic bags on the counter and opened the trash can.

"No!" I hollered to stop him. "I reuse those."

He closed the lid and stared at me. "Whatever for?"

"The small trash can in my bathroom, picking up Judge's poop when I walk him, or when I need to carry something."

"You know they make bags for all of those, right?" Lucian quirked his eyebrow.

"Yes," I shrugged. "But why pay for something when you can reuse what you have?" I motioned for him to join me at the counter. "Drop them, buddy."

Lucian smiled and placed the bags on the counter. "Where are you going to put them, my little tree hugger?"

My heart did a stupid flip. *Did he just call me his? Did he even notice?*

"Uh," I stammered, "I'm gonna turn them into footballs and put them in a drawer."

He blinked. "What the hell are you talking about? How are you going to turn these into a football?"

"Pull up a chair and watch the master at work." I hopped onto a stool and nudged the other out with my foot. "Then you can help me."

I flattened the plastic bag on the counter, smoothing out the air before folding it lengthwise four times into one neat long strip. Then, I bent the bottom corner up at a ninety-degree angle, continuing the same fold over and over again, until only a tiny piece of the plastic remained. Tucking it into the side pocket, I sealed the whole thing in place.

"Voila!" I held up the perfect little plastic triangle. "A football. Make a goalpost with your hands."

"Are you shitting me right now?"

"No, make a goalpost." I showed him how. He mimicked me, and I placed the triangular football on a corner and flicked it with my finger, aiming for his goal post. "Woo hoo!" I screamed when it flew through the middle, between his fingers, hitting his chest, and sliding down to his lap.

"Where did you learn to do that?" He reached for the football and placed it on the counter.

"My dad. When I was little and bored at restaurants, he would make them from the paper surrounding the straws. It's how he entertained me until our food arrived. One day, Mom and I were trying to figure out where to put our plastic bags because they didn't all fit in a drawer. Dad came over and made a football with a bag, and history was made. Now you try."

Lucian turned out to be a quick learner, but his bag was still a little lumpy. I held up my fingers in a goalpost, and he flicked the triangle with confident precision. Unfortunately, it veered left, sailed over the counter, and plopped onto the floor.

"I think I need a little more practice," he said wryly.

I laughed and hopped off my stool to retrieve his sad little football. "Come on. Let's do it together. Once you've got it down, we'll have a competition."

His eyes sparked with interest. "What are we wagering?" He lifted a brow—slow, deliberate, teasing.

"If I win, I want a kiss," I blurted.

I had no idea where that came from—maybe adrenaline, maybe exhaustion, maybe the way he'd held me earlier—but the words tumbled out before I could catch them. And for once, I didn't want to take them back.

"And if I win?" Lucian asked, voice rough around the edges.

"What do you want?"

My breath caught as I waited for his answer. He didn't hesitate. Not even for a second.

"A smile back on your beautiful face." He grinned—small, soft, but sure.

My heart stuttered. I extended my hand, trying to keep it steady even though my pulse thundered in my chest.

"Deal."

"You're on." He took my hand, his grasp warm and strong, his eyes never leaving mine.

The moment our hands met, a shiver rolled through me—warm, electric, impossible to ignore. I handed him another bag to hide my fluster.

"Okay. Follow me exactly."

We sat shoulder to shoulder, folding the bags in rhythm. He watched me with intense focus, matching each move—flatten, fold, crease, tuck. His manly hands, though clumsy, moved with such determination that it melted my heart. When we finished folding, I split our little plastic footballs into two even piles.

"Okay." I smiled. "Every goal is a point. You go first."

"Nope." Lucian said, shaking his head. "Ladies first. My momma raised me to be a gentleman."

The competition got heated fast—trash talk, near-misses, a few questionable flicks on his part—but in the end, I won by two points.

"I win, I win!" I jumped up and down, arms raised, imitating the roar of an imaginary stadium. "Plastic Football Champion of the World. Pucker up, Detective."

Lucian's grin was slow and devastating as he leaned forward. *Did he want me to win?* I closed my eyes and pressed a quick kiss to his soft lips, intending it to be simple, playful. Except the moment I started to pull back, he followed.

His mouth covered mine. Deeper this time. His hand slid to the back of my neck as he kissed me like he'd been waiting years for this moment. My breath caught, my heart tripped over itself, and I sank into the moment. I didn't want it to end.

But then—

The sound of the sliding glass door snapped through the room like a bucket of cold water.

Lucian stilled.

For a second—maybe less—his lips lingered on mine, like he couldn't quite force himself to break the connection. His breath brushed my mouth, warm and uneven, and his hand stayed at the back of my neck as if his body hadn't gotten the message that someone had walked in.

Then, slowly—so damn slowly—he eased back. His forehead hovered against mine, our breaths mingled, neither of us daring to move. His eyes were half-lidded, pupils dark, chest rising and falling too fast for him to pretend he wasn't affected. My breath returned to normal as his fingers skimmed their way from my neck to my jaw. His voice came out low, rough, barely controlled.

"Josie..."

He didn't finish the sentence. Maybe he couldn't. Maybe the words would've undone us both. Behind us, footsteps approached—Ry's easy stride, Judge's nails clicking on the floor. Lucian straightened, the shift subtle but definite, like he was forcing the armor back over every soft part of himself.

But when he sat back, his eyes stayed locked on me. And everything in them said what he didn't dare speak out loud. His lips curved into a smile. That kiss had affected him as much as it had affected me. *He was into me.* I couldn't help wondering if he'd let me win.

Chapter 18

Bag Folding... Yeah, Right.

Ryker

I slid the glass door open and stepped inside, Judge trotting at my heel. The second the door clicked shut, I caught it—that weird, heavy silence that only shows up when you've walked in on something you weren't supposed to.

Josie and Lucian were standing way too close. Both of them looked flushed. Both of them looked guilty. And both of them snapped their eyes toward me like kids caught with their hands in the cookie jar.

Judge padded straight between them, nose working overtime like he could smell the tension. Hell, I could smell the tension.

I stopped, crossed my arms, and leaned against the doorframe. "You two look... flushed."

Lucian jumped off the stool so fast he had to catch it before it toppled over. I chuckled. Josie didn't say a word—just touched her lips like she wasn't sure if they still belonged to her. Not surprising since he was sucking her face.

"We were—uh—" Lucian cleared his throat "—folding bags."

I glanced at the stacked pile on the counter... then at the one rogue football sitting way too close to where Lucian had been standing.

Right. "Bag folding," I drawled. "Yeah, that'll get the blood pumping."

Lucian stiffened as if I'd accused him of a felony. His jaw locked tight, eyes darting everywhere but at Josie. I might have believed him if his mouth wasn't slathered in lip gloss and swollen, like Josie's. Josie looked everywhere except at me.

"Anyway." I pushed off the frame and clapped my hands once. "Grill's hot."

Judge gave a single bark, like he agreed. I opened the fridge, keeping them in my peripheral vision. They were so entertaining, pretending nothing had happened. I swear, I felt like a father catching his teenage kids necking on the couch.

"Did either of you prep the chicken and veggies?" I asked after I grabbed a bottle of water.

Josie pointed to the large aluminum mount on the counter beside the pile of chicken.

"Looks like you two worked up an appetite," I chuckled.

Neither made a single comment. They remained silent, pretending not to look at each other. Like I cared if they liked each other and sucked face in my kitchen. I grabbed the chicken and pointed to Lucian.

"Hey Casanova, grab the veggies and follow me.

Lucian followed me out to the grill like a man heading to his own execution. Judge trotted out between us, happy as ever, oblivious to the hurricane of emotions I could practically see ripping through Lucian's skull.

I lifted the lid, and a wave of heat hit me. Lucian froze, hands gripping the foil, staring toward the ocean. He looked guilty as sin—like a guy who'd just been caught kissing someone he wasn't ready to admit he liked. And being the dutiful smart-ass friend I was, I couldn't resist yanking his chain.

"So..." I said casually, grabbing the tongs. "How'd the bag folding go?"

Lucian froze. Like statue-level still.

"I don't know what you think you saw," he said stiffly.

"Uh-huh." I set the chicken on the grill, letting the sizzle fill the silence. "Looked a lot like a warm-up to me."

I reached my hand out for the foil. His jaw tightened.

"A warm-up for what?" He glared at me and handed me the foil.

"Cardio," I said innocently. "Hand–eye coordination. Totally normal bag-folding stuff."

A muscle in his cheek twitched. Judge plopped down at his feet, tail thumping, staring up at him like he knew something too.

Lucian ran a hand over his face. "Ryker..."

"What?" I asked, flipping the chicken. "You two were standing close. Real close. The kind of close that happens after—oh, I don't know—you finally get your head out of your ass and kiss the girl you like?"

Lucian shot me a look that could've melted steel.

"Relax, man," I grinned. "I'm not judging. I'm just saying...if you're gonna kiss my friend, maybe don't look like you regret it afterward."

His head whipped toward me. "I don't regret it."

Bingo.

I kept my eyes on the grill, trying not to smile too wide. "Didn't figure you did."

Lucian stepped closer, voice low. "But you need to keep this between us."

"Of course," I said. "But Lucian?"

He let out a slow breath. "What?"

"I love Josie—" Lucian stiffened, and I raised my hand to stop whatever stupid-ass thoughts caused that reaction —"down, Detective. I love her like a sister. She's my best friend. Don't mess with her heart or I'll fucking kick your ass."

"Fair enough." Lucian cracked a smile. "But just so you know. She won a bet, and her wager was a kiss. Not that I'm complaining. I'm falling for her."

"Noted." I grinned.

Lucian's eyes snapped toward the sliding door—staring at Josie. The detective had it bad, and knowing Josie, she was pretending the kiss didn't just scramble her entire world. As her best guy friend, I knew better. They both needed a little push, and I was the guy to give it.

"I have an idea to help you along." I glanced behind me to make sure Josie was still inside. "Will you go along with it?"

"Depends." Lucian frowned. "What is it? Will it hurt Josie?"

"No, it won't fucking hurt her." I scoffed. "I'd never hurt her, even to help you."

"So what's your plan?"

"You'll find out soon enough. I need to talk to someone first."

"Okay. Now I'm intrigued."

"You should be," I smiled. "Because once I implement my plan, your ass is gonna thank me."

"We'll see." Lucian gave a dramatic eye roll. So out of character for him. Josie must be getting to him. She loved her eye rolls.

"Just promise to go along with it." I pointed at him. "No questions. The only thing you have to do is be nice to Josie and protect her."

"Done."

"Good. Because if you hurt her, not only will I kick your ass, but Judge gets first bite."

Judge barked in agreement. Good dog.

***

During dinner, they circled around each other like wolves—slow, tense, waiting for the other to make the first move. I don't know how they didn't see it. Hell, anyone with eyes could see how badly they wanted each other. It was written all over their faces, in the way they looked at each other and kept pretending not to.

I'd volunteered to be Josie's roommate for her safety, and I meant it. I loved that girl—she was the big sister I never had, the one I'd always been responsible for. She was a kind soul, and men always took advantage of her kindness. Protecting her wasn't just a job; it was instinct.

But watching them at that table...seeing the way Lucian watched her like she was the only person in the room... I realized something I didn't want to admit—I should've let her stay with him, not me.

At the time, I'd thought Lucian would put up more of a fight. *Asshole!* Not that I minded Josie staying with me—I didn't, but I wanted Lucian to fucking stop circling around her and ask her out already. He was acting like a pussy, and I was sick and tired of the game.

After we loaded the dishwasher, I excused myself and stepped outside. I needed privacy for what I was about to do. The night air was cooler than I expected, but it cleared my head enough to stick to the plan forming in my mind.

We'd run plenty of ops with the Jones County Sheriff's Department over the years, so I pulled out my phone and scrolled until I found the number I needed. Griff—one of their undercover guys, the one who always had our backs. If he answered, he wasn't deep into his "Cain" persona tonight.

He picked up on the first ring. "Hey, Dog Man, what's up?"

Good. Not working undercover.

"I've got a favor to ask," I said. My stomach tightened. This whole thing could blow up in my face, but if it worked... it could give Lucian and Josie the opportunity to realize how much they liked each other.

"Ask away."

"Do you need a K9 assist?"

There was a beat of silence. Then—

"What the fuck are you talking about? You want to leave HiPD?"

"Not forever," I blurted. "Just for a week or so."

"Why?" Griff sounded genuinely confused. "I thought you loved it there. You islanders never seem to want to jump ship to the mainland."

"I'll explain everything later. I can be there tonight."

Another pause. "Are you in trouble? You know I might look like some hoodlum gangster, but I walk the straight-and-narrow."

"No, Griff." I rubbed my forehead. "I'm not in trouble. I'm trying to help out a friend, or two. I'll tell you all about it later."

I glanced through the sliding glass door. Lucian and Josie were flicking those stupid plastic paper-bag footballs again. Laughing when they missed. Cheering when they didn't. And damn if that sight didn't make everything click into place.

This—this—was why I needed to back off and let Lucian take the lead. She wasn't mine to protect anymore, not like that. She'd softened toward him, and he'd opened up to her. Tonight was my chance to step aside and let their love bloom.

"Okay," Griff said finally. "We can always use you and Judge. I'll call Captain Jay and tell him you want to watch, learn, and assist until next weekend. It shouldn't be a problem, and you can crash at my place."

"Thanks, Griff."

"Sure thing. But when you get here, you'd better start talking. You owe me an explanation, Dog Man."

"I'd expect nothing less."

We hung up, and I let out a long breath. Judge ran around the backyard before sprinting toward me, tongue hanging out. I crouched to scratch behind his ears.

"C'mon, buddy," I murmured. "Time to head back inside and interrupt the Football Wars. Or..." I snorted. "Maybe the Denial Wars."

Either way, tonight would be my last night being used as a middleman between the two of them. And honestly—it was time.

Chapter 19

Feeling Lucky

Lucian

Making those footballs—and goofing off with Josie—made me feel like a damn kid again. I couldn't remember the last time I'd laughed like that. The last time I'd let myself. Life, work, deployments—hell, my own expectations—had a way of shutting that part of me down.

But with her? It came naturally—too naturally.

I was the oldest in the Warrick clan, the unofficial second father to my sister and my cousins. Responsibility was not something I pretended to have—it's a fundamental part of who I am. Even Sawyer, my cousin, who was only a year younger, still looked to me whenever shit hit the fan.

Every decision. Every crisis. Every burden. It all landed on my shoulders by default. And most days, that was fine. I thrive on helping my family and friends. But tonight? Sitting at a kitchen island folding stupid plastic bags into triangles?

I'd forgotten what it felt like to be just a man. Not a detective. Not a protector. Not the oldest Warrick expected to keep everyone else in line. Just a man... having fun with a woman who lit something up inside me I hadn't felt in a damn long time.

Josie brought that out of me without trying. Or maybe she didn't even know she did. But I knew, and I wanted more of her magic. And that scared me more than anything I'd faced in fifteen years on the job. Ryker came back inside after his important phone call.

"So," Ryker came over and picked up one of my footballs that had fallen on the ground. "I wanted to talk to you guys about something."

"Okay. What's going on?" Josie took a sip of her wine. I had poured her another glass after dinner before we played with the footballs again.

"I have to go work with JCSD for a week." Ryker blurted and tossed my football to me.

"When?" Josie dropped her hands and faced him.

What the hell was he talking about? I didn't hear about the JCSD needing our K9 officers. Hell, they had six of their own. *Why the hell was he leaving Josie?*

"I need to leave tonight." Ryker cleared his throat.

"Ry!" Josie cried out. "Why didn't you tell me earlier?"

"I just found out when I made that call." Ryker pointed outside. "Griffin had left me a message asking me to call him back. Something about a missing child."

I didn't hear an Amber Alert. I would've known if a kid went missing on the mainland—news like that travels fast, and we'd all be pulled in, not just one K9 officer. *So what the hell was Ryker doing?* I didn't say a word, letting the scene play out, but something wasn't adding up.

I'd worked with Griffin before. If JCSD had an active case involving a child, he would've called me before Ryker. It would've been all hands on deck, no exceptions. *But Ryker? Slipping out for a "K9 assist" with zero warning?* Yeah, something fishy was brewing.

I shot Ryker a look. He answered with wide eyes and a slow, knowing nod. Damn it. I excelled at solving crimes, but when it came to my love life? Apparently, I was clueless. That—right here—was what he'd been hinting at. That was why he'd said I'd end up thanking him.

"What am I supposed to do?" Josie's eyes lifted to mine—wide, watering, pleading. It went straight through me. "Go back to my apartment? Is it safe?"

"Uh...no." I pushed off the counter and stood tall. "You can stay with me. I'll keep you safe."

"I'm sorry, Josie," Ryker said, pulling her into a hug while she sat on the stool. "I'll make this up to you. Besides..." He shot me a knowing look. "Lucian will guard you with his life. Right, Detective?"

"Absolutely," I said without hesitation.

Josie pulled back from Ryker and turned to face me. "Lucian...are you sure I can stay with you?" Her voice dropped to a soft, uncertain murmur. "I still have to go to work. Are you going to... come with me?"

"Yes." I didn't even blink. "I'll bring my laptop and work while you're at the hotel or showing houses. It'll be fine."

"Okay," she whispered. "I guess."

"I'm gonna go pack," Ryker announced, slipping out of the kitchen.

I turned to her. "Go grab your stuff too, Josie. We'll head out whenever you're ready." I gathered the little footballs and stacked them into a neat pile, giving my hands something to do.

"Okay." She slid off the stool, still shaken, and walked out of the room.

When she left, I let out a slow breath.

Ryker had done me a huge fucking favor—and he damn well knew it. I wouldn't forget it.

*** Josie ***

Since I had been sleeping in Ry's room, I joined him there to pack my stuff. The door was ajar, so I knocked in case he was changing.

"Ry, it's me. Can I come in?" I hollered. "I need to pack up my stuff."

"Come in. I'm almost done," his voice floated out of the bathroom.

The weight of everything crashed down on my chest. My hands shook as I pulled my suitcase out from under the bed and laid it on top.

Stay with Lucian. Work with Lucian. Live in his house. Sleep under the same roof. My breath stuttered. I held my chest, willing the rhythm to slow.

"Josie." Ry came out of the bathroom carrying his hygiene and dropped them into a duffel bag on his bed. "If you feel more comfortable, you can stay here with Lucian. He'll take the couch."

"No, I'm sure he'll be more comfortable at his house. It's fine."

This is fine. I can do this. It was either that or go back to my house and hope Thomas wasn't lurking in my closet with a knife and more notes. Nope. Absolutely not.

I grabbed the few clothes that were on hangers and tossed them into the suitcase without folding them. My brain was a mess, my thoughts spinning in panicked circles. Lucian said he'd protect me. He kissed me tonight. *Did he like me? Or was it just the wager?*

My face heated, and I pressed my hands to my cheeks. God, that kiss. I could still feel it—soft at first, then deep and hungry, like he'd wanted me for a long time but waited until I said, *pucker up, Detective* to do something about it.

My stomach fluttered and tightened all at once, like fear and desire were trying to wrestle each other to the floor.

As soon as I finished tossing my clothes into the suitcase, I zipped it up and sat on the edge of the bed, taking several deep breaths to calm my nerves. Judge sat in the doorway, watching me like he knew I was two seconds away from a full-blown meltdown.

"I'm okay," I whispered to him.

"What's that?" Ry walked out of his closet holding several police uniforms.

Judge tilted his head.

"Nothing. I didn't say anything," I said with a shaky exhale.

"Are you okay?" Ry placed the uniforms on the bed and crouched in front of me.

"Mostly okay. A little okay. Okay-ish." My throat tightened, eyes burning. *What if Thomas comes after me again? What if Lucian gets hurt because of me? What if staying with him is a mistake?*

"It's gonna be okay." Ry helped me up and gave me a hug. "Lucian will take good care of you."

Ry's words settled me. Safety-wise, I knew Lucian would do everything in his power to protect me. But opening my heart to him terrified me, especially if I discovered he didn't feel the same way.

"I know he will." I wiped my eyes and grabbed my suitcase handle. "Thanks for taking care of me, Ry. Stay safe on the mainland."

"Always," Ry grinned and winked at me.

I stooped to give Judge a hug. "Thank you for watching over me, too."

Judge yelped and licked my face. I stood, grabbed my suitcase handle and followed Ry into the living room. Back to Lucian. Time to face him. Time to trust him. Whether I was ready or not.

Chapter 20

My New Temporary Home

Josie

I didn't realize Lucian lived in the northern part of our island, near the marina. We were at opposite ends. Other than when I came to visit Silver at the Marina, I never drove into these older neighborhoods. It made sense that the Warrick brothers lived there since their family was one of the OGs of the island.

Lucian's house was a light-blue, two-story place with shiplap siding. The kind of coastal home you'd expect to find on the cover of a beach-town travel magazine. Clean lines, white trim, and a porch meant for lingering summer evenings. And of course, it backed right up to the private stretch of beach this neighborhood seemed to treat like a birthright.

As we pulled into the driveway, I couldn't help feeling a strange sense of calm settle over me. Maybe it was the soft crash of waves in the distance. Maybe it was the seclusion. Maybe it was him.

"I didn't realize you lived in Haven Cove."

I looked around, unable to hide my awe. I'd always wanted to see these homes up close, but the gate kept non-invited visitors out. Plus, properties here almost never became available.

"Yep. My mom saw the for-sale sign years ago and urged me to buy it. It's too big for a single guy like me, but I always hoped to fill it with a wife and kids."

Lucian clicked his garage door opener and parked inside.

"I'll get the door for you." Lucian hurried around the car and opened my door.

"Thank you." I followed him to the trunk to grab my suitcase, but he stopped me.

"I'll bring it in for you."

I followed him through the connecting door into the house.

"Sorry, we're going in through the laundry room, but it's clean."

"That's fine." *Was he a neat freak?*

The laundry room door led into the breakfast nook next to the kitchen. His kitchen had white countertops and cabinets with light blue décor—very beachy.

"This is really nice."

"Thanks. The original owners had cherry cabinets, but I wanted a beach look, so I changed the entire look of the kitchen. Make yourself at home."

He placed the suitcase by the stairs.

"Did you hire a decorator?" Turning away from the kitchen, the house opened up into a wide living room with giant windows that framed the beach like a moving painting.

"Uh, no, my sister, Carolyn, helped me. Well, and my mom. She loves to decorate and spend my money." Lucian imitated his mom and said, "My son will not live in a bachelor pad. It's bad enough he's not married." Then he grinned. "Mind you, I was only thirty when I bought this place."

"Too funny. My parents didn't want me to start a family until their tour of the US was over. Although secretly I think they would end said tour and run home if I gave them a grandbaby." I chuckled.

"You're probably right." Lucian smiled.

He wasn't moving. He stood still, staring. *Did I have something on my face? Did I say something wrong?*

"So, will you give me a tour of the rest of the house? I love looking at homes."

"Oh...," Lucian's body jerked into action. "Sorry. Yes, of course. I have two guest rooms upstairs for you to pick from."

Lucian pivoted and walked to the left. "Here is the formal dining room, the front door."

He turned and ran into me. His hands landed on my waist.

"Sorry," he mumbled.

"No problem." I stepped back, and he motioned me toward the back of the house. *Was he nervous about having me in his home?* He always seemed so in charge, not rattled like he was now.

"Past the kitchen is the living room."

We walked through to a door off to the right.

"Here is my home office. The bathroom leads outside to the pool."

"You have a pool?"

"A small one, yes."

"Wow, a pool and the beach. That's nice."

His office, with a wooden desk and cabinets, smelled of old wood—very masculine, very him. I walked through to check out the pool bath, which was a full bathroom with a shower. Lucian waited for me by the door to the living room.

"The pool." Lucian pointed out as he slid open the sliding glass doors. "All three glass doors slide so the living room flows into the backyard."

Trifold doors. Wow. The small pool, as he called it, was big enough to have a hot tub inside. It looked so inviting. I wished I'd brought my bathing suit.

"Do you use the pool or hot tub a lot?" I asked and dipped my hand in the water. It was the perfect temperature.

"I do," Lucian said with a nod. "I swim to stay in shape, or I hit the hot tub when my muscles need a break. And if I need more space, I head for the ocean."

"Decisions, decisions." I smirked.

"You can use it while you're here. I can heat the hot tub for you anytime you want."

"That would be so nice," I sighed. "Unfortunately, I only grabbed work clothes from my closet. I don't have a bathing suit."

"That's an easy fix." Lucian shrugged. "I can take you to Sammie's boutique and buy you one."

"You don't have to buy me a bathing suit." I chuckled. It was sweet of him to offer.

"I know I don't have to." Lucian slid his hands into his pants pockets. "I want to. You've been through a lot, and you deserve something nice. I can take you shopping on Saturday."

"We'll see." Such a sweet gesture, but he didn't owe me anything, especially since he was giving me a place to stay and protection.

"Are you ready to see the rest of the house?"

"Yep." I stood and followed him to a room off the living room, opposite his office.

"Here's my bedroom with the bathroom." Lucian walked in and made room for me to squeeze past him.

His bedroom was...unexpected. The first thing that caught my eye was the sleigh bed—dark wood, solid, commanding the room like it knew exactly who it belonged to. And the sheets...black satin. *Black satin.* Well. Okay then. Nice.

"Very nice," I mumbled.

The thought of Lucian and me doing sexy things to each other on those sheets sent a flush rising, igniting a fire in my cheeks. I tore my gaze away and stepped into the bathroom before my imagination ran too far ahead of me and I begged him to make love to me. The bathroom was enormous, like something out of a luxury resort suite. It had a walk-in shower large enough for two with several showerheads, some of which were detachable, a deep soaking tub, and double sinks embedded in a long marble counter.

Only one sink held anything—a toothbrush, a razor, his cologne, all lined up like a man who didn't leave messes. The other sink was untouched. Empty. Available.

"Thanks." He cleared his throat. "Let's go upstairs. You can choose which bedroom you want."

When we reached the top of the stairs, I noticed one room on the right and another on the left with a bathroom at the end of the hall. I froze the minute I saw the long hallway leading to the bathroom.

"This room is the bigger of the two." Lucian said as he opened the door to the left.

I wanted to follow him—I really did—but seeing the bathroom at the end of the hallway messed with my mind. A knot tightened in my stomach. A chilling fear crept through my body. My breath hitched, and the hairs on the back of my neck prickled with an icy awareness. The blood in my ears pounded a frantic rhythm against my skull, and a wave of nausea threatened to overwhelm me.

My chest tightened, each breath shrinking in duration until I gasped for air. Dots crowded my vision, and the edges blurred. I reached for the wall. My fingers scraped it as I fought to stay upright. My knees wobbled, and the hallway tilted.

Chapter 21

Best Jungle Room Ever!!

Josie

"Josie?" Lucian's voice sounded so far away, like he was in a tunnel. "Josie!"

I couldn't answer. Couldn't force my lips to move and release the sound through my throat.

Lucian? Where was I? Footsteps thundered toward me, and then firm hands were on my arms—steadying, anchoring, pulling me back before I fell into the darkness swallowing my vision.

"Josie, breathe."

What did he say?

"Josie. Breathe with me. In. Out. In. Out."

I followed his instructions until my breath returned to normal. Lucian stared at me with concern in his eyes. His hands cupped my face.

"Are you okay? What happened?"

"I...I don't know," I whispered. "I saw your bathroom at the end of the hall, and it reminded me of the one at the house on Leonard Street."

"Shit," Lucian growled. "Then I don't want you staying here. We'll go to a hotel."

"No, no." I grabbed his arms and shook my head. "That's ridiculous. This isn't the same place. I can't let him have this power over me. I'm stronger than that." Not sure whether I tried to convince Lucian or myself. "Show me the two rooms and the bathroom. I'll pick one."

Lucian kept his arm around my waist as we stepped into the larger room. The walls were a soft, calming green, and a quilted comforter lay draped across the queen-sized bed. A small closet and a chest of drawers sat against the far wall. Nothing about it resembled the room Thomas tried to assault me in—and that alone helped me breathe a little easier.

"My sister and her husband usually sleep in this room when they visit. I know they don't live far away, but during family nights that go late in the summer, they stay over to enjoy the beach."

"It's very nice."

"The other room is the one Sophie, my niece, uses. I painted the walls purple since it's her favorite color."

I kept my gaze focused on the other room instead of down the hall. Lucian opened the door to a beautiful little girl's room. The walls were lavender, with a white twin bed and matching dresser set. I hope he has a little girl someday because this room wouldn't be a little boy's dream. Well, not a frogs-and-mischief boy.

"I bet she loves staying over at Uncle Lucian's house." I grinned.

"She does." Lucian gazed into my eyes, looking for any signs of distress. "Are you okay checking out the bathroom?"

"Yes." My body stiffened as if I were walking toward my death. I needed to be strong. My parents taught me right. Self-confidence and facing my fears were my motto. Lucian opened the door, and I released my breath. This was nothing like that bathroom. That bathroom had been devoid of any character with tan walls—as it should be when you were selling a house.

But this one—oh, this one had jungle print wallpaper from the ceiling to the floor. A mini jungle, complete with a monkey toothbrush holder and cup. I inhaled the scent of coconuts and cedar from a couple of candles on the counter, adding a soothing balance to the fun, kid-like décor. Light-green towels hung on the towel bars, and chocolate-brown floor mats covered the floor.

"Sophie loves animals," Lucian said, a small smile tugging at his mouth. "The zoo's her favorite place in the world, so...I brought some of it to her." He glanced down, almost sheepish, like he wasn't sure if he should be embarrassed or proud.

"That is so sweet." My lips curved into a crooked smile. "I bet she loves this room."

"She does," Lucian grinned. "Every time she visits, she runs in here like it's her kingdom. Except she wishes the monkeys were real," he said wryly. "That's where I drew the line."

"You are so mean." I gasped at him with my hand over my heart. "A real monkey would make this room come to life."

"Of course you'd agree with her." Lucian flicked off the light and left the bathroom. "She'll love you."

"You did a fabulous job," I praised him. "It's... thoughtful. And honestly? Kind of adorable."

He huffed out a soft laugh, rubbing the back of his neck. "Don't say adorable. I have a reputation."

"Too late." I nudged his shoulder. "You've just been exposed as the true softie you are."

His eyes warmed, lingering on me for a second longer than necessary. "Guess I can handle that... with you."

The air shifted—gentle but unmistakable. Something deeper beneath it. *Did he feel it?* Something that made my heart flutter in ways I was still trying to make sense of. I swallowed, aware of how close we were standing.

"I'd love to stay in the room your sister uses if that's okay with you."

Lucian blinked, then lifted a single eyebrow and cocked his head. "Are you sure? I can sleep on the couch if you want to use my bedroom."

"No, I'll stay up here." I nodded. "I'm good."

How could I ask him to sleep on a couch when he had two perfectly good rooms upstairs?

"Okay, but let me know if you feel uncomfortable or change your mind." Lucian's eyes traced over my face, searching for any hint of doubt.

"I will."

A few seconds passed, just the two of us looking at each other. Then he finally smiled.

"I'll bring up your suitcase."

"Thanks."

I went back into the green room and opened the drawers. They were all empty. Perfect. The closet had a couple of jackets and coats, but other than that, it had plenty of hangers for me to hang my clothes. I grabbed a few and placed them on the bed.

"Here you go." Lucian placed my suitcase on the bed. "I'll leave you to unpack. When you're done, if you want, come downstairs and we can put on a movie."

"It's getting late." I unzipped my bag. "Don't you have to go to work tomorrow?"

"Nope," Lucian said, leaning casually against the doorframe. "I'm gonna be your bodyguard for at least the next week. Wherever you go, I go."

"Oh."

A thrill shot up my spine at the thought of Lucian guarding my body. Totally different reaction than when Ry said he'd protect me. Ry's protection felt brotherly. Lucian's? Lucian's was... hotter. *What else could he do to my body?*

"Okay," I muttered and got my mind out of the gutter.

"What time do you go in tomorrow?"

"I start at six in the morning and work until noon." I took a couple of dresses out and slid them onto hangers.

Lucian checked his wristwatch. "It's already nine. Would you rather go to bed early?"

"Not really." I scrunched up my nose. I wasn't tired. "I'd rather watch something...if that's okay with you." I hung the dresses in the closet.

"It's fine." He shrugged. "I don't require a lot of sleep. Comes with the job."

I'm sure it came with the job and his previous stint in the military, which he never talked about.

"I wish I didn't. I'm a night owl. I stay up late and then hate myself in the morning." I pulled out a couple of shirts and hung them next to the dresses.

"I'll meet you downstairs so you can finish unpacking." Lucian said as he turned to go. "Hell, I'll even have the coffee ready for you in the morning."

"My hero!" I called after him, unable to stop the smile spreading across my face.

After Lucian left, silence settled around me, thick and humming with all the things I didn't want to think about... and all the things I couldn't stop thinking about. I hung another shirt in the closet and stared at it like it might offer advice. Of course it didn't. Shirts were useless like that.

He's going to be with me all week. Wherever I go, he goes. Bodyguard. My stomach fluttered. Again.

I sat on the edge of the bed and ran both hands through my hair. Every time I tried to focus on the clothes in my hands, my brain shoved Lucian's kiss into the center stage spotlight. The warmth of his mouth. The grip of his hand on my neck. The way he only pulled away because Ryker walked in. And the way he looked at me afterward—like that kiss rattled him just as much as it rattled me.

I swallowed hard. My chest tightened. Because right underneath the butterflies and nerves was fear again. Genuine fear. I hadn't forgotten about Thomas, his attempted assault, and the notes he left on my bed. He'd violated my home. I stared at my half-unpacked suitcase, unable to move. Those spine-chilling thoughts attacked me from all sides every time I was alone. Part of me wanted to curl up in the guest room, lock the door, and pretend it hadn't happened.

But another part understood why Lucian insisted I stay with him—why he placed himself between me and danger without a second thought, and why that kiss still lingered on my lips like a promise. Sharing his bed would have made me feel safer... calmer... maybe even hopeful. I zipped up the empty suitcase, pushed it into the closet, and released a deep sigh.

"Okay," I whispered to myself. "You can do this."

I gathered up my courage and headed downstairs. Time to face Lucian. And whatever this thing was between us.

Chapter 22

Too Much... Too Soon?

Lucian

Nights like this made me wish all the damn bedrooms in my house were upstairs. Knowing Josie was up there—alone, still shaken from that panic episode—while I lay down here in my comfortable bed? Yeah, sleep wasn't happening anytime soon.

But she'd been adamant that she wanted to face her fears. And who the hell was I to take that choice from her?

I moved into the kitchen and grabbed a bottle of her favorite wine from the counter. Ryker had handed it to me before we left his place, muttering something about how she'd "appreciate the gesture." He wasn't wrong. My momma didn't raise a fool—I took the bottle and tucked it into the car before Josie finished packing.

I popped the cork and poured her a generous glass. If anything could help her unwind after the scare she'd had upstairs, this would do it. Then I grabbed myself a beer from the fridge and settled onto the couch to wait.

She brought only one suitcase with her, so I knew she'd be down soon. The TV played low in the background—some late-night movies on cable—but if she didn't like any of them; I had plenty of streaming options. Honestly, I didn't care what we watched. As long as she sat next to me.

I leaned back, beer in hand, listening for the slightest sound on the stairs. And for the first time in a long time... I hoped like hell she liked me as much as I liked her.

"Hey, is that glass for me?" Josie asked, pointing to the wine.

"Yup. Your favorite."

Her brows lifted. "How did you know?"

"Ryker had an extra bottle and thought you might need it tonight." I grinned as she took the glass and curled onto the far end of the couch, legs tucked under her.

"Figures," she said, smiling into her wine. "Ry always has bottles in his fridge for me. He's a great friend. Always there when I need him."

"Yeah." I took a slow swig of my beer. "He's a great guy."

Wait—did she say friend?

Ryker lived in her friend zone. And now that I knew they only cared about each other that way, relief loosened something tight in my chest. If he was "a great friend," then I could aim for something more. *Appreciate the help, brother. My night just got a whole lot better.*

I tossed her the remote. "Put on whatever you want."

"Seriously?" She gasped dramatically, placing a hand over her heart. "You're going to hand me the all-powerful remote?"

"Don't be so dramatic." I snorted. "Not all men are remote hogs. I can share."

"Uh-huh," she teased. "We'll see. Oh—wait." She pointed the remote at me. "I get it. You were the older brother who had to give in to the younger, sweet little sister." Josie arched a brow, all smug and knowing.

"Guilty as charged." I gave her a half bow. "To be fair, I didn't mind. We usually watched the same shows. It wasn't such a hardship."

"Are we talking about the same Carolyn that was in several of my classes?" Josie laughed. "The bossy, sassy never take no for an answer?"

"Yep," I chuckled. "That would be her."

Yeah, my sister was spoiled. I wouldn't deny that because I played a major part in spoiling her.

"She was my best friend growing up aside from my cousin, Sawyer," I said, leaning back into the couch. "If she wanted to play baby dolls, I carried them around as her personal assistant. When I wanted to be Lightning McQueen, she insisted on being Sally. Even though there was a six-year age gap, we balanced each other out... but she definitely won most of our battles."

"How is she? I haven't spoken to her since she went to the mainland for college."

"She's good. She married Stephen Beaumont, an accountant on the mainland. Their daughter, Sophie—queen of the jungle room upstairs—turned five in July, so she's in kindergarten."

Josie's eyes lit up. "Five, wow. Time flies."

"It does. My cousin Rosie, who teaches at Hi Prep, gives Carolyn shit about not moving back to the island. If Sophie was at Hi Prep, Rosie could see her every day." I shook my head, smirking. "It's a whole family argument at every Sunday dinner when they both attend."

"I remember Rosie," Josie grinned. "She was a freshman when I was a senior. Rosie teaches third grade, right?"

"Yep," I nodded. "How did you know?"

"Rosie's Hallie's teacher. Sammie is always talking about how much Hallie loves her."

For a moment, I'd forgotten that Sammie and Josie were friends. Yet another reason not to mess around with Josie if I wasn't serious about her. Chief would stand in line behind Ryker and Judge to kick my ass if I hurt her.

"You'll have to tell Rosie when you meet her along with the rest of my family this Sunday for dinner. It'll make her day."

Her head snapped toward me. "What are you talking about?"

"You'll still be with me this weekend," I said, like it was obvious. "And Warricks don't miss Sunday dinner unless they are working—it's an unspoken rule."

"But technically... you are working. As my bodyguard."

"That is not a technicality my mom or aunt will accept," I laughed. "Since I can keep an eye on you just as easily at their house as mine."

"True." Josie took a sip of her wine and looked down at her lap. I could see the wheels turning in her head.

"You're not scared of the Warricks, are you?" I raised an eyebrow.

"No," she said—even though she squinted her eyes at me like she wasn't fully convinced. "But I need more information. Start talking."

Josie muted the TV, turned to me, and gave me her full attention.

"My father, Charles, and Sawyer's father, Rhett, are brothers. Our—"

Josie held up a hand, stopping me. "Wait. The brothers' names are Rhett and Charles?"

"Yep," I sighed. Of course she would make the connection—most women did. "My grandmother loved Gone with the Wind. Imagine her surprise when my father married a woman named Melanie."

Her laugh was instantaneous and joyful. "Wow, I bet she was thrilled. What's your aunt's name? Please tell me it's not Scarlett?"

"Not quite." I chuckled. "It's Ruby."

"Well, that's close," she teased.

"Yeah, sometimes my grandmother calls her Scarlett anyway. Aunt Ruby doesn't mind—she laughs it off." I took a drink of my beer before continuing. This was going to take a while.

"Anyway, back to my story. The Warrick clan isn't just a family—it's a small, chaotic army. Our parents raised us as one big family. Weekends meant someone's backyard, someone's grill, and all of us kids running around until we were sunburned, dirty, and exhausted."

Josie leaned in, so focused on my story she'd forgotten to drink her wine. And damn if that didn't make something in my chest go warm and tight.

"Some traditions stuck, like Sunday dinner at Aunt Ruby's, for one. She's got the only kitchen big enough to feed the entire clan without someone sitting on a cooler or on the floor. Every Sunday—rain or shine—you'd find at least a dozen Warricks crowding her table."

"Wow," Josie sighed. "I bet she likes that."

"Aunt Ruby and my mom both love Sunday dinners." I took a gulp of my beer. "It's a chance for them to inquire about our love lives. Since Carolyn is the only one married and with a child, the rest of us are fair game."

"I know all about that." Josie rolls her eyes. "My parents do that to me when they're home. But hey, now I get a free pass until they return.

"Lucky girl," I smile.

"Okay." Josie sipped her wine and placed it on the coffee table. "Go on. If I'm meeting your family in two days, I need to be prepared."

Josie turned to face me, hugged a pillow tight, and settled in for the rest of my story. I couldn't remember another woman ever listening to anything about my family with so much intensity and care.

"Carolyn studied to be a teacher. She taught at Hi Prep until she married Stephen and they moved to the mainland. Shortly after she had Sophie, she left teaching and became a stay-at-home mom. My beautiful niece has all of us wrapped around her little finger. If she tells you to act like a zoo animal, you pick your favorite one and do it. No questions asked."

Josie chuckled, and damn if that sound didn't hit me right in the chest.

"Of course she does." Josie arched an eyebrow. "Which one do you pick?"

"A stallion." I grinned at her. "I love to sit Sophie on my lap and bounce her on my knee while I make clopping sounds."

"I'd love to sit on your knee," Josie mumbled.

"What was that?" I heard her but pretended not to.

"Nothing." She waved her hand at me in a circular motion. "Go on."

"Ronin, one of my cousins, also moved to the mainland. He's an Internal Affairs officer with JCSD and takes way too much pleasure in riding our asses. According to him, I'm "too soft" on people," I snorted. "According to me, he can be a hard-ass with no heart. But he's my cousin, and I love the bastard, anyway."

Her lips curved, amused.

"Roman, the youngest cousin, recently became the Youth Resource Officer at Hi Prep. Roman and Rosie seem to enjoy working at the same school. And

Sawyer, an ex-Navy SEAL... he's our diver and Marine Unit Sergeant. If the man could grow gills, he would."

I took a drink before going on.

"My mom and Aunt Ruby were teachers before they had kids. Warricks tend to follow the public-service path except for Uncle Rhett. He's a land developer who somehow convinced my dad, after he retired from being a police officer, to join his business."

When I finally paused, Josie's expression was a little hazy, eyes glazed like I'd given her the entire encyclopedia set in one breath.

"You good?" I asked.

"I am never going to remember all that," she muttered.

"You don't have to." I laughed. "I'll help you out on Sunday, no worries."

"For tonight?" I nodded toward the TV. "Just pick a movie or show... and let's relax."

Chapter 23

Heaven

Lucian

Josie kept channel surfing. "I have paid channels if you want to check them for movies."

"Which ones?"

Josie tossed the remote back to me. I opened the TV dashboard and showed it to her.

"Can we find a Christmas movie? I'm in the mood for something sappy and sweet."

"Sure." I went into one of my channels and found a movie. "This is one of my sister's favorites. Have you ever seen it?"

"No. I usually watch horror movies, but I'm not in the mood for them tonight."

"I can understand that."

"Have you gotten any more updates about my case?"

My stomach tightened. "Uh, no."

Not a lie. Just not the whole truth. She was calm again, and I didn't want to send her back into a tailspin. Not tonight. I'd tell her about the underwear and cameras another night. I found the movie and hit play.

"What's this movie about? An overview, don't tell me the entire story." Josie took another sip of wine.

"A pretend runaway bride who needs a story for her editor." I placed the remote on the coffee table and tapped the couch next to me with my hand.

"Why don't you put your feet up and relax?"

"Thanks."

Josie set her glass next to the remote, grabbed a throw pillow, and lay down. When she stretched out her legs, her foot brushed my thigh—light, warm, tentative. Something in me loosened. I pulled her feet onto my lap and massaged the arch of her foot with my thumb.

"Wow," she let out the softest, dreamiest sigh and closed her eyes. "A movie and a massage. Where have you been all my life?"

"You've had a long day." I chuckled. "You deserve a little pampering."

With her eyes still shut, on a soft murmur, Josie said, "Can I take you home with me when I have to go?"

"Yup. Have couch and a movie, I will travel." I grinned, glancing at her. "Are you falling asleep already? The movie just started."

"No," she whispered, opening her eyes. They were glassy. Shiny. That wasn't sleep. Those were tears.

"Hey, come here."

I shifted, leaned my back against the arm of the couch, and tugged her toward me. She settled between my legs, her head resting against my chest like she belonged there.

"Just relax," I murmured and wrapped my left arm around her waist as my right hand drifted into her hair, combing through the soft strands. "It's gonna be okay."

"Other than Ryker... no man has ever been this nice to me." Her voice cracked on the last word.

My hand stilled. *What kind of men had she dated?*

"Didn't any of your boyfriends treat you right?" I whispered. Not wanting to break this moment, but needing to know more about her.

"Not really," she sighed. "I mean—" she pushed up and turned to face me "—they never hurt me or anything. They just... didn't do things like this. Foot rubs. Hair massages." She shrugged.

Our eyes locked. And everything else faded—movie, wine, the whole damn room. A charged stillness filled the space between us, thick with unspoken words.

I wanted her. God, I wanted her. And for the first time in years, the wanting scared me. She wasn't just some woman I found attractive. She'd slipped under my skin in ways I hadn't expected—her sass, her fire, her stubbornness, and now this softness that wrecked me.

I leaned in—slow, careful, giving her every chance to pull back. Her breath hitched, and her pupils widened, but not in fear—in desire. A burning flame flickered in her eyes, drawing me in, causing me not to care if I got burned. I was in deep trouble.

When my lips brushed hers, she let out a helpless sound that went straight to my cock. We stayed like that for a breath—eyes open, searching, falling—before I pressed my mouth on hers.

I closed my eyes and let myself savor the moment she parted her lips for me—so open, so trusting, yet still a little unsure. It felt unreal. Like stepping into something sacred.

Heaven. It had to be.

Her taste lingered on my lips, a blend of her and the wine she loved, sweeter and more intoxicating than anything I'd touched in years. I hadn't been drunk in a long time, not on alcohol, not on anything—but one kiss from her sent me spiraling, anyway.

I wanted more. God help me, I needed more. And the thought settled deep in my chest, heavy and undeniable. This wasn't just desire. This was the kind of thing that rewired a man. The kind that lasted. Forever, if I was lucky.

Josie placed her hands on my chest and gave me a gentle nudge.

"Lucian," she whispered.

"Josie," my voice was low, rougher than I meant it to be.

"I think we should stop."

I pulled back. "Okay."

She licked her lips—I groaned—and she looked at me with guilt clouding her eyes. "I'm sorry."

"Sorry for what?" I frowned.

"Leading you on. Being a tease."

I huffed out a soft laugh. "I'm a big boy, Josie. I stop when you want me to stop." I dipped forward and gave her a quick, gentle kiss on her swollen lips. "Besides, I haven't made out on a couch in forever."

"I find that hard to believe." She rolled her eyes. "Women are always throwing themselves at you."

"I never catch them. But I would catch you," I conceded. "I haven't wanted to kiss them like I just kissed you."

"Yeah, right?" Josie tapped my chest and turned back around, settling against me like she'd been doing it for years.

"It's true," I murmured, resting my chin lightly on the crown of her head. "I haven't had a long-term relationship since my twenties."

"That one hurt, huh?"

"Dagger to my heart," I admitted. "But I'm over it. Learned my lesson and have the scars to prove it. Not going to stay with a manipulative, jealous girlfriend and try to make it work."

My fingers followed the silken fall of her hair, and I understood then how easily I could get lost in her. Touching her hit a hunger inside me that demanded more.

"I hate being manipulated," Josie whispered. "If you can't trust the person you're with, then you shouldn't be with them at all."

"Yeah," I grumbled. "She proved that theory with all her mind games. She manipulated me into believing she loved me."

"How long did you date her?"

"Two years. I'd left the military and was starting my new career as a patrol officer. I worked a lot of overtime so I could afford to buy her a nice engagement ring."

"What happened?"

"She complained about my long work hours. On my days off, she always wanted to go out instead of staying at home and relaxing with me. It was a no-win situation because when we went out, she accused me of flirting with other women, and when we stayed home, she said I was boring. She swore once we got engaged, and she knew I was serious about her, she'd stop. But after two years of constant fighting, I wasn't buying that load of crap. Jealousy and drama were part of her personality. I'd had enough. I didn't want to fight for someone who wasn't willing to meet me halfway, and I hated fighting with her, so I ended it." Bitterness crept into my tone despite how long it had been. "After we broke up, I used the money I'd saved to put a down payment on this house."

"Much better investment." Josie muttered.

"Yep."

Thinking about my past with Lisa was not something I wanted to bring into my relationship with Josie. What Lisa and I had wasn't love. My feelings for Lisa were nowhere near as strong as my feelings for Josie.

"So, what have I missed with this movie so far?"

"Oh, hell no." I leaned over and reached for the remote. "I am not recapping it." I rewound it back to the beginning. "You're gonna have to pay attention to the whole thing to find out."

"Meanie."

"Yep. Now be quiet and focus."

Josie shifted onto her side and burrowed deeper into me, one hand sliding across my chest, the other tucked between us. I wrapped an arm around her and held her close, her breath syncing with mine.

We stayed like that throughout the entire movie. Her wrapped around me. Me wrapped around her. My own little piece of heaven.

Chapter 24

Dirty Talker... Who Knew?

Josie

"**W**ake up, sleepyhead." Lucian's voice drifted into my dream. All warm and husky.

"What?" I rolled toward the sound and blinked my eyes open. The light-green walls welcomed me back to the land of the living.

Lucian sat at the edge of the bed holding a cup of steaming coffee.

"I didn't know how you liked it, so it's black," he said, waving it under my nose.

The coffee bean aroma woke me up faster than any alarm clock. I sat up with a groan. A jolt of black coffee would help, even though I liked a splash of cream and stevia.

"You said last night you needed to be at work at six. I'm about twenty minutes away from Ocean Breeze," he reminded me. "You've gotta get up if you want to shower and eat something."

I reached for the coffee, but he lifted the cup to my mouth instead. Instinctively, I cupped his hand to steady it. The second my lips brushed the rim, I heard him moan. My gaze snapped to his.

Lucian's pupils dilated, and he licked his lips. His jaw clenched and his eyes darkened when I licked a stray drop of coffee off my bottom lip. Coffee was my new love language if I got this reaction out of him every morning.

"It's strong," I managed. "But good."

"You got that right," he groaned.

For a moment, neither of us moved. We just stared—caught in that thick, electric pull that made last night's kiss feel like a spark compared to the wildfire building now.

I didn't want to break the spell. But I needed a shower to help me wake up and start the day. He blinked first and eased his hand back.

"You want to keep the coffee?" he asked, clearing his throat.

"Can you... take it down and add some creamer?" I whispered. "And a packet of stevia if you have it?"

"Sure." His smile was slow and warm, like the sun coming up. "I put a clean towel in the bathroom for you."

"Thanks," I whispered.

He stood, and I watched him go—broad shoulders, easy stride, every inch of him trouble.

I waited until Lucian's footsteps faded down the stairs before I threw off the covers. One stretch... and then I froze. Wait... I was naked... from the waist down.

"What the hell?"

I stared at myself, mortified. *Did Lucian... undress me? Carry me upstairs like some helpless damsel?* I don't remember climbing the steps—let alone removing my pants.

Oh God. He'd seen my landing strip. Fantastic. Kill me now.

"Did we do anything?" I muttered to myself.

I touched my lady bits—no tenderness, no sensitivity. Okay. Okay. We didn't sleep together. Unless I blacked out. But I never got that drunk. Right?

Shit. I don't remember the end of the movie. So not only did I flash the poor man, I also had no clue how the movie ended. Now I'd have to rewatch it. From the beginning. Again. I groaned into my hands.

The chemistry between us was getting dangerous—like volcano-under-the-surface dangerous. At some point, we were going to erupt. Literally. And honestly... the thought turned me on.

I showered fast and got dressed—again, sans underwear. This was getting ridiculous. I needed to hit a store today before I ended up going commando for the rest of my life. I put on my makeup, leaned my palms on the sink, and stared at my reflection.

Okay, girl. Time to face the music. And the man who's seen your hoo-ha hair preferences.

The smoky scent of bacon hit me like a warm embrace with every step I took toward the kitchen. My stomach growled. I hadn't realized how hungry I was.

Lucian stood at the stove in his usual detective uniform, looking fantastic for six in the morning. His crisp white button-down, pulled tight across his chest and arms, tucked neatly into black pleated pants that hugged his thighs and ass, showcasing his beautiful body. The only casual part of him was the black work boots he wore instead of his usual dress shoes.

And there he was, stirring eggs in a pan like some kind of off-duty, too-hot-for-TV chef. My coffee sat on the kitchen island, along with silverware and napkins. Next to him, on the counter by the stove, were two plates loaded with bacon and buttered toast. Wow, he'd been busy. I'd never gotten up early enough to have time for this much breakfast in my life.

"Hi." I slid onto the stool in front of my coffee.

"Hey," Lucian glanced over his shoulder at me before he slid the eggs onto the plates and carried them to the island. "Are you good with coffee? I also have orange juice."

"Just coffee."

Lucian poured himself some juice and sat next to me. I took a bite of eggs—my eyes rolled back in ecstasy, not condescension.

"This is delicious. Thank you."

"No problem." He took a bite of toast. "Breakfast is the most important meal of the day."

"Yeah, yeah, yeah. You and Ry must be twins because he says that to me all the time. If I didn't hit the snooze button so many times, I would have time to eat something." I bit into the bacon and moaned. "Perfectly crispy. You can cook for me anytime."

"Not a morning person, huh?" Lucian's voice dipped low, pulling my gaze to him. He wasn't looking at my face. He was staring at my lips.

His thumb brushed over the corner of my mouth—slow, deliberate—and he brought it to his own lips. And licked it. My brain short-circuited.

"What... uh... what did you say?" I croaked.

"Can I kiss you?" He didn't look away. "I'm dying to savor those lips again."

His hand slid to the back of my neck, tugging me toward him.

"I don't think that's what you asked," I whispered, leaning in.

"So, can I?" he mumbled against my lips.

"Yes," I murmured back. "Please."

He smiled. "So polite." His lips brushed mine in soft, teasing kisses. "If you only knew what I wanted to do to you with my mouth... I don't think you'd be so polite."

"Promises, promises," I hummed.

His words made me feel bold. Daring.

He stood, turned me toward him, and stepped between my legs. One hand tightened in my hair, the other angled my face, and then—God—he kissed me deep. Hot. Hungry. Our bodies pressed together, and—oh yeah—he was hard and ready. My nipples pressed against his chest. The kiss shot straight through me. I wanted more. I wanted him. All of him.

"You are delicious." Lucian groaned into my mouth. "But we've gotta stop if you want to finish breakfast and get to work on time."

"Okay..." I blinked, breathless, staring into the wildfire burning in his eyes.

He stepped back, sat, and we both pretended to focus on food. Every few seconds, our gazes collided and darted away again. I had never wanted a man more in my life, and I prayed tonight picked up right where this left off.

"Think you can take me to a store after my house showing?" I asked, aiming for casual, while everything inside me burned.

"Sure. Where?"

"Siren's Boutique." I swallowed. "I need to buy underwear."

He froze. Then leaned in close.

"Don't buy any on my account." His voice dropped to pure sin. "I loved seeing you pantyless on my spare bed. The only thing better would be seeing you naked on my bed... gripping my black silk sheets while I have you for breakfast, lunch, dinner, and a snack."

I inhaled a piece of egg. Wrong pipe—death imminent. I fell into a coughing fit.

"You okay?" Lucian patted, then rubbed my back. "Too early for dirty talk?" He smirked.

"No... I just..." I coughed again. "Wasn't expecting that from you."

"What can I say?" He shrugged, with a wicked smile in place. "You bring it out of me."

How was I supposed to finish breakfast now? I wasn't sure my legs even worked. His words made me want to march into his room, toss myself naked across his black sheets, spread my legs, and dare him to keep every promise.

The rest of my meal might as well have been cardboard. My brain was too busy melting to register anything else. Lucian took our plates, loaded the dishwasher, and nodded toward the door.

"Ready?"

Not even close. But I nodded anyway, and we headed out.

Chapter 25

Badge Bunnies

Lucian

I loved the blush on Josie's cheeks when I told her I wanted her naked on my bed. The way she choked on her eggs wasn't ideal—but hell, at least I hadn't scared her off. That blush? That was a fucking fantastic sign.

I couldn't stop thinking about how she had looked last night when I stripped her naked and pulled my t-shirt over her sexy body. Work was the last place I wanted to take her right now. I'd rather take her on my bed, in the shower, and on the counter, for starters.

The last woman I'd talked dirty to accused me of being a pervert with deviant behavior, which was laughable considering I was a by the book officer of the law.

Josie wasn't like her. She didn't recoil at my honesty. She flushed, looked breathless and faced me head-on. For a woman like her? I'd make time. I'd make as much time as she needed.

I sat in one of the lobby chairs, close enough to keep an eye on her while she worked at the guest services desk. In the early morning hours, most guests were early morning check-outs with the occasional guest who wanted to check in early. A few guests dropped off their keys and thanked her. Every guest received her soft, professional smile that made something in my chest twist.

When things slowed, she walked over to me.

"If you want coffee or something to eat," she said and motioned toward the breakfast buffet. "You can grab whatever you want. Gene won't mind."

"You know what I want to eat." I cocked my eyebrow at her. "I can't get it there. Well, I could. But somehow I don't think you would let me drape you over the buffet table."

Her blush bloomed, pink and perfect, and I wondered if her skin flushed like that everywhere. A dangerous thought for later.

"Shh," she whispered.

Her eyes widened before she darted a glance around the lobby, even though no one was close enough to hear.

I couldn't help the slow grin that spread across my face. Standing, I set my laptop on the chair and leaned down close enough that only she could hear me.

"Relax," I murmured before I nipped her earlobe. "I'm just saying you look... very hard to ignore this morning. I bet you're drenched and your clit is throbbing. Ready for me to play."

Her breath caught. Her lashes fluttered once. Oh yes, she loved my dirty talk enough to make my pulse kick up. I brushed a chaste quick kiss against her cheek—innocent to anyone watching, but the way she inhaled? The way her hand tightened on my arm and her thighs clenched. Oh yeah, she wanted me as much as I wanted her.

My only regret was that we were standing in a resort lobby instead of my bedroom where I could take her—us—to the next level. *Hold it together, man. At least until tonight.*

"You are so naughty."

"You ain't seen nothing yet, Baby." Out of the corner of my eye, a customer approached her desk and glanced around. "You'd better go. I can wait my turn, but that customer needs your attention."

"Uh," she cleared her throat. "Yeah." She turned away and headed for the desk.

I chuckled to myself and headed for the coffee station, needing something strong. The cup hadn't reached halfway before a hand settled between my shoulders. *Josie*, I thought, *she must enjoy my dirty talk to be back so soon for more.* I pasted my best smoulder look on my face and turned—and froze. It wasn't Josie.

A long-haired blonde stood there in a tiny sundress with her too-large-for-her-frame chest spilling out of the top. She brushed her breast against my arm, and she smiled up at me.

"Hello, officer," she purred, lifting her coffee. "Mind if I sit with you?"

Officer? My badge must've caught her eye since I wasn't wearing a blazer. Some women had an unhealthy fixation with badges.

"I'm sorry." I stepped back. Over her shoulder, Josie stood behind the front desk—arms crossed, hip cocked, and an amused look on her face. *Aww, fuck me. She was going to think I was flirting—I was not. This woman approached me. I was not interested.*

"I'm working," I added.

"You can work on me anytime," the blonde said, and before I could react, she slid her room key card into my front pocket. *What the fuck!* "Come find me... I promise I'm worth the trouble."

She dragged her hand down my chest and sauntered off to a table.

I stood there stunned. No woman had ever been that bold with me—at least not in public. *What the hell had just happened?* And now Josie looked ready to murder me. She probably thought I was lying when I said I would only catch her. That I only wanted her.

I could see the headline now on the front page of Hi News. 'Detective did not detect his death by coffee stirrer at Ocean Breeze Resort'.

Oh, hell no. I would not lose Josie. Not now, when I was so close to making her mine. I pulled the card out of my pocket, marched over to the blonde's table, and set it down.

"Change your mind, officer?" She drawled.

"No. I'm taken." I pointed toward the desk. "That's my girlfriend behind the front desk, and I will not disrespect her."

"The hot ones are always taken," she sighed dramatically. "But if you change your mind... I'm in room 2516. She doesn't have to know."

Damn, this girl was bold.

"Yeah, that's not happening. I'm not a cheater." I'd like to give her a piece of my mind, but as an officer for HiPD, I have a reputation to uphold. I had to remain civil, so I pasted a smile on my face. "Have a good day and enjoy your time on Haven Island."

"I would've had a better one with you for breakfast," she called after me.

I ignored her and headed straight to Josie before she exploded.

"I had nothing to do with that," I blurted before her wicked tongue cut me to the quick. We've argued in the past, but now that we're in a good place, I didn't want to ruin it.

"Right," she muttered and rolled her eyes.

"How is that my fault?" I frowned and placed my hand over my chest.

"I saw the sexy look you gave her when you turned around," she accused.

"I thought it was you," I said, throwing my hands up. "Why would I flirt with a stranger when I'm literally here for you?"

"Yeah, cause I'm your job," she huffed.

"You are more than that, and you know it." I pointed at her and glared.

"So you said nothing to lead her on?" Josie planted her hands on the counter and leaned toward me. "She gave you her room key."

"I didn't ask for it." I met her halfway across the counter, keeping my voice low.

"Right." Her eyes darted around my face. *Was she looking to see if I was lying?*

"Dammit, Josie," I said through clenched teeth. "I didn't instigate a damn thing. Hell, I told her you were my girlfriend and gave her the damn key back. What else was I supposed to do?"

"Don't play with my feelings, Lucian." Josie whispered, tears in her eyes.

"I'm not." I reached out for her hand. "I swear."

"Okay." Josie nodded. She released my hand, leaned back, and straightened her shirt. "I don't want to make a scene."

"Okay." I gazed into her eyes. "But we're talking after your shift because you are the only woman I want."

I stormed back to my chair, opened my laptop, and forced myself to focus on case reports. That damn woman would not come between Josie and me.

Every few minutes, my eyes drifted back to Josie. *Did she believe me?* I'd just told her about my ex and how I didn't mess around when I was in a relationship. *Had she forgotten everything I said last night?* I was not going to be accused of doing something I didn't do. And I sure as hell would not waste years convincing her to trust me. Been there... Done that.

Dammit, I had to let this anger go. Josie wasn't like that. She understood. The resort lobby was not the place for a personal conversation. We'd talk about what happened when we got home. Until then, I had reports to read. Soon enough, I'd be able to hold her in my arms and reassure her she was the only one for me.

I focused on the new reports about break-ins. It sounded like those damn teenagers again. Something needed to be done about them. Buried in the files, I jerked when fingers brushed my shoulder. I looked up and found Josie watching me.

"Hey," she mumbled. "I'm done."

Shit, was it already noon? I'd been so wrapped up in the break-ins case, I wasn't watching the time. Which was stupid because the numbers glared at me from the top right of my computer.

"Okay." I saved my notes, shut my computer, and slid it in my backpack. "Where to? Are you hungry?"

"We can eat here in the restaurant since my showing isn't far away."

"Lead the way." I stood and followed Josie.

We went to the restaurant and ordered lunch. Silence stretched between us until I finally reached across the table and took her hand.

"Can we talk about what happened?"

"Sure," Josie sighed.

"I swear to you," I gazed into her eyes. "I didn't do anything to lead her on. Tourists and some locals like to flirt with cops—it's a thing. My buddies and I call them 'Badge Bunnies' as a joke."

"Why do you call them Badge Bunnies?" Josie frowned.

"Because they want to fuck as many cops as they can," I grumbled. I didn't want to talk about this. I wanted to talk about our relationship.

"Does that happen often?" She smirked.

"With tourists yes, locals not all." I shook my head. "Anyone who lives here knows I don't fuck around. I'm too damn busy, especially after Chief made me his second in command."

"Okay." The word came out of her mouth, but her eyes were still leery.

"I mean it, Josie." I squeezed her hand. Time to lay it all on the line and hope she didn't hate me. "I want to date you and only you."

She blinked, surprised. "Do you honestly mean that?" Josie whispered.

"I do." I grinned. "So... what do you say? Will you be my girlfriend?"

Josie got a reprieve from our conversation as the server placed our lunch in front of us. When she finally looked at me again, her smile was soft and real.

"Yes," Josie smiled. "I'll be your girlfriend." Then her smile dropped, and she pointed her fork at me. "But if you flirt with another girl, I'll take you both out."

"Possessive little thing, aren't you?" I grinned.

"Yep, so don't forget it." She put her fork down and sighed. "And... I'm not your ex. I trust you. I was just having a weak moment."

"I'm sorry I made you feel that way." I pressed my hand to my heart. "You have my word that I will only flirt, date, and fuck you and only you."

And there it was—that blush I loved so damn much.

Chapter 26

Where is She?

Thomas aka Cade

"**W**hat the hell do you mean you lost her?" I snapped the second Vincent's call came through. He was supposed to grab Josie and bring her to our rental. We got one that was secluded on the beach. The perfect place to disappear without a trace, and no one would hear her scream as we took turns.

"She's not staying at the K9 officer's place," Vincent muttered.

My pulse spiked. "Well, where the hell is she?"

"I don't know," he bit out. "His house has been empty all morning. No car, no movement. Nothing."

I ran my hand through my hair. She was at the resort yesterday with the K9 officer. I even followed them to the showing and his house, but I left when the detective showed up. Cursing under my breath, I paced the living room, every step heavy with frustration.

"You got inside, right? I asked him. "Anyone see you?"

"I was in," he said. "Picked the lock in under a minute. But I had to hightail it out the back sliding glass door after an officer showed up. Announced himself and everything."

"Did you trip an alarm? Did you wear gloves?"

"If I did, it was silent. And yes, I wore fucking gloves. Give me some damn credit. I'm not some fucking amateur."

"After the last time, I wasn't sure if you'd stuck to the plan." I raised my voice.

"I told you I was sorry. What more do you want?"

"Fine." I rubbed the back of my neck. "Where are you now?"

"Driving to the resort. She works mornings. I'll let you know if she's there." The line went dead.

Motherfucker! Where the hell was she?

I stood there, jaw clenched, staring at nothing. She was slipping through our fingers—again.

We'd hoped that the K9 officer had gone to work and left her at his house. It would've been easy pickings because she didn't know how efficient Vincent was with locks. There wasn't a door in this country he couldn't get through. And me? With my training, tracking people was second nature. Together, we made the perfect team—until her.

We'd traveled through several states already—testing security, watching people, finding out which places were too easy and which ones took finesse. Florida, with all its laid-back tourists, had made it easy until we met Josie. She turned it into a challenge. She made us think. Adjust. Strategize. She was clever, cautious, unpredictable.

Which made the chase even sweeter. I smiled to myself, slow and sharp. She could run. She could hide behind all the officers she wanted. But sooner or later? We'd catch up. And when we did—she'd finally understand who she was dealing with. The hunt was on. I couldn't wait to catch my prey.

**** Vincent aka Aubrey aka Garrett ***

After all the wasted time watching that officer's house only to find out she wasn't there. My anger boiled every time I thought about catching her, but I loved the chase. That's why Cade and I got along so well. We loved watching them and planning a way to get them. Most girls woke up surprised and begged for their lives. They didn't fight because their terror paralyzed them. *Which was fucking perfect.* I wasn't just a computer nerd—I had sexual kinks that needed satisfying.

In the resort lobby, Josie stood behind the front desk, locked in a heated conversation with some guy in a dress shirt and slacks. Watching as I approached, he turned, and I recognized him as the officer who found my camera, whom I called the lion.

I strolled toward the desk, taking my time so they could finish. I'd told Thomas I would find her, which I did, but now I had to come up with a story she would believe because I didn't want to stand in the lobby looking stupid. If the lion noticed, he would seek me out and question me. That could not happen, so I stood in line waiting my turn.

Behind the scenes, picking locks, and computer stuff encompassed my skill set, not face-to-face encounters with victims before Thomas brought them home. If Thomas hadn't screwed up at the house on Leonard Street, I wouldn't have to be here. Then again, seeing the lion up close and personal had its advantages. He didn't know who I was, but I sure as hell knew who he was.

She finally glanced my way and waved me over. The man turned, his eyes flicking between us before he stalked off. As he passed, I caught the badge at his hip and the gun on his belt. He must be Josie's bodyguard now—fucking perfect. He was a tough one. His stone-cold demeanor and eagle eye made it impossible to get anything past him. I stepped up to the counter.

"Good morning, how can I help you?" Josie's smile seemed forced. Whatever the lion said messed with her usual sunny self.

"Everything okay?" I asked, nodding toward him with what I hoped looked like concern. "Was that officer bothering you?"

Stupid question. As if I would confront him. This was why Thomas was better at small talk.

"Oh, no, he's not bothering me. I'm okay." She swallowed. "He's... uh... my friend." Her wince said more than her words.

Friend, huh? Interesting. If he was her friend, why did she say it like that?

"How can I help you?" She asked again, this time more professional with a real smile.

"I wanted to check in."

"What's the name on the reservation?"

"Aubrey Beardsley," I gave the name of my other favorite artist, who created images that were dark, detailed and twisted in all the right ways. I loved Beardsley's work. He painted erotic images with pen and ink. Several of them are about beastiality.

"I'm sorry, Mr. Beardsley." Josie continued to click away at her keyboard. "I'm not seeing a reservation under that name. Are you sure it was for today?"

Of course, she didn't. I hadn't made one. I just wanted the chance to hear her voice. See her face up close again. Watch how she moved, how she talked. Play the game. And report everything back to Thomas.

"I... uh... I thought it was." I pulled out my phone as if I were checking something. "I'll text my girlfriend and see what's happened."

Josie gave a polite smile. Nice. I pulled that off and sidetracked her with the whole girlfriend bit. Inside, I smiled too and texted Thomas.

Garrett aka Vincent aka Aubrey: Girl is at resort. Gonna hang for a bit.

Cade aka Thomas: Perfect.

Josie Hale could run circles, build walls, surround herself with law enforcement all day if she wanted. But eventually? Everyone slips. And when she did... we'd be right there... waiting.

"Mr. Beardsley," Josie's voice interrupted my thoughts. "We have rooms available if you need a place to stay."

"You are so kind." I pointed to the buffet. "May I get some coffee while I wait for her to answer me back? I don't want to book a room if she has a reservation for me elsewhere."

"Of course. Feel free to enjoy our complimentary coffee and something to eat while you wait."

"Thank you so much." I leaned closer, pretending to read her badge. I already knew her name—she didn't need to know that. And besides, her sweet perfume drifted toward me, a reward all its own.

Ah, the scent of roses. I loved to play with roses. Not only were they silky, but the thorns left nice little blood marks when pressed against skin with just enough pressure. Pleasure and pain were an arousing combination.

"Josie." I grinned.

All I could think of was Josie and the Pussycats. How I would love to stroke her kitty.

"Of course," Josie smiled. "Enjoy your breakfast. Please let me know if there is anything I can do for you."

You can drop to your knees and open your mouth. I would love to drive my cock inside that mouth and hold your head still while you take every inch down your lovely throat. You'll gag from my size, and tears will roll down your face, turning me on even more because I'll love every minute of pain it will cause you.

"Mr. Beardsley," Josie frowned. "Are you okay? Is there anything else I can do for you?"

The sound of her brought me out of my dirty thoughts and back to the moment. No, my little kitty. But soon, very soon, you will be doing a lot for me.

"No, Josie," I smiled. "Thanks again."

I headed to the buffet, and my stomach growled. I'm always hungry. Thank fuck I had a fantastic metabolism otherwise I'd be as large as a cow. In my line of work, staying fit was crucial, so I ran several miles a day to help me keep up with my prey—in case they attempted to make a run for it.

At the buffet area, I picked a table facing Josie and the lion. Pulling out my cell phone, I opened up social media and pretended to be interested in my screen. On her previous shifts, she had worked until noon. That was a couple of hours away. I could sit here for thirty minutes, let her know my reservation was at another hotel and then wait for her to leave from my car.

Going by the amount of glances they gave each other and the way he scanned the lobby, I was certain not only was he her bodyguard, but her boyfriend. Friend, my ass. No one looks at their friend like he looks at Josie. That's okay. I knew how to recon without being noticed. I was a master at it along with my other skills.

Thirty minutes later, I stood and headed back to the desk.

"Hi, Mr. Beardsley. Any news from your girlfriend?"

She smiled—warm, polite. And damn, she remembered the fake name. Smart girl. Smart enough to pay attention... but not smart enough to see me for what I was.

"Hi, Josie. Looks like I'm booked at another hotel," I lied easily, slipping the phone back into my pocket. "But thank you for checking."

"No problem." She gave that professional brief nod, the one she gave every guest—but I liked to pretend it was just for me. "Please consider our resort next time you're on Haven Island."

"Oh, I will," I assured her, and meant it—for reasons she'd never imagine. "Thanks again."

"You're welcome. Have a great day, and a fantastic stay on our island."

I nodded, calm and collected, then turned and walked out through the sliding glass doors like any other harmless tourist. But once I reached my car, the smile dropped. She thought I was leaving. She thought that was the end. I unlocked my door, got in, and settled into the seat with a clear view of the lobby windows.

Let the surveillance begin.

Chapter 27

Sold

Josie

A ndy and Jane Cormant were an absolute joy to work with. They'd finally decided they were done with the long, brutal Michigan winters and wanted something smaller—and much warmer—to settle into once Andy retired in six months. I couldn't blame them one bit. The thought of driving in snow gave me hives. Give me Florida sunshine, ocean breezes, and sand between my toes any day. I loved this island with my whole heart. I couldn't imagine living anywhere else.

Lucian did a full sweep of the house before I even stepped inside—every room, every closet, every shadowed corner. Only when he finally gave me a tight nod did I bring Andy and Jane through the front door. Then he slipped back outside to keep watch. Calm. Cool. Collected. Just another day at the office.

I was grateful when the couple didn't ask a single question about the detective's behavior. No curious looks, no raised brows—just polite smiles and an eagerness to explore the house. I dreaded having to tell the Cormants about my stalker. It would scare them, and I knew Lucian would keep us safe.

This was the third house on our list. They preferred to keep things simple—two houses in the afternoon per day. They had a reasonable wish list. A house with two bedrooms, two baths, an open floor plan, a screened-in back porch, and a small yard for their little dog. Easy enough, at least compared to some of my other clients.

Andy and Jane explored the house, dreaming aloud. I stayed in the kitchen, fingers on the cool island, letting their voices settle around me.

No strange sounds.

No cold rush of dread.

No sense of someone lurking where they shouldn't be.

Just a normal showing. Thank God.

I let out a slow breath I hadn't realized I'd been holding, grounding myself in the ordinary murmur of their voices as they moved from room to room. When their footsteps finally circled back toward the kitchen, I straightened, smoothed my shirt, and fixed my realtor smile in place. Even though Lucian searched the house, giving me a sense of safety, a part of me still stayed on edge and couldn't wait to go back to Lucian's house.

That feeling had to stop, or my real estate career would be dead in the water. I couldn't have Lucian following me everywhere so I could sell a house.

Andy and Jane came back with the easy excitement of people imagining a future.

"So?" I asked, turning to face them. "What do you think?"

"This is our favorite so far," Jane said, glowing as she looked up at Andy. "Right?"

"Yep, I agree, sweetheart." Andy held her hand, their fingers intertwined as if they'd been doing it forever. "But I'd still like to see the next one today. After that, I think we can decide."

"We can definitely do that." I gave them both a smile. "Let me lock up and turn off the lights, and we'll head over."

I walked past Jane toward the hallway light switch, but she caught my arm with surprising speed and strength for someone just under five feet tall and old enough to be my grandmother.

"Who is that handsome man, dear?" she whispered conspiratorially.

I blinked. "Who?"

"Oh, don't be daft." She swatted my arm. "The one waiting outside. The one who checked every room before you let us in. The dressed in work clothes, wearing a badge and making googly eyes at you." She wiggled her eyebrows like a matchmaker who'd just hit the jackpot. "Is he your personal officer bodyguard?"

"Sweetheart..." Andy sighed fondly and tugged her gently back to his side. "Stop teasing the poor girl. My wife loves a good romance, Josie. Pay her no mind."

"It's fine," I laughed. "He's a friend who wanted to tag along today. Is that okay? I can ask him to keep his distance if it makes you uncomfortable."

"Oh no, dear." Jane winked. "Quite the opposite." Her eyes sparkled with mischief. "He's very easy on the eyes."

Oh. My. Heavens. This sweet little grandmother was a full-on flirt—and, I kind of adored her for it. She had more game than I did.

"Yes, he is." I burst out laughing. "I'll be back in a minute. You can stay in here or with Lucian."

"Andy, you wait here for Josie. I'm gonna go talk to the officer." Jane announced, already floating toward the door like a woman on a mission.

I shook my head, amused, and turned off the lights before stepping out behind Andy. I locked the door and turned to see Andy glance at me over his shoulder.

"Josie," Andy whispered, "you know Jane is teasing you because she likes you, right? I hope she's not overstepping."

"No," I chuckled. "I like her too."

Lucian drove us to the next house. Same routine. He checked every room while we waited in the foyer.

"All good." Lucian gave us a thumbs-up.

"Officer." Jane stepped in his path like a five-foot-nothing general. "Why don't you stay here with Josie while we look around? So she isn't alone and bored."

Lucian blinked. "Uh, sure. If it's okay with Josie."

"Of course it is," Jane answered before I could. Then she turned to me, eyebrow arched. "Isn't it, Josie?"

"Yes," I grinned. "I'd love the company while you guys look around."

"Perfect!" Jane beamed, hooked her arm through Andy's. "We'll be back in a few minutes." With a backward wave, she pulled Andy toward the bedrooms.

Lucian leaned down, voice warm against my ear. "She is a force to be reckoned with. If you want me to give you space while you work, I can wait outside."

"She is," I agreed, turning toward him. "You can stay. It's fine. I don't mind the company."

"Whew." Lucian wiped imaginary sweat from his brow. "I'd hate to piss off Jane. Thanks for saving me."

"You know," I teased, walking into the kitchen and sitting on a barstool. "You can be quite charming when you're not bossing me around."

He followed, leaning against the island with his hip against the counter and his foot crossed over the other.

"You forgot, panty-melting sexy body, excellent kisser, devastatingly handsome, best—"

I held up my hand to stop him from continuing his rant. "Uh, I wouldn't know about panty-melting since I don't have any panties on."

"Don't remind me." Lucian groaned, planted his hands on his hips, closed his eyes, and dropped his head.

"And," I whispered, reaching for his hand. "A gentleman. Thank you for not taking advantage of me last night when I fell asleep on the couch. Not many men would carry me upstairs to the guest bedroom, leave me half naked in a bed, and walk away."

Lucian lifted our joined hands, brushing a kiss to the back of mine. His eyes heated as they met mine.

"I would never do anything to hurt you," he murmured. Then, with a slow, wicked smile, "Besides, I don't want to fuck a corpse. I want you to be panting for me. I want you so worked up you can't imagine not being with me." He leaned down and kissed me. The kiss started soft, but grew more intense within seconds. A slow burn crawled up my spine.

A throat cleared. We broke apart to find Jane standing in the archway, beaming at me, while Andy smirked behind her like he'd just walked in on a soap opera.

"Sorry to interrupt, but we've made a decision," Jane announced, practically vibrating.

"You're good." I slid off the stool. Lucian didn't release my hand, so I stood in front of him. "Which house do you want to put an offer in on?"

"The other one we saw today." Jane turned to face Andy. "Right?"

"Yes, sweetheart." Andy gave me a warm smile. "We loved that one. It was perfect for us and for when our daughter comes to visit. Thank you for all your hard work."

"It's my pleasure," I said, already buzzing with excitement for them. "Let's go back to the office and talk numbers before I call the seller's realtor."

"We're willing to offer full asking price," Andy added.

"I'm sure they'll be happy to hear that. Now cross your fingers they don't have other offers."

"I'll cross everything," Jane snorted.

I left them in the living room discussing décor possibilities. Small houses were quick to lock up, so the process didn't take long. Lucian placed his hand on my lower back and guided me outside behind Jane and Andy.

He drove us to Haven Realty, our small office space on Main Street, tucked beside the bank. Three realtors, one secretary, and a rotating schedule—simple, cozy, and perfect for island life.

"Hi, Angie," I said, leading the group inside. "Jane and Andy are ready to put in an offer, so we'll be in my office."

"That's wonderful news! Can I get you something to drink?" Angie asked, directing the question at our buyers.

"Water, please," Jane replied.

"Coffee," Andy added.

"Of course." Angie stood. "Black or with cream and sugar?"

"Just black, please."

"I'll bring it to you." Angie smiled and turned. "Detective, anything for you?"

Jane nudged me and whispered, "Detective, huh?"

I rolled my eyes but didn't respond. I was too busy watching Angie flirt with Lucian.

"Black coffee would be great." Lucian smiled and answered. "Thanks, Angie."

"Follow me." I blurted and stepped away from Jane before she made any other comments about Lucian.

My office was the last one down the hall—newest Realtor meant furthest from the door, but I enjoyed the quiet. Jane and Andy took the seats across from my desk while Lucian lingered behind me, a steady presence.

I called the seller's agent, and he accepted. The sellers were ecstatic about the full list-price offer, and my clients were thrilled to land the house they wanted. A win all around.

I stayed thrilled right up until I logged into my computer and spotted the folder labeled *Buyer's Paperwork*... ugh. A necessary evil—and a time-consuming one. I opened the contract file and started typing in the seller's address when Lucian's phone rang.

"Chief, what's up? Okay... give me a second." He held up his phone. "I need to take this. I'll be right outside your office."

"Is everything okay?" I frowned.

"Yeah," he said with a too-casual smile that didn't fool me for a second. "Just need some privacy while I talk to the boss."

I wasn't buying his song and dance, but now wasn't the time to question him. I had contracts to fill out and a house to sell.

He congratulated Andy again with a handshake. When Jane extended her hand, she tugged him down, whispered something in his ear, and Lucian nodded before heading out and closing the door behind him.

I blinked. *What was that about?*

"I'm going to print the contract, and then we'll go over it before you sign."

"Perfect," Jane said, practically glowing.

Chapter 28

Perverted Alias

Lucian

"Sorry, Chief, I was in Josie's office with a client." I stepped farther down the hall, away from her door. "What's going on?"

"There was a break-in at Ryker's house early this morning," Chief said.

"Fuck." My pulse spiked. "Do you think they were looking for Josie?"

"I do. I watched the camera footage. He got in fast."

"Did Ryker's alarm go off?" All of us had alarms and cameras on our homes—the job required it.

"Yep, but since it's a silent alarm, the fucker didn't realize he'd tripped it," Chief exhaled heavily.

"Leave it to Ryker to turn it to silent mode." I scrubbed a hand over my jaw. "Judge hates that alarm sound, and God knows he hears everything."

Chief snorted. "And Ryker loves to set Judge free on an intruder or perp."

"Yeah, he does." Despite the situation, I let out a short laugh. "Have you told Ryker yet?"

"No need. He told us. His alarm is synced to an app. When it went off this morning, he called it in. Sean responded and found the front door ajar. He went inside the front at the same time a blond man ran out the back. Unfortunately, he didn't catch him."

I stiffened. "Anyone we know?"

"No. But we ran facial rec on him from the camera footage. His name is Garrett Stein. He's wanted in a couple of states for sexual assault and murder. A real gem."

My stomach dropped. "Serial rapist and killer?"

"Yeah," Chief sounded bone-deep tired. "I think so. We've gotta find this guy."

"Send me the footage and his photo. I want to ask Josie if she's seen him."

"Sending now."

My phone buzzed. I swiped up, opened the message—my blood boiled.

"Fuck," I muttered.

"What?" Chief pressed.

"He was at the resort today," I ground out. "Talking to Josie about a room. There was something wrong with his reservation, so he sat in the complimentary food area drinking coffee and checking his phone." I rubbed the back of my neck, fury and fear colliding in my chest.

"Do you think he's still there?"

"I thought he left, but let me ask Josie." My voice clipped, urgent. "I'll call you back."

I hung up and shoved my phone into my pocket. That fucker had been within arm's reach. If I'd seen that video sooner, I could've arrested his ass and kept him away from Josie for good. My jaw locked as I pushed open her office door.

"Josie, I'm so sorry to interrupt, but can you please step out here for a second?"

"Sure." Josie frowned. "I'll be right back," she told Jane and Andy. "Look over the contract. I'll double-check everything when I return."

I closed the door behind her and lifted my phone, turning the screen toward her.

"Do you remember this man at the resort today? Is he staying there?"

"Yes." Josie's face paled. "I remember him. That's Mr. Beardsley. And no, he's not staying at Ocean Breeze. He said his girlfriend booked him at another hotel. Why?"

"Was this the same guy that assaulted you at the Leonard Street house?"

Beardsley didn't fit Josie's earlier description of Thomas Kincaid. *Could there be two of them?*

"No." She shook her head.

"He could've changed his appearance."

Please, dear God, let there not be two of them.

"No." Josie pinched the bridge of her nose. "I would've recognized Thomas Kincaid."

Motherfucker! I calmed my racing heart. I didn't want to let her know what she'd confirmed until she finished with Andy and Jane. Going into detective mode, I got more info for when I called Chief back.

"What's Beardsley's first name?"

"Aubrey." Her brows pinched. "Lucian, what's going on?"

"What hotel?"

"I didn't ask." She crossed her arms, posture stiff—bracing. Trying to look strong, but she wasn't fooling me.

"Did he say anything else?"

"You're freaking me out, Lucian." Fear crept into her eyes. "What's going on?"

"How much longer until you're done with Andy and Jane?"

"Thirty minutes, max. Why?"

"I don't want to talk about this here." I lowered my voice, glancing down the hall. "Finish up. Then we'll head to my house. I'll cook you dinner and explain everything."

"Lucian." She gripped my forearm. "Please. Just tell me."

"I will," I said, looking her dead in the eyes. "Later."

She swallowed, nodded, and slipped back into her office.

I called Chief the second her door clicked shut, relayed everything Josie told me.

"There's fucking two of them!" Chief hollered into the phone. "Fuck!"

"My sentiments exactly," I murmured.

We were both pissed beyond measure by the time we promised to keep each other updated and hung up.

How the hell had they known she was at Ryker's house? Was it just the two of them or were there more involved in terrorizing Josie?

I hadn't seen anyone tailing us from the resort, but clearly, I needed to focus on a tail instead of how to get Josie into my bed. Those bastards were circling us. Now was not the time to let my guard down. Over my dead fucking body would they touch Josie.

While I waited, I ran a quick search on Aubrey Beardsley. Only one result—the historical artist. Every piece of artwork I found was disturbing as hell: twisted erotic drawings, demons, and animalistic depravity.

My gut went cold. For the first time in Haven Island's history, we had a deranged sexual serial killer, maybe two—with a fetish for the grotesque. And the worst goddamn part?

They were hunting my girlfriend.

Chapter 29

What Did I Do?

Josie

On the drive home, I learned Lucian's personality had several sides. He could be sarcastic, a dirty talker, sweet, attentive... and the hyper-focused detective who shut out the world when he was on a case. Right now, I got the last version—with a heavy dose of barely contained anger. His silent treatment made my nerves worse. *What information was he keeping from me that required complete privacy?*

"Will you please talk to me?" I blurted.

"When we get to my place," he muttered, and gripped the steering wheel so tight his knuckles were white. His eyes scanned the mirrors, the road, the sidewalks—everywhere but me.

My nerves snapped tighter than a rubber band being released after being stretched to the max. I spun around, looking out all the car windows.

"Is someone following us?"

"No."

"Are they after me?" I needed to know if I was their sole target or if they were victimizing other realtors. His one-word answers were driving me bat-shit crazy.

"Yes."

"Lucian!" I yelled, the sound bouncing around the car. "Will you please say more than yes or no!"

He exhaled hard, muscles tense. "I'm gonna answer all your questions," he glanced at me, "as soon as we get home."

"My imagination is running wild," I snapped. "I'm two seconds away from a full-blown panic attack. Can you at least give me a hint?"

"I know," he groaned, dropped one hand onto my thigh, and squeezed. "I'm sorry. But I want to give you my full attention and support when I explain."

It didn't help. Not really. But the sincerity in his voice kept me from spiraling out of control. He pulled into his driveway, opened the garage, and parked. Before I could gather my purse, he was out, hustling me inside like we were being hunted. The moment the door shut, he reset the alarm with quick, practiced movements.

"Do you want something to drink?" He took two steps toward the kitchen.

"No." I grabbed his arm and yanked. "Stop avoiding this. Talk to me."

Lucian froze. The tension in his shoulders shifted—less defensive, more resigned. He nodded and guided me to the couch. He sat first, then pulled me down beside him, holding both my hands in his warm, steady grip.

"This is bad, isn't it?" I whispered.

"Yes." His voice was low. Final. A truth dropping like a stone.

My stomach plunged. My heartbeat throbbed in my ears. I was right to be terrified. My phone rang. It was Ry.

"Hey, Ry," I answered, staring straight at Lucian. Before I could blink, he lowered my hand and hit the speaker button.

"How are you holding up after what happened today?" Ry asked.

"Lucian hasn't told me what happened today, but you're both freaking me out." My breath stalled. "Would one of you please tell me what the hell happened?"

"Someone broke into my house this morning," Ry blurted. "We think they were looking for you."

"What?" The scream ripped out of me. I dropped the phone like it burned me and slapped both hands over my mouth. "How did he know I was there? Why do you think they were looking for me?"

"Shit, I'm sorry, Jo," Ry sighed. "I wish I was there with you."

"Ryker, I'll take it from here," Lucian cut in, voice tight.

I stared at the phone like a snake ready to bite. Lucian hung up and placed the phone face down on the coffee table.

"Maybe they were after Ry, not me," I whispered, desperate for another explanation.

"After reviewing the evidence of the Leonard Street attack, your ransacked lingerie, and the break-in," —Lucian cleared his throat— "we believe the perpetrators are targeting you specifically."

"Did you say perpetrators? As in plural? More than one?" I stood so fast the room spun.

What had I done to deserve this in my life? I was nice, and I stayed out of everyone's business. I wasn't overly flirtations. I always helped people in need. Why me?

"Josie. Stay with me." Lucian held me steady in front of him. "Are you positive Mr. Beardsley couldn't pass for Thomas, with some makeup and dyed hair?"

"No," I shook my head. "I mean yes, I'm sure Mr. Beardsley is not Thomas Kincaid. I guess you could alter body type with a muscle suit, but you can't change height. Mr. Beardley was taller than Thomas."

"Fuck," Lucian muttered and pulled out his phone.

"Who are you texting?" I glanced at the screen.

"Chief. He needs to know there are definitely two."

"Oh. My. God." I stumbled back. "I thought the worst was over."

Lucian slipped his phone back into his pocket and pulled me into his arms. My mind reeled as I spoke my fears.

"Lucian, what did I do? Was it something I wore?" I looked down at myself—nothing was low-cut or revealing. "Was it something I said? Did Thomas think I was flirting when I showed him the property? Is he angry because I fought back? Did I cross a line and say the wrong thing to Mr. Beardsley?"

"Don't do that." Lucian pulled me from his embrace and fixed me with a hard, protective stare—not anger at me, but anger on my behalf. "You did nothing wrong. These men are two seriously warped individuals. Do not blame yourself. You have done nothing wrong. Do you hear me?"

"H-how did they know where I was?" I nodded, but the tears were blurring my vision.

"They must've been following you."

"Oh, my God…" I crumpled in on myself, hugging my ribs. *How did I not notice someone watching me? How had they gotten so close?*

"I need you to know," Lucian said softly, "Ryker and Judge would've kept you safe. And so will I."

"How can you?" I pulled away from his hands, pacing, panic blistering under my skin. "They seem to be everywhere!"

"Josie." Lucian stood and caught my face in both hands, gently tilting it until our eyes met. "I'm damn good at my job. I'm not leaving your side. I will protect you with my life."

"I don't want anything to happen to you either," I choked out. Tears surged and overflowed. "I hate this feeling. I'm not weak. I've never been helpless. But this... this is too much."

Lucian pulled me into his arms, and I broke. I sobbed into his shirt while he held me tight, steady, unshakable. His warmth seeped into me, calming the tremors. We stood there for what felt like forever, though it could've only been minutes.

"Why don't you lie down, and I'll make dinner?" he murmured. He eased me onto the couch and tucked a blanket around me. "I'll cook on the stove so you can see me the whole time."

I nodded and curled up. He turned on the TV to the game show channel and set the remote beside me.

"Thank you," I whispered.

I stared at the screen, hoping mindless noise would drown out the fear clawing at me. Men flirted with me all the time at the hotel—but no one had ever taken it this far.

*** Lucian *****

I was going to kill that motherfucker when I got my hands on him. Seeing Josie so defeated shredded something in me. I loved her strength—even when she argued, especially when she argued. She always stood her ground. She never let anyone walk over her.

But now? She looked small. Scared. Hurt. And that was unforgivable. I'd never let him near her again. Never.

I cooked the chicken on the stove instead of the grill—I wasn't stepping outside, not tonight. Not with every part of me wired to protect her. I roasted pre-seasoned potatoes in the oven, poured her favorite wine, and set the glass on the coffee table. Then I sat on the edge of the couch, leaned down, and kissed her forehead.

"Dinner will be ready in twenty."

"Okay."

Chapter 30

Heart Pounding Fear

Josie

I'm sure the chicken and potatoes were delicious—Lucian cooked like a man who knew his way around a kitchen—but my taste buds were nonexistent. I chewed and swallowed only because he watched me with those quiet, steady eyes, gently urging me to put something—*anything*—in my stomach. I didn't want to disappoint him, so I forced down most of it. But fear knotted my body too tight for hunger to stand a chance.

And God help me... I wasn't in any rush to go upstairs alone.

If I asked him to stay with me—just until I fell asleep—would he? Or would that make me look pathetic, weak, needy? I didn't want him to see me as someone breakable.

"I'll clean up if you want to go to bed," Lucian said, standing and taking my plate.

"Okay." My voice came out thin. I stood on shaky legs and walked toward the stairs. Halfway up, I froze and turned.

He was elbow-deep in sudsy water, scrubbing the plates so hard the enamel might scrub off.

"Lucian?" My voice squeaked out.

He looked over his shoulder. "Yeah?"

"Nothing," I muttered. My courage fizzled. Heat rushed to my face. God, I sounded ridiculous. "Never mind."

He stopped scrubbing and faced me. His brow dipped with concern as his gaze cut straight through me—of course it did.

"Are you sure? Do you need something?"

"No," I lied through a shaky smile. A crooked, pitiful attempt at reassurance. "Good night."

"Good night," he muttered.

His voice wrapped around me, warm... protective... almost enough. Almost.

I could feel his eyes on my back as I climbed the stairs—like he was willing me to turn around and just ask. My chest ached. I wanted to. I really did. But fear and pride made a mess of my voice.

A shower sounded wonderful... but the moment I stepped into the upstairs hallway, the image of the hall bathroom in the Leonard house clawed at me. The one with the latch he tried to break. The one where I hid, shaking. My body locked up.

Not tonight. Please, not tonight. Hadn't I gone through enough in one day?

Instead of taking a shower, I walked into the light green bedroom and shut the door. I undressed and pulled Lucian's t-shirt over my head. The fabric swallowed me whole, soft and warm, smelling like him—soap, clean cotton, and Lucian's musky scent. The hem brushed just above my knees, reminding me how he towered over me.

I crawled under the covers, curled on my side, and tugged the blanket up to my chin. But no blanket could do what I wanted. No blanket could keep the nightmares away. No blanket could guard the door the way Lucian could. And that was the problem—I didn't want sheets or fabric.

I wanted him.

***

I crouched in the corner, spine scraping the tile, trying to disappear into the wall. The doorknob exploded into motion—jerking, shaking—each violent rattle slamming dread into me like a blow.

"Open the fucking door, bitch!" Thomas yelled.

I slapped my hands over my ears, curling tighter into myself. My heart hammered against my ribs—an uneven, panicked rhythm—each pound echoing in my skull like gunshots.

Bam. Bam. Bam.

Was he throwing himself against the door?

"Open it! I swear to God I'll make your death more painful if you don't!"

Death. He wasn't just going to assault me—he was going to kill me.

Terror flooded me so fast my limbs trembled, but the thought of dying broke through the icy paralysis strangling me. My eyes scanned the tiny room.

The window. A small rectangular window above the toilet. It wasn't big, but I was small. I could make it. I had to.

I scrambled up; my sock-covered feet slipped on the porcelain tile as I climbed onto the toilet. My hands shook as I threw the window open. Fresh air hit my face—a cold reminder that escape was inches away. I slammed my fists against the screen until it popped loose, metal scraping my knuckles.

CRACK.

He was kicking the bathroom door. Hard.

"Oh, my God..." I whispered, breath heaving.

I heard the bathroom door groaning, cracking, and splintering behind me. I hooked my hands onto the window ledge and pulled. Harder than I'd ever pulled in my life. I'd never done a pull-up, not even in high school—it didn't matter. I would do it today or I would die trying. My torso slid through. Half of my body dangled outside, swallowed by the pitch-black night.

The door exploded inward. He barreled into the room.

"Where the hell do you think you're going?"

His hands clamped around my ankles like a vise and yanked. I screamed and kicked—wild, desperate blows. My legs were stronger than my arms, but he didn't budge. My hands were slipping, sweat mixing with blood. My grip broke. I caught the torn window screen, the sharp wire slicing my palms open. Warm blood tracked down my wrists.

"Help!" I sobbed. "Someone, please—help me!"

The screen tore with a sickening rip. Arms snaked around my waist from behind, trapping me. His rank, rotting breath hit my cheek as he leaned in close.

"Gotcha."

A bloodcurdling scream tore out of my throat. And the world snapped. I jolted awake.

Lucian was on the bed, gripping my arms in a tight, but gentle hold, voice low and urgent.

"Josie! Josie—wake up. I've got you. It's okay. Wake up."

My vision cleared in patches—the room, the shadows, the familiar warmth of his hands. The nightmare clung to me like spiderwebs, suffocating, sticky, too real. I could still feel the phantom arms around my waist, the stink of his breath, the helpless terror tightening my chest.

An icy chill sliced down my spine. Lucian brushed my hair off my damp forehead and cupped my face with both hands, grounding me in reality.

"Josie, you were having a nightmare. I'm right here," he whispered, voice rough with worry. "You're safe. I swear to you—you're safe."

"It felt so real," I whispered, voice trembling. "He chased me into the bathroom and—and he caught me before I could get out."

"Oh, baby..." Lucian's voice broke around the edges. He gathered me into his arms and held me tight, one big hand rubbing slow circles down my spine while the other massaged the back of my head. "I'm so damn sorry."

That was all it took.

The tears came again—harder, hotter, as if my body had been saving them for this moment. I pressed my forehead to his shoulder, shaking, while he rocked me, grounding me with every slow stroke of his palm. He didn't rush me. Didn't shush me. Just held me as if nothing in the world mattered more than giving me a safe place to fall apart.

When the sobs finally ebbed, Lucian tipped my chin up with careful fingers. "What can I do for you?" His eyes searched mine—raw worry, fierce protectiveness, and something heartbreakingly tender.

"C... can I sleep with you?" I swallowed, my voice low. "In your bed?" Embarrassment crawled up my neck, but my fear of repeating the same dream was stronger. "I don't want to be alone."

"Absolutely." His answer was immediate. Firm. Certain.

Before I could say another word, he slid one arm behind my knees, the other around my back, and lifted me as if I weighed nothing.

"You don't have to carry me," I said softly, meeting his eyes.

"I want to." He kissed my forehead—slow, lingering, gentle enough to undo me all over again.

I rested my head on his shoulder, letting the steady rise and fall of his breathing soothe the leftover tremors in my limbs. After that nightmare, I wasn't sure my legs would even hold me. And the thought of falling on the stairs... no thank you.

Lucian set me down beside his bed but didn't step away. He kept an arm around my waist until he was sure I was steady. Then he pulled the sheets back, but I hesitated.

"I need to use the restroom."

"Okay." His thumb brushed my hip. "I'll go check every door, window, and the alarm system again. I'll make sure the house is locked down so you can sleep without a worry in your head."

That simple promise should not have made tears prickle again—but it did. I nodded and slipped into his bathroom. No long hallway. No shadows to trick my mind. Just a clean, bright space connected to his bedroom.

I splashed water on my face, hoping to wash off the lingering fear. When I reached for his toothpaste, a faint smell—stale breath, coarse and sour—flashed through my memory, hitting me like a physical blow. My stomach twisted. Tomorrow I'd bring my toothbrush and other hygiene to this bathroom.

I rinsed my mouth, banishing the phantom scent, and hurried back into the bedroom.

Lucian's sheets were cool and soft against my skin. The scent of clean laundry and him—warm, crisp, masculine—wrapped around me. I buried my face in his pillow, breathing him in, letting that familiar comfort push back the monster clawing at my nerves.

When Lucian came back into the room, the mattress dipped under him, and the entire space shifted—warmer, steadier—my pulse easing on instinct because he was close again.

"Josie," he murmured, voice a low rumble, "I'm right here."

And for the first time that night, the fear loosened its grip. Nothing could reach me, not with him right there, steady and unshakable at my side.

Chapter 31

Be Her Friend

Lucian

Josie slept peacefully, her mouth slightly open against my neck, her breath warm and steady on my skin. I was grateful she was finally resting—but I was anything but calm. My eyes snapped open. I had to get up and clear my head, because lying beside the most gorgeous woman I'd ever met—who was curled into me like I was her anchor—was too much temptation.

I wanted to slide my hand under her shirt and claim her as mine. But I couldn't. Not tonight. Not when what she needed more than anything was comfort, safety, and a friend she could trust.

Who the hell had I pissed off in a past life to earn a punishment like this? Because damn, this was one hell of a penance. Holding her, wanting her, and not being able to do a damn thing about it.

Shit, who was I kidding? I'd do this penance for the rest of my life since it meant I got to hold her safe in my arms. But if I didn't get up and calm the chaos pounding in my chest, sleep wasn't happening.

Not with her this close. Not with my heart trying to claw its way out of my ribs just to reach her.

I eased out of the bed, careful not to disturb her. The house was dark and quiet, so I headed for the kitchen. A cool glass of water was calling my name, something cold to shock my system back into sanity.

I leaned against the counter, condensation sliding down the glass, and replayed the last hour in my head.

I'd put on a movie to distract myself from sprinting upstairs like a lovesick idiot—just something loud enough to drown out the silence and keep me from hovering outside her door like a creep. But then, her scream cut through the house.

A sound no human should ever have to make. A sound no man who cared about her could ever forget.

I was up the stairs in seconds. Josie's body thrashed on the bed—kicking, gasping, twisting like she was fighting for her life. I tried waking her gently, calling her name, but she didn't hear me. She was trapped wherever her mind had dragged her. So I grabbed her by the arms and hauled her upright.

"Josie! Josie—wake up. I've got you. It's okay. Wake up."

Her eyes snapped open, but she wasn't fully there—not at first. Terror clung to her face. And in that moment I knew if I didn't find that bastard soon, if I didn't stop him, he would terrify her forever. Night after night.

No. Hell no. Over my dead body.

My upstairs wasn't identical to the house on Leonard Street, but the bathroom being at the end of the hallway was close enough for her brain to make the connection. Close enough to twist her stomach. Close enough to yank her right back into that terror. Close enough to send her into a panic attack under my roof. And I missed it. Like a fucking rookie. Like a man more buried in a case file than in the woman sleeping in my house.

She had been so brave for attempting to sleep upstairs. That must've been what she wanted to ask me earlier when she hesitated by the stairs. I should've caught it. Should've read her body language. What kind of detective was I? I excelled at my job, so why had I failed her? I should've insisted she stay with me from the start. That was on me. And I wasn't making that mistake again.

While she was in the bathroom, I double-checked every lock, every window, every alarm setting while reminding myself I had to pull my shit together. Her safety—physical and emotional—was on me now. And I wasn't about to half-ass that responsibility.

By the time I returned to my bedroom, she was curled up under my sheets. I thanked all the gods that all I could see of her was her head because the truth was—if I saw too much of her in that damn T-shirt of mine again; I wasn't sure how strong my self-control was. Her panties were all at my office. She was going commando underneath it. Commando. In my bed. Right next to me.

"Snap out of it," I murmured to myself. "You were supposed to get water to calm your libido, not rev it up."

I rinsed my glass and stuck it in the dishwasher before I dragged my ass back to bed. When I reached the doorway, my stomach dropped. The bed was empty. *Where was she?*

"Josie?" My voice was low but sharp.

Nothing but the bathroom door was closed. *Should I check? Should I knock? Should I kick the door in?*

Her previous nightmare had been so vivid she woke up screaming. *What if she had another one and instead of screaming she was curled up against the wall of my bathroom? PTSD and fear attack everyone in different ways.*

I cracked the bathroom door open and heard the shower. *Thank fuck.* After taking a huge sigh of relief, I sat on the bed, leaned back against the headboard, and closed my eyes.

Don't picture her naked. Don't picture her naked. Don't—Yeah. Useless. But underneath all the restless heat, one truth hummed stronger. I wasn't moving from this bed until she was right there beside me, safe. And God help anyone who tried to hurt her before I caught him.

The bathroom door finally clicked open, and I let out a breath I didn't realize I'd been holding in my chest. She hesitated for a few seconds. Long enough to make sure I wanted her in my bedroom.

"I couldn't sleep," she whispered. "So I took a quick shower. I hope it's okay that I used a couple of your towels. Can I borrow another one of your t-shirts?"

I blinked and stared at her. She stood in the doorway with a towel wrapped around her head like a soft white turban, another cinched between her breasts, the knot nestled right where my eyes had no business lingering. The hem skimmed her upper thighs, leaving her legs bare—pale, clean, still damp from the shower.

But it wasn't the sight of her body that punched the air from my lungs. It was the way she held herself. Uncertain. Exhausted. Fragile in a way Josie Hale never let herself be. Something in my chest tightened so sharply it damn near hurt. Every instinct I had—the cop, the soldier, the man—wanted to wrap her up and swear no one would ever touch her again.

"Of course." I croaked.

I opened a drawer on my dresser and pulled out a navy-blue Haven Island PD t-shirt and handed it to her.

"Thank you."

I nodded because I'd lost the ability to speak. She went back into the bathroom. I sat on the edge of the bed and took several deep breaths. Get it together, man. She doesn't need to see your desire for her right now. To get my mind in order, I recited laws and their corresponding numbers. My breathing returned to normal, as well as my dick.

Better. I could do this. The head on my shoulders could control the other one. Piece of cake. Until she came out of the bathroom and my heart rate spiked.

"I'm done. It's all yours." Josie grinned.

She walked around the bed and lifted the covers. *Oh shit!* My shirt rode up, and I got a breathtaking view of her spectacular round ass. I turned my head away and waited until she slid under the sheet. My sheets rustled around her, swallowing her whole. She looked over at me—just a quick glance—but that was all it took. The trust in her eyes almost took my knees out.

Normally, I slept in the nude, but I didn't want to freak her out. Earlier, when I woke her up from her nightmare, I had been in my jeans. Pajama pants would be a hell of a lot more comfortable for her and me. So I grabbed a pair and headed to the bathroom, keeping my eyes forward. No glancing in her direction.

I took a cold shower, wrapped my towel around my waist, and was brushing my teeth when Josie came up behind me.

"Is it okay if I sleep on the side I chose?" Her fingers slid along my back, slow and steady.

I sucked in air so fast I swallowed some of my toothpaste. My coughing frenzy was not sexy at all as my face turned red.

"Sorry." Josie was patting my back. "Oh my God, are you okay?"

I nodded my head, leaned over the sink, and rinsed my mouth. The knot on my towel loosened, but I grabbed it before it unraveled and tied it again.

"I'm fine." I cleared my throat and wiped my face. "You can stay on whichever side you want." Out of the corner of my eye, I saw her eyes focused on my abs.

"I don't want to take your side." Josie bit her bottom lip.

No, no, no, no. I'd just gotten the fucker to go down. If her tongue licked me like she just did her lips and her mouth wrapped around me, I wasn't going to get any sleep. I straightened and grabbed my pants. "I'll sleep on the left side."

"The left side facing the bed or when you're on the bed?"

"Uh... the left side facing the bed." I held my pants against my abs, obstructing her view. Josie blinked, looked at me and blushed. Fuck, I loved her blush.

"Okay," Josie said before she left.

That was awkward. *Did she want me to make love to her? Or only comfort her?* I groaned and stared at the ceiling. It was going to be a long fucking night. I stepped into the toilet area of my bathroom, shut the door, and changed into my bottoms.

She was under the covers when I entered the bedroom. I slid in beside her, careful, controlled. Every muscle in my body coiled too tight. I lay on my back, giving her space, even though every instinct in me screamed to pull her against my chest and keep her there.

She shifted closer in the dark. One inch. Then another. And another. Until her thigh brushed mine.

Heat shot straight through me like a live wire under my skin. Her bare leg. Her warmth. Her body right fucking there. I froze. Completely. Don't move. Don't react. Don't even breathe wrong.

She didn't mean anything by it. She was scared. She needed comfort. She needed safety. Not the detective with a hard-on next to her. Then her hand slid across the sheet searching for me, shaky and unsure, until her fingers curled lightly around my forearm.

"Is this okay?" she whispered.

My throat locked up. "Yeah," I managed. "It's more than okay."

She exhaled, a tiny, relieved sound that hit me dead center. Then she inched even closer until her head rested on my shoulder and her body molded to my side.

And that was it. I was done for.

Her heat seeped into me, all soft curves and warm skin. Her thigh draped over mine, her breath fanned my neck, and every nerve in my body shot to life like someone threw gasoline on it.

I clenched my jaw. Tight. Tighter.

My body reacted at once, too fast to hide, and I had to rein it in—lock down every instinct that reached beyond protection. She trusted me. She was scared. She needed peace, not pressure. She deserved restraint. She deserved the best part of me, not the part currently losing its goddamn mind.

Don't move. Don't grind. Don't even think too loud.

She burrowed in as if she belonged there. Like I was shelter—not temptation.

Her hand slid across my chest, fingers curling into the hair on my chest as she whispered, "Thank you, Lucian."

I swallowed hard. "Always."

Her muscles relaxed, breath evened out, and her body melted against mine like she finally felt safe.

Me? I laid there stiff as a goddamn statue, praying to every deity in existence to help me keep my shit together. Because Josie was pressed against me—again—all warm and trusting, her bare legs brushing mine, her soft body draped over my side... And I had never wanted someone—not like this. Not this badly. Not this fiercely.

I should've taken a fucking sleeping pill with my damn glass of water.

***

Again, I stayed awake long after she fell asleep, her breath steady on my neck, her hand still curled over my heart. Protecting her. Calming her nightmares. Fighting mine. Trying—really damn hard—not to react to the woman I was falling for.

After a couple of hours of forcing myself not to toss and turn, the nightmare wasn't hers—it was mine. Josie was still wrapped around me like she'd been poured into the space I left for her. With one of her legs thrown over mine, her arm across my stomach, breasts against my chest, cheek warm where it rested on my collarbone. With every inhale she took, she pressed her body closer. Every exhale brushed the sensitive spot on my throat.

And every tiny shift she made was... fucking lethal. I had to get out of bed and distract myself with work. Okay. *You can do this, Warrick.* Slow. Smooth. Don't wake the sleeping angel draped all over you.

The problem was she felt too good—her warmth, her scent, her soft breath fanning my skin. She made a soft noise in her sleep, something between a sigh and a hum, and instinct had my hand twitching toward her waist.

No. No touching. No indulging. No fucking. I slid my hand out from under her. Her fingers tightened around my waist. *Shit.*

"Lucian..." she whispered, half asleep, voice soft and wrecking me. She nuzzled into my side, her leg tightening around mine. "Don't go."

My whole body went rigid. Focus. Focus. Don't react. Don't let her feel it.

"I'm just...," I whispered, "I'm right here."

And God help me, I didn't move. Couldn't move. It felt like gravity itself was pinning me to the bed. Her breathing slowed again. She drifted back under, unaware she was the reason I might need an ice bath.

Okay. Operation Escape, round two or was it three? Who the fuck was counting on the longest night of my life? I slid my arm out from under her neck millimeter by millimeter, moving like a fucking ninja on a tightrope. When her head dipped, I slid my pillow under her cheek.

She didn't stir. Good.

Next: her leg. Her bare, warm, smooth-as-hell leg hooked over mine like she owned me.

I angled my leg, held my breath, and gently moved hers off. It landed with a whisper of movement on the mattress. I almost sagged in relief.

Okay. Just roll out. Quiet. Easy. Like you're not a six-foot-two man trying to escape the softest, sweetest human in existence.

I eased onto my side. Her fingers brushed my stomach, searching. Like she sensed I was leaving. I froze. Not breathing. Not blinking. Not thinking. She sighed and settled again, her hand landing near my hip—but not on it. Close enough that my entire body lit up like a firecracker ready to explode on the Fourth of July.

I finally rolled out of bed, feet hitting the floor as quietly as possible. Tension held my spine in place, every muscle braced. I took the blanket and drew it up over her, shielding her from the cold.

She curled into it, pulling it to her chest, her face soft and peaceful. Thank God. I backed toward the bathroom, adjusting myself in the least obvious way possible—not that she could see, but my dignity insisted.

"Lucian?" her sleepy voice mumbled.

I froze in the doorway. "Yeah?" I whispered.

Her eyes stayed closed. "Don't leave."

My heart damn near split open.

"I'm right here, sweetheart," I whispered back. "Just using the bathroom."

She hummed in response, relaxed, and drifted off again. I let out a breath I'd been holding for what felt like an entire year and slipped into the bathroom, shutting the door with the softest click imaginable. Then I braced both hands on the counter, dropped my head, and whispered to myself:

You're in so much fucking trouble.

Chapter 32

I Want More

Josie

"Lucian?" I rolled over and put my arm out. The space next to me on the bed was empty. *Where was he? Did he leave?*

I jumped out of bed and checked the bathroom. He wasn't there. The moon illuminated the room enough for me to see my way around, which I appreciated because I didn't want to turn on any lights. *Did he leave me alone?* Ry would never leave me alone.

I headed into the living room. A beam of light came out of his home office. I pushed the door open. Lucian sat at his desk staring at the computer. His hair looked rumpled, strands pushed out of place and tangled from restless fingers combing through it.

"That photo, Lucian!" I screamed at him. "What the hell is that?"

He froze mid-click—like someone had pulled a gun on him. His jaw clenched, the muscle ticking hard. He closed the image. He didn't turn around. Didn't say a word. That scared me more than the damn photo.

"Lucian." My voice cracked, sharp and trembling. "Don't lie to me. Not now. Not after everything."

He shifted and looked over his shoulder. His shadowed, tired eyes were full of something that twisted my stomach into knots—guilt? Or pity? Neither one was acceptable.

"Josie," he said carefully, hands up like I was a skittish animal. "Please... don't work yourself up."

"Work myself—?"

I barked out a laugh, wild and too loud in the quiet room. "There were photos of my underwear on your computer. And a man's underwear. Why are you hiding evidence from me?"

His throat bobbed.

"You said you'd tell me everything." I stepped closer. "You said you'd keep me safe. That means telling me what you know. Not hiding things like—like whatever the hell I just saw."

He exhaled hard and dragged a hand through his already wrecked hair. "You weren't supposed to see that."

"But I did see it." My voice dropped to a whisper. "So tell me the truth."

He hesitated... too long. And something in me snapped. My hands shook. Cold sweat crawled up my spine. "Why were those photos next to mine? Are they... from my house?"

Lucian's eyes softened, which made it worse.

He stepped toward me with deliberate steps. "Josie—"

My breathing hitched. Tears pricked my eyes. My chest tightened, panic squeezing hard and fast.. "Those are mine, aren't they?"

"Baby—"

"Stop." I shook my head. "Please stop calling me that unless you're actually being honest with me."

He flinched. Good.

"Are those photos from my bedroom?" My voice trembled. "All the underwear the police took? The ones the pervert touched? All those pictures—were they all mine?"

Lucian swallowed and shut his eyes for a beat. "Yes."

The floor seemed to tilt under me. My hand flew to my mouth. No, no, no. Images of both monster's hands—touching my clothes, my bed, pieces of my life—slammed into me so hard I wanted to throw up.

"And the black underwear?" I whispered. "The man's underwear? Why—why was that there too?"

Lucian stepped closer again, hands extended, palms up—pleading. "Josie, please. Let me explain."

"Explain?" I shook my head hard. "You should have explained hours ago! You said you didn't want to upset me before, but THIS? THIS is upsetting! What else haven't you told me?"

"Josie—"

"What else, Lucian?"

"The black underwear," he sighed, shoulders slumping in defeat. "It's the suspect's. The dried substance on it..." he paused.

"Is his," I whispered, finishing for him. My stomach lurched. "From what he did in my bedroom."

Lucian's hands curled into fists at his sides. "I didn't want you to see that. I didn't want you reliving any of it."

"But you saw it," I whispered. "You looked at every single piece of evidence. You studied them. You... saw them."

"I had to," he mumbled.

"I didn't."

He stepped in close, palms warm against my shoulders, anchoring me in place. "Josie. You weren't supposed to wake up alone. I couldn't sleep. I need to find him. You weren't supposed to see any of this—I'm so sorry."

"But I did." Tears finally spilled over. "And now I can't unsee it."

He pulled me into his chest, his chin resting on my head. I let him, because I didn't have the strength to push him away. My hands fisted in his shirt.

"Josie," he murmured, holding me tight. "I swear on my life—I'm doing everything I can to keep you safe. I wasn't hiding it to deceive you. I was hiding it to protect you."

"I don't need to be protected from the truth," I whispered into his chest. "I just want the truth."

He cupped the back of my head and exhaled into my hair. "Then tomorrow... I'll tell you every detail. Everything we know. Every piece of evidence. I'll walk you through it all. You'll know everything I know."

I nodded against him. "Okay."

"Tonight," he whispered, "let me take you back to bed."

I swallowed hard. "But don't leave."

His arms tightened around me. "I won't."

We went into the bedroom and crawled back into bed. Lucian turned to his side with his back to me.

"Will you hold me, please?" I whispered, needing to feel his arms around me.

"Yeah," Lucian sighed and rolled onto his back.

"You don't have to if you don't want to."

Lucian raised himself off the bed on an elbow and leaned over me.

"Let's get something straight." He reached over and ran his fingertips from my forehead to my jaw. "That sigh wasn't because holding you is a hardship. It's because it's going to take all of my self-control to only hold you when I want to do so much more to you."

"What makes you think I don't want more?"

Lucian's smile grew. "I'm glad you want more, but for tonight, let me be a gentleman and just hold you. You've had a lot thrown at you today."

"Okay."

Lucian gave me a sweet kiss before he lay on his back and pulled me into his arms. I laid my head on his chest, wrapped my arm around his waist, and tucked my leg between his. He was more comfortable than any bed I'd ever laid on. The sound of his steady heartbeat mixed with the rise and fall of his breath lulled me to sleep.

Chapter 33

Fort Knox

Thomas aka Cade Gaines

I t had been almost an hour since Garrett had called to tell me the lion cop was glued to Josie today. *Shit—could the bitch just stay put for once?* Every time we got close, somebody in a uniform came sniffing around. And where the hell was that K9 officer? I didn't mind dealing with cops, but the dog? That beast was a different story. Fast. Smart. Loyal. A problem. I dreaded not knowing when he would turn up.

I cracked open another beer, dropped onto the couch, and flipped through channels. Boredom was its own kind of torture. We never stayed in one place this long—too risky. We usually kept moving every few days, leaving nothing behind but a new state line between us and whoever was dumb enough to chase.

The front door slammed. Finally.

"Where the hell have you been?" I sat up.

Garrett dragged a hand down his face. "That lion cop lives in a gated community. A real one. Guard shack, name-check, the whole nine yards. We either catch her by surprise or befriend someone inside."

"Can't you linger by the keypad and listen for the code?" I scoffed, taking a long pull from my beer.

"No," he snapped. "There's a guard posted at the front gate. He asked for a name. I gave him a fake one. He couldn't find it. So he asked me to call the homeowner so he could verify I was on the approved list."

"Holy shit," I muttered. That was a level of security I didn't expect from a beach-town development. "What did you do?"

Garrett shook his head. "I acted like I misread my text, told him it wasn't today, and drove away."

"Quick thinking." I grinned. "You're getting better."

"Whatever." Garrett grimaced. "How are we going to get her? We have no way of knowing what block she's on or which house she's in. Could be the first street or the fifteenth."

"We'll follow her together next time," I said easily. "I'll drop you off before we turn into the neighborhood. You tail 'em on foot."

"What if they recognize me? I'm supposed to be a tourist named Aubrey Beardsley. What would I be doing in that neighborhood?"

"Make something up." I shrugged. "You're better at bluffing when you're under pressure."

"Nope." Garrett shook his head. "I'm not doing that."

"Fine." I threw my hands up. "We'll have to catch her when she's not in that super-duper gated community you don't want to walk around in. But she's protected every second of the day. If not the dog guy, then the detective. They're on rotation." I opened the fridge to get another beer and tossed him one.

"Then we grab her somewhere else." Garrett huffed. "The resort. A showing. Whatever's easiest." Garrett twisted the cap. "Fuck!" he screamed and held the beer away from his body as the suds flowed out.

I slapped my leg and laughed so hard I thought I would piss my pants.

"You asshole!" Garrett glared at me. "You did that on purpose."

"You're the one who opened it after I tossed it to you. You should know better." I grinned and took a big gulp of mine.

Garrett came back with a towel and wiped the floor, his shirt, and the beer bottle before he took a swig.

"Are you sure you want to keep pushing this?" He stared at me. "There are other women. Easier ones. Ones who don't hang out with cops and can pick you out of a damn lineup."

"You losing your nerve, Wendy Whiner?" I glared at him. Hard.

His jaw clenched.

"I like a challenge," I said, dropping onto the couch again. "And I thought you did too. Admit it—we wouldn't be having this much fun if she were boring. She can ID me, not you. You just need to stand around looking pretty and stupid."

"I don't want to overstay our welcome," he exhaled through his nose. "And... I've done all the work."

"Look," I laughed. "If we hadn't spent half our time relaxing on the beach, we'd have her already."

Garrett rolled his eyes. "I didn't think we were working this trip."

"We weren't," I sighed. "But then I saw her. And I'm not passing up a prize like Josie."

"Fine." Garrett took a swig. "So what's your brilliant plan?"

"How about we grab her at the resort?" I said, leaning forward.

"Bathroom is off limits." Garrett shook his head. "It's too exposed, and there are customers everywhere."

Garrett knew the layout better than I did because he'd scoped it all out when he had coffee in the buffet area. I trusted his opinion. The only time I'd ever been inside the resort, I didn't notice the layout. The lobby served one purpose—a shortcut to the beach.

Then her laugh cut through the noise. Low. Warm. Enough to make me stop mid-stride and track the sound. She stood behind the desk, beautiful in a way that froze me in place. I watched as she handed a card to a guest. When he left, she disappeared into the back.

I needed that card. I moved past the desk and swiped one before anyone noticed. My pulse kicked when I turned it over. Her photo stared back at me with her name printed beneath it—followed by the word *Realtor*. I knew it then. She wouldn't be just another face. She would be our next catch. I hurried home, and Garrett agreed.

"Okay, then we create chaos." I snapped my fingers. "Pull the fire alarm. Everyone funnels out in a panic. You separate her from the crowd. I get the car ready."

Garrett blinked, then grinned. "That... might actually work. People freak out during fire drills. And the cop will be busy trying to control the herd."

"Exactly," I smirked. "Nine-thirty tomorrow morning. Right before checkout. People will scramble like cockroaches, angry about the fire alarm and fearing a late checkout charge."

"Wish I could stay to watch them lose their shit." Garrett barked out a laugh. "But I'll be busy escorting the lovely Josie to my car for a little extracurricular activities."

"Our car," I corrected, lifting my beer in a toast.

He clinked his bottle against mine.

"Can't wait till you grab her," I said. "Then... we'll have some fun."

"When we're done, we head north?" Garrett asked.

"Exactly." I leaned back, already imagining her screams. "Goodbye Florida. Hello Tennessee."

Chapter 34

My Naughty Girl

Lucian

The first thing I felt when I woke up was Josie. She was curled against me, soft thigh thrown over mine, her face tucked under my chin like she'd been made for that exact spot. Warm. Peaceful. Breathing slow and deep. And for the first time in days, she wasn't shaking. She wasn't crying. She wasn't waking up screaming. She was safe. With me.

My sheet had slid down below my knees. I'm not sure how it got there. I don't remember her being restless after we went back to bed. I lay there for a long minute, watching the rise and fall of her back beneath my arm. The morning light spilled across her back, causing her blonde hair to glow like an angel. When she shifted, the hem of my T-shirt—the only thing she had on—slid up her thigh, exposing smooth skin I'd been trying not to think about since the moment she'd walked into my arms last night.

Christ. The things I'd do to her if she asked.

Josie stretched like a cat, soft and sleepy. Soft, plump breasts with perky nipples rubbed across my chest. A smooth leg slid higher across my hip. Her thigh brushed past my cock. My body reacted before my brain did.

Her eyes fluttered open. She caught me staring. And instead of pulling away—like she had every right to after everything she'd been through—she gave me the smallest, shyest smile.

"Morning," she whispered, voice rough from sleep.

My heart did a goddamn somersault. "Hi, beautiful."

She shifted again, her thigh pressed against my hard cock, showing her how much I wanted her. Her breath hitched. Her eyes dropped. Then lifted. Then softened with something I didn't expect this morning:

Want. Desire.

"Lucian..." Her voice trembled—but not with fear this time. "Can I kiss you?"

I cupped her cheek. My thumb brushed the warm skin under her eye. "You never have to ask."

I leaned in an inch at a time—I didn't want to rush. I wanted to savor every moment. But when my lips brushed hers, she surged forward like a spark catching gas. Her hands slid up my chest, fingers curling around the back of my neck.

I groaned.

Her mouth opened for me, sweet and hot and willing. The kiss deepened, slow but heady, like we were relearning how to breathe with someone else's air. When her tongue slid against mine, I swore under my breath, gripping her waist as she climbed over me. The T-shirt rode up to her hips. I could feel her heat pressed against my belly. My lungs forgot how to function.

"Josie," I groaned.

She rested her forehead against mine, breathing harder now. "No nightmares," she whispered. "Not with you. I want... I want to spend the day with you and feel good before dinner. Before seeing people. Before I have time to think too much."

I searched her eyes. "Are you sure?"

Her answer was a small, desperate nod. "Please. I want you. I want to remember this morning like... like I chose something good."

Fuck. My chest cracked open. Such a humbling moment to know she wanted me to give her something good. And I aimed to please. I tore off the t-shirt and ran my hands over her breasts up to her neck.

"You are so fucking beautiful. I can't wait to sample every inch of your body."

Josie's body shivered. My words added to her pleasure—I was so fucking glad she liked my dirty talk. I flipped her onto her back, keeping my weight on my forearms so she never felt trapped. She guided my hand down her stomach until it slipped between her thighs.

Fuck. She was already wet. Warm. Ready.

Her breath stuttered when my fingers slid along her. "Oh God, Lucian..."

"That's it," I murmured against her jaw. "Let me take care of you. Your body is my new favorite playground that I can't wait to explore and fuck."

"Yes," Josie moaned. "Please."

I kissed my way down her throat, past her collarbone, and between her breasts. Her nipples tightened, and I cupped one breast while I savored the other. Her back arched, feeding me more of her luscious breasts. I lavished attention on one before I gave the other the same attention. Her hands gripped my hair, smashing my mouth against her breast. I tweaked one nipple while I swirled my tongue around the other.

"Lucian—"

"I've got you," I promised, sliding my hand down her body until two fingers slipped inside her, slow and steady so she felt every inch.

She gasped, back arching off the bed. "More... please... I need more."

I gave her more. My fingers rubbed against her sweet spot while my thumb teased her clit, causing her body to tremble and jerk up into mine. Every sound she made went straight to my cock. She moved against my hand, hips rocking, breath hot and broken. She was so close.

"Look at me," I whispered.

Her eyes opened—wide, trusting, wanting.

I kissed her again, and she moaned right into my mouth as her thighs trembled and her muscles clenched around my fingers. Her release hit hard, fast, like her body had been waiting days for this moment of pure, unfiltered pleasure. I held her through it, kissing her trembling lips, whispering how beautiful she looked when she came.

When the aftershocks faded, she exhaled, pulling me down for another kiss.

"My turn," she breathed against my mouth, rolling her hips into mine.

"Not yet." I kissed my way down her body and brought her back to another orgasm. Except this time instead of her climaxing on my hand, I shoved my mouth between her legs and lapped up all her juices. When her breathing returned to normal, she sat up and pushed me down.

"Now... it really is my turn." She grinned, with a glint in her eyes.

Who was I to stop her from having her own fun?

She ran her hands down my abs and into my pajama pants. *Oh shit, that felt good.* I arched my back. Josie took that as a good sign and pulled my pants off. Flinging them behind her. I looked down at her and grinned.

"You won't be needing those anymore." She smiled and stared at my cock. "Somebody's happy to see me."

"He's not only happy to see you. He wants to fuck you. From above, beneath, or behind." I cocked my eyebrow. She needed to know I would take her, however she wanted.

"Mmm, let me think about that." Josie crawled up my body until her lips lined up with my cock. Her eyes lifted to mine. I remained still, awaiting her next move. She lowered her mouth and licked the pre-cum off the tip. *Fucking hell!* I squirmed but continued to stare at her as she lowered her mouth, taking me deep into her mouth. Her throat opened up to me, and her lips met my skin.

I'd never been this deep inside a woman's throat. I could feel her throat tighten around me every time she swallowed.

"Fuck, Josie!" I gripped her hair and held on while she worked her magic tongue around my cock. "You feel so damn good."

She wrapped one hand around my balls, and I thought I was going to shoot my climax in her mouth. My breath was coming out like a freight train. I wanted to come inside her, not in her mouth. I cupped her head and pulled her off. "Stop. I need to be inside you."

I'd planned to go slow. Careful. Gentle. But with the way her mouth worked me over, I was holding on by a thread. I got her under me again and angled myself between her thighs, and paused long enough to search her face again.

"You still sure?" I panted.

"I'm on the pill and I'm clean." She wrapped her legs around my hips. "But most of all, I need you to fuck me, please. "

Well, that did it. My girlfriend was a dirty-talking naughty girl.

"I'm clean too," I smirked. "And since you asked so nicely."

I pushed inside her in one slow, deep thrust—her tight heat surrounded me until I had to squeeze my eyes shut and breathe. I'd never gone bareback before. Her tightness assaulted my senses.

"Fuck... Josie... You're so fucking wet... and so damn tight. Fuck! You feel good."

Her fingers dug into my shoulders, and she wrapped her legs around my hips, driving me deeper inside. "Don't stop. Please don't stop."

I didn't.

I moved with her, slow but strong, giving her everything she asked for, everything she leaned into, everything she moaned for. Her nails raked down my back as we found a rhythm that made her cry out into my neck.

Every sound, every breath, every tremble told me the same thing. She wanted me as much as I wanted her.

Her climax tightened her heat around me as she broke apart beneath me. I pumped into her a couple more times before I came with a groan against her shoulder, holding her tight, grounding both of us.

I rolled to my side and pulled her against my chest. We were both breathing as if we'd run a marathon. When our breathing returned to normal, I lay on my back with Josie sprawled out on me.

"What time is dinner with your family?" She mumbled against my chest.

"Five, but I usually show up around three to hang out with everyone."

"Okay," Josie sighed lazily. "How far is it from here?"

"A couple of blocks. I usually walk." I closed my eyes and enjoyed the feel of her body on mine. "But I can drive if you don't want to walk."

"Nope. I'd love the walk." Josie pulled away and looked at me. "Is it safe to walk?"

"Yes." I gave her a quick nod. "I won't let anyone near you."

"When you say it like that, I believe you." Josie smiled and laid her head back on my chest.

"You should." I ran my hand over her back and through her hair.

"What should we do until then?" Josie kissed my chest.

"Oh." I rolled her under me and smiled. "I can think of several positions I'd like to explore with you." I winked. "You know to give you something good."

She laughed. And for the first time in days... she looked happy and unafraid.

Chapter 35

Shower

Lucian

We'd dozed off after round two of something good. I woke up first, with her still wrapped around me. I didn't want to move, didn't want to break the moment. I loved her. She was my future. Contentment settled deep in my chest, steady and sure.

"Lucian..." she yawned into my chest. "What time is it?"

"One-thirty."

"We should probably shower before we meet your entire clan."

"Probably," I said and kissed her forehead. "They'll smell sex on us a mile away."

She smacked my shoulder, laughing into my skin. God, that sound. I'd bottle it if I could. She lifted her head, her hair a sleepy mess, cheeks flushed, lips swollen from kissing. Beautiful.

"Come on," she whispered and slid out of bed, tugging my T-shirt down her thighs.

Whose idea was it for her to put the shirt back on? *Oh, yeah, mine.* I thought she would feel more comfortable waking up with something on. It didn't matter to me. She looked like sin with the shirt and without the shirt. I sat up and watched her walk toward the bathroom doorway, hair tumbling down her back, legs wobbling from what we'd done. My pride swelled like a damn balloon.

She glanced over her shoulder when she realized I hadn't moved. Her smile was shy, warm and devastating.

"You coming?"

"I'm all about conserving water." I got up and followed her.

She had already taken off my t-shirt and stood naked, opening the glass shower door.

"I love a thoughtful tree hugger," she said as she tested the water temperature with her fingers.

"Oh baby, I'll hug your tree, run my fingers through your leaves, play with your knot, and suck the sap out of you."

"You're crazy." She laughed.

"No, what's crazy is standing here holding myself back while you bend over checking the water temp. Get in the damn shower so I can fuck you against the wall."

"Not until it's at the right heat."

"I'll give you all the heat you need," I said seductively while I thrust my hips forward against her ass.

"You're on a naughty-mouth roll this morning, aren't you?" She glanced at me over her shoulder with her eyebrow arched.

"What can I say? Your sweet body turns me on." I reached out and ran my hand down her spine. Her shivers let me know she was enjoying my naughty mouth.

"Perfect," she sighed and grinned before stepping in.

"Yes, you are." I stepped in behind her and slipped my arms around her waist.

Her hands wrapped behind me, cupping my ass, pushing me into her from behind. My hands slid up the front of her body until they reached her breasts. I massaged and tweaked them until she groaned and leaned her head back onto my shoulder.

"God, Josie..." I moaned into her neck. "You are so beautiful, inside and out."

She felt right in my arms as she continued to push back into me. My mouth latched onto her neck, and I sucked so hard, I knew I was leaving a mark. She was mine, and I wanted everyone to know it. Hot water cascaded over her breasts, heightening her pleasure.

"Lucian... please."

"Please what? I want to hear you say it." I ran one hand down her body and slid my finger where my cock wanted to be. She was so wet, and it wasn't from the shower.

"Please fuck me," she sighed and squeezed my ass.

"My pleasure." Those dirty words were music to my ears.

I took her hands off my ass and placed them flat on the shower wall. Then I pressed her breasts against the cold tiles. She gasped. I spread her legs and whispered in her ear— "Do... Not... Move" —then I grazed her ear with my teeth.

Stepping back, I admired her body—so fucking sexy and perfect. I could look at her like this all day, but my girl needed her release, and I couldn't wait to give it to her. I entered her in one quick thrust. Her body slid higher, nipples dragging along the tile, increasing her pleasure.

"Oh... my... God," she murmured and leaned her cheek against the tile.

I grasped her hips and continued to thrust into her. My assault was ruthless. The more she moaned, the harder I thrust. She tightened around me, and I knew she was close. I reached one hand around and stroked her clit. She went wild. Her body pushed back into me so hard, I released her hip and braced my hand on the wall. She stiffened and screamed as her orgasm ran down my cock.

I grabbed her hips and thrust into her again and again, prolonging her orgasm as long as I could. My legs shook. I was so fucking close. Her fingers curled on the tiles before she went off again and took me with her. I wrapped my arms around her, sat on the tile seat in my shower, and leaned against the wall. Wrapping my hand around her cheek, I pulled her against me. Thank fuck, the previous owners were smart enough to put a seat in the shower because I needed a minute before my legs could hold me up.

"That was..." I breathed heavily into her neck.

"Amazing," she finished breathlessly.

We stayed like that until we could catch our breath.

"Best shower sex ever." I turned her head and kissed her.

"Ditto," she murmured against my lips.

"Stand up." I tapped her hip. "I'll wash you."

I helped Josie stand and led her under the showerhead. While the water ran down her body, I reached for the shampoo and massaged it into her hair, working slow circles into her scalp. Her eyes fluttered shut, and she let out a soft moan that almost brought me to my knees.

"You keep doing things like that," she murmured, "and we'll never make it to dinner."

I chuckled and rinsed her hair before I applied conditioner. With the soap in hand, I washed her shoulders, arms, legs, and her back, staying in the safe zones.

"I think you should wash the other parts—" I gave her a peck on the lips. "—or else you're right. We're never getting out of this shower." I smiled and handed her the soap.

She washed her other areas while I watched and groaned.

"Are you okay?" she giggled.

"Just imagining watching you pleasure yourself," I murmured.

"Would you like me to do that while you watch?"

"Fuck yes." No doubts, no questions. I would love to see her with her hands between her legs and her mouth open moaning.

"Then we'll do that someday." She gave me a lop-sided grin. "For right now, can I wash you?"

My heart raced. Did she say she would fulfill one of my fantasies? Josie was perfect for me.

I nodded, stepping forward.

Her palms slid across my chest, slow and tender, followed by warm suds while her fingertips traced the lines of my muscles like she was memorizing them. I closed my eyes, letting her touch sink deep in places even I didn't know were hungry.

She washed my shoulders, my arms, and the scars on my ribs from old cases. She handled me like I wasn't breakable—but I mattered. When she leaned in and pressed a soft kiss to the center of my chest, right over my heart, I lost the air in my lungs.

"Lucian," she whispered. "Thank you... for last night. For this morning. For staying."

I cupped her face, thumbs brushing water off her cheeks. "I'm not going anywhere."

We finished rinsing off in comfortable silence—her small smiles, my gentle teasing, water running warm over both our bodies.

I turned the water off and wrapped a towel around her, rubbing her arms to warm her. She looked up at me through damp eyelashes.

"Think your family will like me?"

I kissed her forehead.

"They're going to adore you."

Because I already did.

Chapter 36

A Warrick Dinner

Josie

I knew Carolyn, but I hadn't seen her since high school. Not that we were best buds, I hung out with Ry, Cassie, and Silver. I don't know who Carolyn's friends were.

I got dressed in record time, and we walked hand in hand to Aunt Ruby's house. Lucian gave me a refresher on who was who in the family. I thought I had it straight, but only time would tell.

We stopped at a yellow, two-story colonial, its windows framed by white shutters with a perfectly trimmed lawn. Cars parked along the circular driveway, leaving little open space.

"Now I see why you walk." I stared at all the cars.

"Yep, there's not much room left since everyone else lives farther and they drive."

Lucian walked right in.

"Aunt Ruby, Mom, I'm here!" he shouted from the foyer. "And I brought a guest."

I pulled his arm. "You didn't tell them you were bringing me?"

"No," he shrugged. "With everything going on, it slipped my mind."

"Oh my God, Lucian." I smacked his shoulder.

"Oooh, someone's in trouble," a young lady said in a singsong voice.

"Hey, Rosie." Lucian hugged her. "This is Josie Hale, my girlfriend," I said proudly.

"Your what?" An older woman screeched from around the corner.

My body jolted closer to Lucian.

"Hey Mom." Lucian hugged the woman standing there with her mouth open. "Josie, this is my mom, Melanie. Mom, this is Josie."

"Well, isn't this a special surprise?" Another older woman wiped her hands on a dishtowel as she approached us.

"Aunt Ruby." Lucian kissed her cheek and gave her a hug.

"Luc," she hugged him back and then pushed him out of the way. "Welcome to my home, Josie. It's nice to meet you. Luc hasn't brought a girl to Sunday dinner since... well, never."

She shrugged and pulled me into a hug.

"Isn't that right, Mel?" Aunt Ruby nudged Lucian's mom.

"Yeah, wow." Lucian's mom snapped out of it, and she smiled at me. "Come in, Josie. It's very nice to meet you."

"Thank you, Mrs.Warrick. It's a pleasure to meet you as well." I put my hand out to shake hers, but she pulled me in for a hug.

"Please call me Mel. If you say Mrs. Warrick, Ruby and I won't know who you're talking to."

"She's not wrong," Rosie giggled. "And if you say Ms. Warrick, then I'll think you're talking to any of us. Call me Rosie."

"And I'm Aunt Ruby. Come," Aunt Ruby waved her hand, motioning us to follow her. "Luc, your cousins are in the backyard playing football. Go join them and leave Josie with us. We'll take good care of her. Won't we, Mel?"

"We sure will," Melanie winked at her son.

"Oh, shit." Lucian leaned down and looked at me. "Are you going to be alright?"

"Of course." I frowned. "Why wouldn't I be? You go play with your cousins."

"I'd rather play with you." He wiggled his eyebrows.

"Okay, Loverboy," Rosie shoved Lucian from behind. "I'll make sure the moms play nice with Josie."

Lucian gave me a peck on the lips and jogged through the house out the back.

"He's smitten." Rosie wrapped her arm around mine. "But you look smitten too, so I'm guessing it's mutual?"

"I hope so." I smiled and stepped into the kitchen.

"Ladies, start chopping." Aunt Ruby took out two cutting boards and placed them on the counter. "We have a lot of salad to make and apples to cut."

"What did you make for dinner, Mom?" Rosie grabbed a couple of knives from the drawer.

"I made two lasagnas, and we are going to bake two apple pies. So, more cutting and less talking." Aunt Ruby waved her knife at us. "Well, except Josie. We have a lot of questions for you."

"Oh...kay."

I must've looked nervous because the mom's laughed and Mel draped her arm around me.

"Don't be so nervous, Josie. We're glad you're here. We want to get to know you better."

"Who's the hottie, Aunt Mel?" A tall, dark and handsome man stared at me with questions behind his eyes.

"Don't be an ass, Ronin." Rosie smacked his chest. "This is Luc's girlfriend, so leave her alone."

"Does she have a name or do I call her Luc's girlfriend?" He arched an eyebrow at me.

"My name's Josie." I glared at him. "But Lucian's girlfriend will work just fine."

"Yes, it will." Lucian came in and wrapped his arm around me, pulling me against his chest. "Don't be such a dick." He smirked at Ronin.

"She's quick, sassy, and beautiful." Ronin slapped Lucian's shoulder before he glanced at me. "Let me know when you tire of him—" Ronin pointed at Lucian "—and want a nicer dressed, smarter Warrick."

"Asshole." Lucian shoved Ronin.

"Boys," Aunt Ruby shouted. "Out. We have a lot of work to do, and you're interrupting our mojo."

"Mojo, huh?" Lucian laughed.

"Don't you laugh at me, or you'll eat cereal for dinner." Aunt Ruby placed her hands on her hips and stared Lucian down.

"Okay, okay," he chuckled and backed up with his arms up. "I came in to ask if dinner would still be ready at five."

"It'll be ready when we tell you it's ready," Melanie glared at him.

"Got it. I'll pass the message along." Lucian kissed my forehead and grabbed Ronin. "Let's leave the ladies alone."

"Don't trust me with your girl?" Ronin laughed.

"I trust her, not you." Then Lucian shoved him outside and followed behind them.

Ronin was everything Lucian had said he was, down to a tee. I couldn't wait to meet his other cousins.

***.

We finished the food and had the pies in the oven when Aunt Ruby called everyone to come in to eat.

Everyone came in and took their respective seats. Lucian introduced me to Sawyer, Roman, Charles—his father, and Uncle Rhett before he sat me next to him.

"Aunt Mel," Rosie tapped her shoulder. "Can you scoot over one so I can sit next to Josie?"

"Of course." Melanie moved one down.

"Thanks," Lucian said low enough for Rosie and I to hear.

"You're welcome. That's two you owe me." She smiled and sat. "But who's counting?"

"You, apparently," Lucian murmured.

I noticed Lucian's dad and uncle sat at the two heads of the table, but their wives weren't sitting next to them. "Doesn't your mom want to sit next to your dad?" I asked Lucian.

"No, she and Aunt Ruby like to sit next to each other."

"They like to gossip," Rosie murmured out of the side of her mouth.

"We do not." Melanie glared at Rosie.

I didn't miss the fact that Ronin sat as far away from me as he could on the other side of Aunt Ruby. I couldn't even see him. But I could see Sawyer and Roman on the other side. Three empty seats faced us.

"Where's Carolyn?" Lucian asked before he grabbed the salad bowl that was being passed by his father.

"She called and said they were running late." Melanie sighed.

"They're always running late," Charles spoke out.

"Maybe if her father bought her a new wristwatch for Christmas," Uncle Rhett chuckled. "She'd actually wear it."

Everyone at the table laughed. I didn't understand the joke, but everyone else did. I glanced at Lucian.

"Uncle Rhett bought her a nice, fancy wristwatch last year." Lucian laughed. "Not that it did any good. She's still late."

"Hey everybody!" A woman's voice came around the corner. "Sorry, we're late."

"Uncle Luc!" Sophie screamed and ran to him. Lucian pushed his chair back and sat her on his lap.

"Hey, munchkin. How's my favorite niece?" Lucian kissed her cheek.

"What am I, minced meat?" Charles grumbled.

"Hi, Grandpa." Sophie slipped out of Luc's lap and over to Charles.

"Go say hi to your grandma." Charles nudged.

"Hi, Grandma," Sophie ran to Melanie for a hug before making her way around the table. Finally settling back on Lucian's lap. "Who's the pretty girl?" She smiled at me.

"Soph, this is my girlfriend, Josie." Lucian placed his hand on my thigh.

"Hi, Sophie." I smiled at her. "I heard you started kindergarten. Do you like it?

"I love it!" She swung her legs back and forth so fast she bounced on Lucian's lap.

"Sophie," Carolyn waved her hand. "Come sit in your seat and let your uncle eat."

"Okay," Sophie grumbled and stomped to her seat across from us.

"Hey Josie," Carolyn said while she helped Sophie into her seat. "I remember you from high school. What have you been up to?"

"I still work the front desk at Ocean Breeze Resort, and I'm a realtor."

Melanie and Ruby held out their hands and placed a helping of lasagna on everyone's plate.

"Josie sold another house yesterday," Lucian announced. Pride in his voice over her accomplishment.

"Congratulations" and "That's awesome" echoed around the table.

Sawyer and Roman were whispering at the end of the table and glanced my way twice. I remembered Lucian telling me they were both HiPD officers, so I'm sure they were discussing my case. I was glad they didn't dampen the mood by bringing it up at the dinner table.

I had too much fun watching them tease each other while they enjoyed their meal.

"You guys are so lucky to have each other," I said to Lucian.

"You can have them," he said wryly.

I nudged his shoulder.

He smiled and said, "You're right. We might tease each other mercilessly, but we love each other." Lucian put his finger up to his mouth in a shhing motion. "Don't tell my mom or Aunt Ruby, but we all secretly love Sunday dinners."

Chapter 37

Perfect Morning

Josie

This time, I woke up with Lucian spooned behind me, his breath warm and steady against my ear. A smile curved across my lips. Relief settled in when I realized I hadn't had another nightmare. Leaning back into Lucian's body, I heard his groan against my ear, warm and familiar. His hand shifted, spreading over my abdomen in a possessive, grounding touch.

"Stop moving," he grumbled. "I can only take so much before I forget my manners and fuck you until you pass out and go back to sleep."

"That sounds like fun." I wiggled back again.

"Woman." He pushed back into me. "What time do you have to go to work?"

"Same as yesterday. I have to be there by six."

"That means we have thirty minutes. What will we do?"

His hand drifted across my stomach in slow circles. I wanted him. All of him. Grabbing his hand, I guided it between my legs.

"Are you sure?" Lucian raised up on his elbow and waited until I turned my face to look at him.

"I'm positive," I whispered.

He leaned down and nibbled on my mouth before he plunged his finger inside me. Pleasure skyrocketed through my veins. I arched and opened my mouth, giving him the perfect opportunity to devour my mouth with his tongue. His tongue mimicked the same actions as his fingers.

He took me from zero to one hundred in seconds. My climax bursting into his hand. Most men would've stopped then, but not Lucian. He was thorough and focused on giving me another one. By the time I'd come down from my second climax, I'd drenched the sheets.

"I need you." I reached for him behind me and wrapped my hand around his wide, long dick. Stroking it several times before I ran my finger over the top, slathering his pre-cum over the head. "And I think you need me."

"I do," Lucian moaned. "But I don't want to rush you. This can be about you. I'll survive."

"I don't want you to survive." I gripped him and stroked harder, faster. "I want you to soar with me."

I scooted under him. "Please." I whispered against his lips.

"You never have to beg me to be with you. I'm more than happy to give you pleasure any time you want it."

Lucian got on top and slid all the way inside me. We both moaned. He stayed still, waiting for me to adjust to his size. I was so wet; it didn't take me long to crave the friction.

"Are you good?" Lucian kissed my collarbone.

"Yes."

He moved slowly at first. In, out, in, and grind. He kept up the tempo until we were both breathing heavy our bodies straining towards each other, needing release. His thrusts were so powerful, I slid across his satin sheets and bumped the headboard with a soft thud. I barely noticed it—didn't care enough to slow down. All my attention stayed on him, on us, on the need to finish what we'd started together.

"Oh, shit." Lucian stopped and rubbed my scalp. "Are you okay?" He was panting.

"I'm fine." I raised my hands over my head and pushed against the headboard, grinding into him. "Don't stop."

"Fuck!" Lucian growled.

He held my hips and pounded into me until I closed my eyes, tightened around him, and climaxed in sweet relief. My body floated on a wave of ecstasy. His movements didn't slow down. He was a man on a mission, seeking his release just as badly as I sought mine.

Before I came down from my climax, he thrust harder and faster, bringing me to another fevered frenzy.

"Josie," he grunted before we both lost control.

When our panting returned to normal, Lucian planted soft kisses on my neck before he braced himself on his elbows and stared into my eyes.

"That was amazing," he murmured against my lips. "I'm gonna shower so I can give you a few more minutes."

"Okay," I whispered and rolled over. I hadn't been with anyone in a long time, and my body was feeling the effects of being entered by a large man often. But I must admit, I loved that kind of sore. One that I hoped to have every day. I curled up in the fetal position and closed my eyes. For the first time in years, I didn't want to think about my finances and go to work. I wanted to lie in bed with Lucian all day. I was dozing off when the bed dipped.

"Hey, Sleeping Beauty." Lucian kissed my shoulder. "You need to rise and shine if you're going to make it to work on time."

"I don't want to go," I murmured into the pillow.

Lucian chuckled. "I'll go start the coffee."

***

The aroma of coffee reached my senses, and I opened my eyes.

"Hey, beautiful." Lucian was crouched on the side of the bed waving the coffee near my nose. "Time to get up and get moving."

"What time is it?" I sat up and brushed my hair away from my face before I reached for the perfect alarm—coffee. I took a long sip, letting it flow into my throat. I loved coffee. It helped me in the morning, at night, and even during the day when I was so damn tired from the hotel and still had to be a realtor.

"It's almost eight."

"What!" I swung my legs out of bed and spilled the hot coffee on them. "Ouch!" I screamed. *How could my favorite vice burn me? Traitor.* "Why did you let me sleep so late? Gene is going to kill me."

"Hey, calm down. It's okay." Lucian grabbed my coffee and placed it on the nightstand. "I called him and let him know you were coming in late."

"Why would you do that?" I shoved him so I could stand, but he wasn't budging.

"Because you were tired and I'm betting with that nightmare, you haven't been sleeping. Besides, you looked so good basking in the afterglow of our fucking." Lucian grinned.

"Jerk." Deep down, I knew he was right. I had enjoyed those few more minutes—hours—of sleep time, but shit, now I had to hurry. I opened my legs, putting them on either side of him, and placed my hand on his shoulder, ready to stand. Lucian growled and, with his hand pressed to my stomach, pushed me back on the bed. His tongue dove toward my clit.

"We don't have time for this?" My voice came out raspy. How did he get me so wet so fast?

"Sure we do." He mumbled and slid a finger inside.

"Lucian," I put my hands on the sides of his head fully intending to push him away, but my hands had a mind of their own and pulled him closer instead. My body was on fire from his talented tongue and fingers. Gene could wait.

What's another few minutes?

Or an hour.

After Lucian worked me over, I showered and was ready to go.

Chapter 38

Fire Alarm... Really?

Lucian

On the drive to the hotel, Josie tried to stay mad at me—she really did. She kept her arms crossed, chin high, refusing to look at me. But every time I caught her sneaking a glance, the corner of her lips twitched up into a grin she couldn't fight.

Fuck yeah. I'd given her a damn good wake-up call this morning—twice—and seeing that glow back in her eyes after the shit she'd gone through these past few days felt like a personal victory. She deserved to wake up smiling. She deserved peace. And if I had to give her an orgasm every morning to make that happen, well... that was a sacrifice I was prepared to make.

When I pulled into the parking lot, Josie didn't wait for me. She rushed out of the car into the resort like a race car driver pulling out of the pit after a tire change. Her frantic run to the front door was adorable as hell, but so unnecessary.

When I spoke to Gene this morning, I updated him on the situation with Josie and looped him into the plan to keep an eye out for her. He'd even offered to give her the entire day off, but that wasn't Josie. My girl needed to stay busy. My girl. Damn, I liked the sound of that—a little too much.

I sat in the resort lobby with a clear view of the front desk. I watched Josie greet guests with a practiced, polished, and professional smile. Opening my laptop, I dove into reports when all hell broke loose.

The fire alarm exploded through the lobby—shrill, deafening, and fucking wrong.

I snapped my laptop shut and stood. Instantly, chaos erupted. Guests panicked and shoved each other toward the exits. Luggage toppled. People screamed. Shoes slapped against the tile in frantic steps.

Gene rushed out from the back and tried to corral the crowd with Josie, but the pandemonium drowned their voices.

This wasn't normal. This wasn't accidental.

My phone was already in my hand as I scanned the room, adrenaline hitting me like a freight train. I texted Chief even though I was sure the alarm had also notified dispatch.

> Lucian: Fire Alarm at Ocean Breeze. Possible Distraction. Josie with me. Send ambulance and backup. Will update.

I didn't send my second thought. Feels like a setup. Because it did. Every instinct I had—the ones that had kept me alive through almost two decades of serving in the military and police work—lit up at once. Someone pulled that fucking alarm. And they did it with one intention.

Josie.

I slid the phone back into my pocket, not waiting for his response, and looked toward the guest services desk. With so many people running around, I didn't see her.

"Everyone!" I shouted and raised my hands. "Exit the building slowly. The fire department is on its way. Please stop running."

They slowed down for about a minute before the next batch of guests came off the elevators and out of the stairwell. I continued to yell at them to slow down as I cut through the crowd looking for Josie.

The lobby desk was empty. She must've gone out through an employee exit. I rounded the corner and saw Gene assisting guests.

"Gene?" I screamed over the sounds of crying children and angry parents. "Where's Josie?"

"I don't know. She went toward the elevators to help an older lady with a walker."

"Is this a false alarm?" A lady yelled at Gene. "My kids wanted to go to the beach, but we had to evacuate before they could put their bathing suits on. This is ridiculous. I'm never coming back to this hotel!"

Gene had his hands full. She wasn't the only guest screaming bloody murder at him. Between trying to help Gene and looking for Josie, I was losing my damn mind.

Gene said in the nicest voice possible. "Ma'am, I'm so sorry for the inconvenience. But it's better to exit the building until the fire department gets here and gives us the all clear."

She was not letting up, and I'd had enough. 'Ma'am, I am a detective with Haven Island PD." I unclipped my badge from my belt and placed in front of her. "Please evacuate the building now."

"Fine," she grumbled and led her kids toward an exit.

"Gene," I put my badge back on my belt. "You need to exit the building."

"I will," Gene nodded. "As soon as the last guest has left my hotel."

"Really?" I threw my hands up.

"Yep, if this resort goes down, I'm going down with it." He turned away from me and kept repeating to the guests to please exit the building.

"Unbelievable," I muttered. Stubborn man, but I didn't have time to argue with him. I tapped his back and said. "I'm gonna go look for Josie."

I had to find her. *Where the hell was she?* Gene said she was helping an older woman by the elevators, but when I got there—no Josie.

The fire station trucks were blaring outside along with our police sirens. I walked the entire first floor near the elevators screaming for Josie, but I couldn't find her. The fire chief and several firefighters took to the stairs. I grabbed the fire chief's arm before he passed me.

"Fire Chief, I'm looking for Josie Hale. Do you know who that is?"

"Yes, Detective." He nodded.

"If you see her, call me ASAP. She could be in danger."

"Will do."

The fire chief got on his radio and told his men to be on the lookout for Josie as he ran up the stairs.

"Josie," I mumbled to myself. "Where the hell are you?"

"Detective!" I turned and saw Ryker and Judge running toward me. "Where's Josie?"

"I don't fucking know." I ran my hands over my head, pushing my hair back. "One minute she's behind the desk and the next she's gone. Gene said she came over here to the elevators to help an older lady, but I've checked the whole fucking floor and I can't find her. The firefighters headed up the stairs, checking every floor. I asked the fire chief to be on the lookout for her."

"Shit. Okay. Judge and I will check outside."

"Thanks."

I paced the shit out of that floor like a trapped animal. My heartbeat was a sledgehammer to my ears. Every face I passed that wasn't Josie's made my stomach twist tighter. *Where could she be? Did she exit with the older lady? Did she double back? Was this a fucking setup?*

"Detective! Lucian!"

I snapped my head up. Chief Alejandro bulldozed his way through the crowd, looking angrier than a wounded grizzly. The sight should've grounded me. Instead, dread crawled up my throat. He was going to chew me out for losing Josie.

"Chief," I said, forcing myself still though every muscle in my body was screaming at me to keep searching.

"Has anyone seen her?" His voice thundered, sharp enough to cut.

"No, sir," I answered.

"What the fuck happened?"

I explained everything. With every sentence, his hands flexed—opening, closing—like he was strangling the air just to keep from strangling me. When I finished, I stood there... waiting. For the wrath. The lecture. The punch to my face for fucking up. But it never came.

"Why are you looking at me like that?" Chief frowned at me.

"Go ahead," I said hoarsely, stepping forward, shoulders tense. "Hit me. I know you want to. I lost one of your wife's friends. I fucked up royally, and I deserve to feel some pain."

I shook out my arms, bracing myself. God, I hoped it hurt. Maybe it would knock loose this suffocating guilt, this terror that wouldn't let me breathe. Chief stared at me like I'd grown three heads.

"Have you lost your fucking mind?" he barked. "I've never hit a fellow officer, and I'm not about to start now." His voice softened just a fraction. "Besides, I'm pretty sure that heart and mind of yours are beating you up enough."

He had no idea. My heart wasn't beating me up; it had shredded itself, each beat sharp and unforgiving.

"You're right," I rasped. "Fuck! I never considered someone pulling a damn fire alarm to get to Josie."

"You don't know that's what happened." Chief looked around at the chaotic lobby, scanning every face with the same desperation I felt. "She might be helping someone as we speak."

I shook my head, a sick twist tightening my chest until it hurt to inhale. My voice cracked when I spoke.

"I don't think so." I swallowed hard, but nothing loosened. "I have a sinking feeling in my chest." I touched my hand there without meaning to. "I think those assholes orchestrated this whole thing..." My voice dropped, raw. "...and they've taken her."

The words soured in my mouth. I hadn't felt this powerless since my worst nights overseas—those moments when the world went silent right before the shitstorm hit, when no amount of training or muscle or grit could change what was coming.

But this? This was the first time as a Haven Island PD officer that the old feeling surged back—dark, cold, and merciless. The same helplessness I thought I'd buried in the sand after my last deployment now clawed its way up my spine, gripping tight.

"Hey!" Chief Alejandro grabbed my shoulders and shook me. "Snap out of it. Let's go talk to the fire chief."

Chief Alejandro had also served. We'd had many conversations about what we went through in the sandbox.

"Fire Chief!" I screamed when he came out of the stairwell. Chief and I ran toward him. I had to know if this had all been a setup. Both chiefs shook hands before the fire chief spoke.

"It was a false alarm. We found an alarm pulled on the fourth floor. We still checked every floor, just in case, but no fire."

"Did you see Josie?" I asked.

"I didn't." Fire Chief got on his radio again as the firefighters were exiting the stairwell. "Anyone see Josie Hale?"

Lots of 'no sir' in person and over the radio.

"Sorry, Detective." Fire Chief placed his hand on my shoulder. "Let's give everyone the all clear. Good luck with the angry guests." He smirked at me and Chief Alejandro.

"Yeah, thanks," I muttered, but the Fire Chief was already walking away—free from the fallout. Must be nice.

The moment the fire chief stepped outside to give the all-clear, I knew in my gut what was coming next. Guests surged back toward the lobby, some muttering, some flat-out yelling. Hudson jogged to my side.

"Well, this is gonna be fun," he whispered before a woman launched into a tirade about how the fire alarm ruined her morning.

I tuned her out, scanning the crowd for even a glimpse of Josie. My pulse hammered in my ears. My chest felt too tight to hold air. *Where the hell was she?*

"Lucian!" Ryker rushed in from outside, Judge practically dragging him by the leash. "Nothing. We checked every exit."

My heart dropped. "Let's check the lobby desk. Maybe she doubled back."

"Right behind you," Ryker agreed.

We pushed through the crowd and into the lobby again. Gene was behind the desk doing his best to calm the growing mob, promising refunds, future discounts—anything to make them stop yelling.

But Josie wasn't there. She wasn't anywhere.

"We need the camera footage." I didn't recognize my own voice—raw, scraped, edged with something close to breaking.

"It might take a minute before Gene—" Ryker motioned to where the man was practically drowning under complaints "—can break away."

"Yeah, well, this is police business. They're gonna have to wait." I stormed my way behind the desk.

"Ladies and gentlemen," I projected, letting command settle into my tone, "we realize this was an inconvenience, but I need to speak with Mr. Helmond privately. Please come back in twenty minutes."

More grumbling. More protests. I didn't care, but I pulled Gene aside and offered a suggestion.

"Give them something so we can talk."

Gene raised his hands. "I will email all of you a complimentary night's stay—or a discount for a future trip. Please, give us a few minutes."

Ryker shot me a look. "Nice save."

"Wasn't for them," I growled.

"Thank you for the assist." Gene turned to us and rubbed his forehead. "That was—"

"We don't have time," my voice cracked. "We need your camera footage. Now."

Gene's eyes widened when he finally looked at me, surprise cutting across his expression. He saw it. The fear. The fury. The absolute bone-deep desperation.

"Follow me."

"Chief?" I turned to see if he was coming.

"Both of you go." He waved his hand toward Gene. "I'll control the crowd."

"Thanks." I nodded.

Ryker, Judge and I followed Gene into his office behind the lobby desk. Ryker closed the door behind us, and Judge planted himself right in front of the monitor, whining—like even he sensed the urgency. I leaned on the desk, breathing hard.

"I'm sure she's in the building," Gene said, trying to reassure me. "She would never leave without telling me."

"No," I whispered, staring at the dark screen, willing it to show me her face. "She's not."

Something in my chest twisted, leaving pain in its wake.

"She's gone."

Chapter 39

Camera Footage

Lucian

"We need to retrace Josie's steps from the moment the alarm went off," I said the second Gene settled behind his computer. My voice was barely holding together—steady enough to pass for professional, but underneath it, panic gnawed straight through my ribs.

Ryker stood behind me, arms rigid, jaw tight. Judge leaned against his leg, ears perked, picking up every bit of tension in the room.

Gene clicked through camera feeds. Behind the desk, Josie helped two guests, smiling, handing out keys. Then, a few minutes later—

"There." Ryker jabbed a finger at the screen. "She's heading toward the elevators."

Gene slowed the footage.

Josie pointed toward the exits near the elevator. Several guests shoved an older woman, who was struggling with her walker, out of their way. Josie fell into step beside her, close enough to shield her if needed. That's my Josie, so trusting and kind.

"Zoom in," I barked.

Gene obeyed.

Then, a man stepped behind her. A man I recognized. Garrett. Motherfucking. Stein. Aka Aubrey Beardsley. The mug shot I'd seen on my computer a couple of days ago.

Garrett kept his head down, but I knew that profile, that build, those shoulders. The same fucker who broke into Ryker's house. The same fucker who lied his way into the resort under a fake name. The same fucker whose underwear we found in Josie's bedroom.

He reached out, grabbed the walker from the older woman, and yanked it sideways, creating a split-second of chaos—just enough for him to shove Josie out the exit doors and out of sight.

I felt the blood drain from my face.

"Fuck." Ryker exhaled.

Gene covered his mouth with his hand. "Dear Lord..."

The fire alarm being pulled not only served as a perfect distraction—it set the trap.

I slammed my fist on the desk. "He pulled the damn alarm so he could walk her out in the panic without being seen." My jaw clenched so hard it ached.

"We need footage from the outside cameras," I said, turning to Gene.

"I only have this view on my screen," he said shakily, "but we can go to the security office. You can see all the feeds there."

"You have a security office?" I stared at Ryker. He stared at me, stunned, mirroring my own shock. "Why didn't I know that?"

"We don't tell many people." Gene hurried to open the door for us.

"Uh, we're the police." Ryker pointed at both of us.

"I know, but we haven't had any trouble here, so it never came up." Gene shrugged. "Besides, it's only monitored by two men who take shifts."

"Great," I grumbled. "So where the hell was he when everyone was evacuating like bats out of hell?"

"I don't know." Gene frowned as we picked up the pace. He stopped at a door near the end of the hall and knocked. "Jim!" he called.

No answer.

I grabbed his arm and pulled him back. "Let us go in first. Just in case."

Ryker and I drew our weapons. Judge stiffened, ready.

We nodded to each other. I turned the knob—unlocked.

"Jim!" I hollered. "Haven Island PD—we're coming in."

Ryker entered first with Judge. The room was small, lit by the glow of dozens of monitors showing every floor and every exterior shot.

A man in a security uniform lay on the floor—face down, unmoving. Blood on the back of his head.

"Ryker, call it in." I knelt and checked for a pulse. "He's alive."

The guard groaned, hand reaching for the back of his head.

"Sir, can you hear me?" I demanded.

The man gave a slight nod and squinted his eyes open. "Yeah... shit...," he groaned.

"I'm Detective Warrick with the Haven Island PD. Can you tell me what happened?" I helped him sit while Ryker called for an ambulance. Judge sniffed around the room, alert.

"I was watching the monitors," Jim rasped, "and I saw this guy pull the fire alarm. Next thing I know—pain radiates through the back of my head—and it's lights out."

"Do you think you can pull that footage before the ambulance gets here?"

"I... I can try." I helped Jim back into his chair. He reached for the mouse, fingers unsteady. "Man, I'm fuzzy."

"Never mind." I steadied him. "Gene, take him to the lobby. The ambulance should be here soon."

"Come on, Jim," Gene said, helping him up. "Lean on me."

As soon as they left, Ryker scanned the room with Judge, and I texted Corey in IT.

> Lucian: I need you to come to Ocean Breeze ASAP.

> Corey: On my way.

"Do you see anything?" I asked Ryker.

"Yeah, come here."

I stepped to where he stood. A metal bat lay on the floor—blood smeared across it.

"Great," I muttered. "We'll dust it for prints." I texted Kyle. I needed him and Jamie now, with their kits.

"Security guard's lucky he was only hit once," Ryker said. "That shit could've killed him."

"I don't think he was here to kill Jim," I growled. "He was here to kidnap Josie."

Ryker's jaw flexed. "I hate to say it. But I think you're right. And that fucking pisses me off."

Judge growled low.

Within minutes, the room filled—Corey at the computer scrubbing footage, Kyle dusting the bat, Jamie taking photos. Ryker, Judge, and I stood pressed against the wall, watching the screens like they were the only oxygen left.

"Wait—there!" I snapped.

Corey froze the frame of the guy pulling the alarm.

"Put that on a flash drive," I ordered. "So we can rewatch it and run facial rec."

"On it," Corey confirmed.

Ryker crossed his arms. "But if Jim saw Garrett Stein pull the alarm, who hit him in the back of the head seconds later?"

"Fuck!" I squeezed the bridge of my nose. "There are two of them. That's why Josie didn't see Thomas Kincaid. Garrett Stein, aka Mr. Beardsley, was watching her, feeding Thomas information. Sorry, I forgot to update you."

"What the fuck, man?" Ryker glared at me. "That's the guy who fucking broke into my house!"

"I know!" Ryker raked a hand through his hair.

I moved behind Corey. "I need you to show me the lobby, elevator hallway, and follow them out the side exit."

I held my breath as people poured out of the stairs and elevators trying to find an exit. Josie came into view.

"Stop it right there and slow it down."

Josie appeared beside an older woman, steadying her, keeping the crowd from trampling them. She held the exit door open while the woman passed through. Then, a man shoved Josie outside and grabbed her arm.

"I already saw this," I barked. "I need another fucking angle!"

Corey scrambled over the keyboard until the outside camera feed filled the screen—the angle I'd been waiting for. Garrett hauled her out of the hotel, his grip tight and unyielding. Josie fought him, twisting and pointing back toward the entrance, trying to break free.

My lungs constricted as I watched Josie fighting for her life.

Garrett ignored her protests and shoved her into the backseat of a car parked along the side of the resort, the engine already running. Josie scrambled to the door, pulling on the handle—it didn't open. Garrett slid into the front passenger seat and shut the door. The last image I saw before they drove off showed Josie's face—pale, terrified—as she banged on the window, screaming.

My rage became a living thing.

"Can we get a shot of that tag?" my voice bellowed.

"Yeah," Corey emphasized. "I'll take everything back to the station. Run facial rec, tag scan, the works."

"Thanks. Please hurry."

"We're done too, Detective." Kyle said as he and Jamie packed up.

The room emptied.

I stood there for a moment, staring at the blank monitor, my pulse pounding in my ears. We all knew the truth. In abductions, the first twenty-four hours were everything.

After that... it turned into recovery instead of rescue. I refused to let that happen to Josie.

"I'm going back to the station," I said, turning to Ryker. "You coming?"

Ryker didn't hesitate. "Abso-fucking-lutely."

Judge barked, ready for war.

And so was I.

We left the room with one mission. Find Josie. And destroy the men who took her.

Chapter 40

We Did It

Thomas aka Cade

"**H**oly Shit! That was fucking awesome!" I hollered, adrenaline still pumping as I checked the rearview mirror. People flooded out of the hotel like ants from a kicked hill—panicked, confused, useless. "Look at 'em scatter."

Josie was in the backseat, pinned between the locks and her fear. Tears streamed down her cheeks, streaking her makeup. She looked small, cornered. Perfect.

"Who are you people? What do you want with me?" she screamed, voice cracking. She yanked at the door handle.

It didn't budge.

"We've got unfinished business," I said, twisting in my seat so she could see my smile—the one she'd never forget. The moment recognition hit her, her mouth dropped open and her eyes went wide.

There it was.

Fear.

Delicious, helpless fear.

"Please," she sobbed. "Let me go. I haven't done anything to you."

"Yeah, right!" I chuckled. "You stopped me from having fun at that house. Not to mention kicking my balls pissed me off. I don't let that shit slide."

She grabbed the handle again, pulled until her knuckles turned white.

"You can't get out," I laughed. "Child safety locks. A beautiful invention for situations like this."

"And your precious officer hasn't even realized you're gone yet." Garrett snorted beside me. "Dumb bastard."

"He's not a bastard." Josie's voice shook, but she had fire. "You're the bastards."

Garrett let out a low whistle. "Damn, Thomas. She's got a mouth on her."

"She'd better shut that mouth or I'll stuff it with my dick to shut her up. My cock needs some TLC after she attacked it," Thomas laughed.

"Stick it in my mouth and I'll bite it off!" Josie hollered.

"Damn, Thomas, we got us a feisty one," Garrett snickered. "I like it."

"Let... me... go!" Josie enunciated each word with a kick to the back of our seats.

"Fucking bitch!" I screamed. "I'm trying to drive. Stop fucking kicking my seat or you'll get us all killed!"

Josie wasn't stopping. She kicked and shoved the seat harder. Then her hand smacked the back of my head, stunning me for a second.

"Holy shit!" Garrett nearly doubled over laughing. "She's got spirit."

"It's not fucking funny, Vincent!" I growled, my temper snapping. "Do something or I'll pull over and put a bullet in her head before you can fuck her!"

Josie stopped. I glanced at her in the rearview mirror. She was panting, but what I loved most was seeing the fear in her eyes. Good. The reality of her situation had finally sunk in. Thank fuck. She wasn't dealing with idiots or amateurs. This wasn't our first rodeo. About fucking time she realized that.

"You should listen to Thomas." Garrett twisted in his seat and gave her a slow grin. "Either settle down... or things are gonna get a lot worse for you real fast."

"I see that got your attention." I laughed. "Did you think we were just going for a joyride?"

Her breath hitched, and she glared at Garrett. "I thought your name was Aubrey Beardsley?"

"One of my many alias'." Garrett grinned and pointed at me. "Did you really think his name was Thomas Kincaid?"

"No," Josie blurted, but she didn't look fully convinced.

"So our toy isn't as smart as we thought." I smirked and glanced at Vincent.

"If anything happens to me, Detective Lucian will skin you alive," she grumbled and leaned back, chest heaving. Her eyes flicked between us, searching for an opening she'd never get.

"Who the fuck is Detective Lucian?" I frowned.

"If it's that officer with the dog," Garrett snorted. "He's not exactly a genius. I broke into his house, and he didn't even know until it was too late."

"He did know, asshole," she shot Garrett a glare. "Silent alarm and cameras. He knows exactly who you are."

Garrett shrugged, unconcerned. "Big fucking deal. I ain't caught yet. We've been at this for what two... three years."

I backhanded his chest. "Shut the fuck up."

Josie's breath hitched. "You... you've done this before?"

Her lips trembled as she said the words. Good. She needed to understand she was in deep shit.

"Yup," I sighed. "And we'll do it again after you. So sit back and relax." Smirking over my shoulder while I glanced at her, I said. "Pretty soon, you won't have any worries at all."

"Yeah," Garrett chuckled and leaned back with a lazy grin. "We'll even give you a good time before you sleep with the fishes."

Josie's face paled, her lips pressed shut. Good. Let her think. Let her simmer. Let her realize she had nowhere to run. We controlled the situation. We covered our tracks. Her precious Detective Lucian and the cop with the dog wouldn't find us fast enough to save her.

Chapter 41

Focus... Plan... Escape

Josie

I couldn't believe I'd let them take me. One minute I was helping an older lady out of an elevator and the next, I was shoved into a car with these two serial rapists, killers or both. At first I'd banged on the window, pushed on the door handle, and screamed for Lucian, but it all proved to be futile. I didn't see Lucian. With all the chaos in the hotel lobby, he wouldn't have noticed my absence.

I'd stopped kicking their seats when I realized how much trouble I was in. I prayed they'd left Lucian a clue so he could find me. They were driving around the island for a while. *Why hadn't they gotten on the highway?*

I controlled my breathing, refusing to let them hear the fear clawing at my chest. Panic wouldn't save me. A plan might. I reached for the door handle again—damn child locks. My fingertips skimmed the window button—disabled. The fire alarm wasn't random. It was planned. They were prepared—I was not.

"What the fuck are you doing back there?" Thomas's voice cut through the air.

My entire body went still.

"Nothing," I whispered.

"She's trying to plot shit." Garrett laughed. "They always do." He twisted in his seat and grinned at me. "It's cute."

I clenched my jaw, refusing to shrink back even though every cell in my body wanted to.

"You won't get away with this," I said, voice shaking but steady. "Lucian is coming for me."

Thomas rolled his eyes. "And when he does? He'll be too late."

"Where are you taking me?" I asked loud enough for them to hear.

They said they loved the fight, but did they really?

I'd read somewhere to fight until your last breath, and that's what I intended to do. Along with clawing the hell out of them so I could leave their DNA under my fingernails. They might take me down, but they sure as hell weren't taking anyone else. I refused to make it easy for them. Surrounding myself with bravado, I continued to bait them.

"I know this island inside and out. I'll run away from wherever you take me. You guys are a bunch of idiots."

"Shut her up!" Thomas yelled at Beardsley. "Now!"

Beardsley reached back to grab me, but I pulled out of his reach and kicked their seats again.

"I'm trying, but I can't reach her," Beardsley growled.

I waited for him to climb over the seat and hit me, but he never did. He was such an idiot.

"Try fucking harder!" Thomas reached his hand back to smack me. "Bitch, stop kicking my seat, dammit!"

Nice try, asshole. Dodging Thomas's hand proved easier than avoiding Beardsley's.

"Wait till I get my hands on you!" Beardsley yelled.

He snarled something I didn't catch—because the next second his fist twisted in my hair and yanked. Pain detonated across my scalp. Before I could scream, he slammed my face into the back of his headrest.

White-hot stars burst behind my eyelids. A vicious shockwave shot through my skull, down my spine, splintering through every nerve. My ears rang. My vision flickered. Something warm slid over my upper lip. Thick. Metallic. Wet. Blood.

A tremor seized my stomach. The coppery scent rushed up my nose and burned the back of my throat. I sucked in a shaky breath and gagged on it.

Did he break my nose?

My fingers shook as I lifted them. When I touched my nose, a bolt of agony exploded behind my eyes. My fingertips came away slick and red. I stared at the blood on my hand as if it belonged to someone else. Every pulse echoed through my face, turning each breath into another spike of pain. Panic coiled tight in my chest, threatening to swallow me whole.

Stay calm. Stay alive. Those were the only clear thoughts in the chaos. I lowered my head, let my body go slack, and pretended to pass out.

"Well, that will shut her up. Why the fuck are we at our rental?" Beardsley berated Thomas.

"Because we need to grab our stuff and get the hell out of Dodge."

My ears perked. *Why were we at their rental?* Getting out of town would've been the smarter exit plan. I'd been kidnapped by Dumb and Dumber except they packed a mean punch.

"Thomas, you were supposed to grab our stuff before you came to the resort."

"Yeah, well, I forgot," Thomas grumbled.

The car rolled to a stop. I lifted my head up enough to peek from the corner of my eye, searching for the rental they meant. The most secluded rental on the island sat at the southern tip, water hemming it in on three sides. Of course they'd pick this one. Only a single road led in or out—unless the ocean sounded inviting.

"Tie her up while I grab our shit," Thomas spat out before he slammed his door shut.

"Fine!" Beardsley got out and walked to the trunk.

The last thing I wanted was to be tied up with these assholes. I turned my knees ready to drop onto my back and kick him when he opened the door. The trunk slammed shut, and he pried my door open.

I kicked out with both legs and landed a solid hit to his midsection. Beardsley staggered back and clutched his stomach, giving me just enough room to bolt out of the car.

"Bitch!" Beardsley screamed and grabbed my hair.

Pain tore through my scalp, and a scream burst from my throat. My feet slipped on the asphalt as he yanked me backward, dragging me like I weighed nothing. He shoved me into the backseat with so much force that he knocked the breath from my lungs. My shoulder slammed into the seat. My knee cracked against the doorframe. Before I could orient myself, a fist drove into my ribs—hard, sharp, exploding fire across my side.

"*No—stop—*" I gasped, the sound barely clearing my throat.

Another blow. This time, to my back. Pain raced down my legs, forcing my back into a sharp arch. He kicked me again—hip, thigh, the soft give of my stomach, anywhere his foot could reach—until my limbs shook.

I curled my legs onto my chest and pushed myself into the seat, sliding in, trying to reach the other side of the seat—away from him. I tried to shield myself, but he wasn't letting me. He forced me flat, shoving my face into the upholstery until the stale smell of cigarette smoke filled my nose.

Terror surged, nausea rising hard and fast. My frantic heartbeat clawed at me, begging me to run, to fight, to breathe—to get the fuck away from him. His fists. His boots. The relentless press of the seat against my cheek as my vision flickered around the edges.

My body stopped fighting first, then my mind. *Oh God, this was it. I was almost free. And now... now I'm gonna die for my effort to escape. I'm sorry, Lucian. I love you.*

Tears burst from my eyes and rolled onto the seat. My fingers twitched against the seat as he pinned me there, and the world narrowed to the sound of my ragged breathing—and the low, satisfied growl of the monster above me.

"Shit! Dammit!" Beardsley kept screaming obscenities at me while he wrenched my arms back and zip-tied my wrists. Then my ankles before he pulled me to a sitting position and buckled me in. "Try to run now, bitch!"

He slammed the door and got back into the front passenger seat.

"What the fuck is taking him so damn long?" Beardsley panted from exhaustion. "Fuck!" He slammed his hand against the dashboard. "Don't fucking move." He glared at me. "I'll be right back."

I kept my mouth shut. How was I going to save myself when he had bound my hands so tight I could feel the zip-ties cutting into my skin? My gaze slid to the floor. A water bottle rolled under the seat. A discarded fast-food bag. Nothing. I saw nothing I could use to defend myself or break the zip-ties.

My phone! I still had my phone. With numb, tingling fingers, I eased it out of my back pocket. My body was bent at an awkward angle as I tried to find Lucian's number.

"Come on, come on," I whispered as I scrolled through my contacts. "There."

I'd never been so happy to see his name. I clicked on his phone number and listened to the ringtone. It rang only once before he picked up. The sound of his panicked voice calling my name boomed over the line.

"Lu—" I started to say, but stopped when the sound of my captors' voices grew louder. They were arguing on the front porch. *Could they see me on the phone?* Beardsley looked up and pointed toward me. I lowered the phone.

"Josie! Where the hell are you?" Lucian's voice screamed.

Thomas and Beardsley were heading toward me. I hung up, lowered the volume and put my phone on vibrate. God, I hoped he could trace my call. Seconds before they reached the car, I slipped it into my back pocket.

Beardsley missed it while zip-tying my wrists. I kept my relief to myself. I didn't want to lose the only lifeline I had to Lucian.

"Let's fucking go," Beardsley barked and slammed his door shut. "No more stops."

"One more," Thomas grumbled. "I'm hungry."

"Are you fucking kidding me?"

"Nope. But I'll go through a drive-thru."

"They're gonna see her if you go through a drive-thru!" Beardsley screeched at him.

"Fuck yeah, you're right. We can put her in the trunk."

"Just drive the fucking car out of town." Beardsley sighed and sat back. "We'll eat when we're far away from this fucking island."

Thank goodness Beardsley convinced Thomas not to put me in the trunk. That would've been more frightening. At least in the back seat, I could hear their plan.

Although in the trunk, I could kick out the taillights and attempt to use my phone. *How crazy was I wanting to be locked up in the trunk of a car while two psychos drove me to a secondary location to kill me!*

Lucian better be good at his detective skills and find me because if their plan was to drive to another state, I could kiss my luck goodbye.

Why didn't I stay behind the desk when that damn alarm went off? Or run to Lucian?

Because the older lady was struggling, her face pale with effort, and I couldn't ignore the possibility of her getting trampled, I had to help her.

In hindsight, I should've grabbed Lucian and then gone to help the lady. If Lucian had been with me, Beardsley wouldn't have shoved me out the exit, and I wouldn't be zip-tied in the backseat of a fucking car with two lunatics.

"Shit," Thomas spoke up and turned to look out the back window. "I think someone is following us."

Chapter 42

So Close

Lucian

I barreled into the station like a man possessed and went straight to Corey's desk.

"Anything?" My voice came out harsher than I intended, but I didn't apologize. I didn't have apologies left in me.

Corey spun his chair around. "Yeah. Got the plate. It's a rental—figures—but our PRs are already tracking it. I sent out a BOLO and a CLEAR Alert to neighboring counties. I contacted our eyes in the sky—they're lifting off now. I also reached out to JCSD and asked their aviation unit to sweep the mainland."

BOLO meant "Be On The Lookout". CLEAR Alerts were alerts for adults as opposed to Amber Alerts for kids and Silver Alerts for adults over 65 years of age. PR's were plate reader cameras that we had installed at our intersections on Main Street. We had everything in place. We just needed a lead in the right direction.

"Thanks, Corey. Let me know as soon as you pick up a sighting. Here—" I extended my phone to him "—Josie tried to call me, but hung up as soon as I answered. See if you can trace the location of the call."

"Did you hear any recognizable sounds?" Corey took my phone.

"No." I shook my head and ran my hand over the back of my neck. "I heard her uneven breathing. She started to say my name, then fell silent. I faintly heard two voices before she hung up."

"Oh, shit." Corey spun back to his computer. "You got it."

I exhaled, but it didn't relieve an ounce of pressure in my chest.

"Call me the second you hear anything." The pieces of the puzzle were connecting in my head. I only wish they'd connected sooner—before she got kidnapped.

"You got it," Corey grunted.

I nodded, turned—and almost collided with Ryker and Chief as they stormed through the doorway. I repeated the updates. Chief didn't waste time.

"I'll call Jay at JCSD," he said, already dialing as he strode away. "Get him up to date."

"We're gonna find her," Ryker muttered, unclipping Judge's leash. Judge barked once, sharp, ready.

"Yeah." My voice cracked. I cleared it. "I'm gonna get some coffee."

I lied. I didn't need coffee. I needed something to do before I shattered. I'd barely taken a step when—

"Detective, wait!" Corey shouted, thrusting his headset toward me.

I ran to him and slapped the headset over my ears. A pilot's voice crackled through the static.

"The white Corolla is heading north on Main Street. About to pass the station."

Adrenaline hit me like a bullet.

"Fuck!" I ripped the headset off. "Tell dispatch to switch us all to the emergency frequency. I want to hear everything that's going on. Let's go!" I hollered to Ryker.

Ryker and Judge sprinted after me as I bolted out the front doors.

"They're about to pass us on Main Street," I shouted as we ran.

I dove into my car, started it before my ass hit the seat, and peeled out of the lot with Ryker spinning his wheels behind me.

I tuned into the emergency channel, the pilot's voice coming through loud and clear.

"Car still headed northbound on Main. Passing Hi Foods. Accelerating. They're aiming for the mainland bridge."

My grip tightened on the wheel until my knuckles went white.

"Where the hell have they been?" Ryker's voice broke through the radio.

"I don't know. Don't fucking care." My nostrils flared. "As long as we find them now."

The pilot spoke.

"They're approaching the bridge. You'll lose PR coverage once they hit the mainland. Recommending immediate intercept."

No shit. The mainland had its own PR cameras we could tap into, but it wasn't our jurisdiction. I slammed my foot harder on the gas. *Hold on, Josie. I'm coming for you.*

I scanned every car in front of me—*white Corolla, white Corolla—come on, where the fuck are you?* Two cars ahead, I spotted them. I clicked on my radio.

"This is Detective Warrick. I got eyes on the vehicle. We're almost out of our jurisdiction. They're going over the bridge now. I'm still in pursuit."

"Detective Warrick, this is Captain Jay from JCSD. We are waiting for them on our side of the bridge. We will continue the pursuit."

"10-4, Captain," I spoke into my radio. "We're crossing now. I see you guys."

The second the Corolla hit mainland asphalt, a swarm of sheriff's patrol vehicles lit up behind it—red, blue, sirens screaming. The suspect floored it, weaving through traffic like he had a death wish. If he didn't slow down, he was going to kill someone—or all of them. More units joined. Still, he pushed faster.

Chapter 43

Lucian!

Josie

I turned my head to look out the back window. Not an easy feat, trapped by the seat belt with no use of my hands. *Was that Lucian several cars back weaving in and out of traffic?*

"It's that fucking lion cop!" Beardsley hollered.

Lion cop, what the hell was he talking about?

"Go faster!" Beardsley rolled down his window and pointed a gun behind us, in Lucian's direction.

"No!" I screamed, picked up my legs, and kicked his seat.

"Bitch, you better stop or I will shoot you!" Beardsley pointed the gun in my face and glared at me.

"Not yet." Thomas blurted. "Not until we've had our fun. I'll lose the cop."

The original developers of Haven Island had envisioned Main Street as a ribbon that stretched from the mainland into our little paradise, connected by our scenic bridge. Locals loved the continuity. Tourists adored the charm and walking access to both.

Thomas hit the gas as we reached the bridge. The car launched into the air—I screamed—and slammed down on the far side. The seat belt cinched tight, locking me in place. Blue and red lights flooded the road ahead. Sirens erupted, then surged behind us as they gave chase.

"Fuck!" Thomas roared. "Where did all these cops come from?"

"Shit!" Beardsley twisted around to look behind us, his wild eyes catching mine for a split second before he faced forward again. "Your driving better be fucking fantastic."

Thomas' evil grin sent chills down my spine. "I have an idea."

Before I could blink, he jerked the wheel hard right. If I hadn't been seatbelted, I would've flown across the back seat. The tires screamed, and so did the pedestrians.

We shot up onto the sidewalk, the car bouncing as people scattered in every direction like terrified birds. My heart strangled itself in my chest.

"Oh... My... God!" I shrieked. "Stop! Stop! Don't kill them!"

"Hey!" Beardsley shouted, leaning toward the window and laughing like a demon. He pointed at a woman clutching her belly. "Two points for the pregnant lady!"

"No! No!" My voice cracked under the weight of pure terror.

Tears blurred my eyes as I saw the woman freeze in place, her face a mask of raw fear. A man lunged from behind and yanked her into a shop doorway seconds before Thomas barreled past.

Their laughter exploded in the car—high, sharp, gleeful.

How could they laugh? How evil did a person have to be to enjoy this horrible game they were playing?

Thomas swerved again, the car fishtailing across the pavement. "Shit, we missed her." He scanned the sidewalk like a wolf searching for prey. His gaze landed on a young mother pushing a stroller. "How about two points for the baby in the stroller?"

"Don't—please—*please* don't—" My entire body locked up.

The mother saw us. Her scream cut through the chaos. She scooped up her baby, abandoned the stroller, and sprinted toward the nearest doorway.

Thank God. Thank God.

Thomas slammed into the empty stroller at full speed. The impact was like a gunshot. Metal snapped. The stroller launched upward and smashed into the windshield, cracking it in a spiderweb of gleaming lines.

"Fuck!" Beardsley yelled, covering his face from the burst of glass. "You were supposed to crush the baby in the stroller, not toss it into the windshield. Now I can't see out of my side," he snapped, batting away shards.

"Never mind the fucking points. I'm getting the fuck out of here." Thomas yanked the wheel, laughing maniacally as he forced the car back onto the street. "Relax. We'll lose them."

I knew—deep in my bones, in the shivering pit of my stomach—that Lucian was somewhere behind us. And he would burn the world down to save me.

Hurry, Lucian, please hurry. I was holding on by a thread. I needed him to wrap his arms around me and tell me it would be okay.

*** Lucian ***

"We need a roadblock," I snarled into the radio. "Or spikes. Now!"

"Done," Captain Jay agreed. "Primary unit, prepare for a pit maneuver."

I knew Jay. We both served in the military and had lunch with Alejandro and Griffin once a month. He was a great friend, but I was shocked as hell that he was letting me take the lead.

"On it." Another officer responded.

My chest tightened. PIT stands for Precision Immobilization Technique. It's when the officer's car intentionally taps the rear corner of a fleeing vehicle to force it into a controlled spin. You shouldn't do a PIT maneuver at high speeds. But when push comes to shove, we do it regardless. Fingers crossed, Josie had her seatbelt on.

"Be fucking careful," I snapped. "They have a hostage. I want her breathing. Not a scratch on her head."

Static—and then an officer snorted. "Aww, sounds like the detective has a soft spot for the hostage."

"Bigger than you know." Ryker's voice cut in, dry as hell. "Plus, she's my best friend, so don't screw this up. Judge is dying for a bite."

Judge barked as if seconding the threat.

"Copy," the officer chuckled. "Attempting PIT maneuver now."

Tires shrieked. Metal slammed into metal. A brutal crash echoed through the radio.

My heart stopped.

*** Josie ***

A police car came out of nowhere and hit the back passenger side of the car—my side—hard enough to knock the breath out of me.

"FUCK!" Thomas roared as the car fishtailed, his hands scrambling uselessly over the wheel.

The impact jolted my body from side to side until my shoulder slammed into the door. The world tilted—swerved—blurred.

Beardsley lurched toward Thomas, grabbing the wheel with both hands. "Hold it—HOLD IT—"

But the car wasn't listening to either of them. It spun toward the park—trees rushing closer, too fast, too big, too dark. My scream ripped out of me just as we hit.

The impact came with several sounds. A deep, bone-shaking *crunch.* Metal folding in on itself. Glass exploding. My skull whipped forward and slammed into the back of Beardsley's headrest—again. I hated that damn thing. White pain streaked across my vision. My head throbbed. Warmth trickled under my nose—blood, again.

The seatbelt slammed into my ribs, locking me in place while the rest of the car screamed and crumpled around us. My teeth rattled. My ears rang.

Then—Silence.

A terrible, eerie silence broken only by the harsh hiss of escaping steam from the ruined engine... like the car itself exhaled a final breath.

*** Lucian ***

"Someone, please—*please*—tell me she's okay."

My voice cracked, and I didn't give a single fuck who heard it. My lungs locked up in my chest. It felt like my entire ribcage was collapsing inward, crushing everything vital inside me.

She had to be okay. I couldn't imagine a world without Josie—without her soft laugh when she teased me, the spark that lit up her eyes when I whispered dirty words in her ear, the way her entire face softened when she trusted me. We weren't done—we were just starting. I wasn't letting fate, God, or some psychotic motherfuckers make this the end of our story. There had to be a fucking happy ever after puzzle piece left to snap into place.

Everyone was silent on the radio. Dead silent. Too silent.

Then—footsteps. Shouts.

"This is the Jones County Sheriff's Department! Come out with your hands up!"

I screeched to a halt, ran out of my car, and drew my gun. The officers were crouched behind their open doors. I didn't join them. I ran past them to the back of another police vehicle parked closer to Josie.

"Detective! Hold up!" someone shouted.

Fuck no. I didn't hold up for shit. Not when I could see the Corolla crumpled against a tree like a crushed soda can, steam hissing, glass fucking everywhere. The front end obliterated.

"We need you to come out with your hands up!" Captain Jay barked.

"Maybe they're all hurt," I muttered under my breath. Or maybe they were fucking dead. They hit that tree fucking hard. No. No. I wasn't letting that thought bounce around in my head. I'm going in.

I didn't wait for permission. Didn't wait for backup. Didn't wait for logic. I darted from behind one police car to a parked car farther up the line on the right.

"Right behind you." Ryker tapped my shoulder. Judge next to him.

I didn't know where they came from, but I was damn happy to see them. They were ready and alert, waiting for my command. Judge was vibrating—every muscle taut, ears up, hackles raised. He knew. He always fucking knew.

We crept forward. Slow. Controlled. My heart slammed against my ribs, wild and frantic. I eased out a breath and looked over the hood of the parked car.

My eyes locked on the back window of the Corolla. And I saw her.

Josie.

Her body slumped sideways, her head resting against the passenger headrest. Too still. Way too still. Ice shot down my spine, freezing my blood.

"I see Josie," I rasped. "She's not moving." My breath shook on its way out. "I think she's hurt. Cover me."

My vision narrowed to a single point. My hands gripped my Glock. This was no longer just a case. It's personal. That's my girl. The love of my life. My Josie. And I was prepared to kill or die to save her.

Chapter 44

One Down... One To Go

Josie

Lucian screamed my name. At first, it sounded so far away—like someone calling to me through water. My head throbbed, and I blinked. My vision swam as I tried to follow the sound that dragged me back to consciousness. *Was that Lucian?*

I forced my head up from where it had sagged against the passenger headrest. Everything felt heavy, thick, wrong. Yet so right when I saw Lucian behind a parked car.

My heart lurched. "Lucian," I mumbled.

"Josie!" Lucian broke cover, sprinting toward me.

Time hiccuped. Then his body jerked—twisted.

"Lucian!" I screamed.

"Fuck!" he shouted, but he kept coming.

Then another shot slammed into him. His chest snapped back. And he flew backwards onto the concrete. Ry stepped out from behind a car and dragged him to safety.

Then, all hell broke loose. Sharp cracks exploded through the air. Metal pinged around me. The back passenger side of the car dropped—the tire must have blown out.

Why were they shooting? Why the hell were they shooting at the car I was in? When the shooting stopped, I looked around. *Where was Lucian?*

"Lucian!" I screamed so hard my throat tore. My foot slammed into the back of the seat. Again. Again. "You killed him! You fucking asshole!"

My vision blurred with tears, everything shaking—my breath, my hands, my entire fucking world collapsing in on itself. Rage and grief surged like wildfire. I didn't care if Beardsley turned the gun on me next—I wanted to claw him apart.

Outside, officers shouted. "Come out with your hands up!"

Sirens wailed closer—the ambulance—thank God, please God, please let them get to Lucian in time. The hospital wasn't far. He just needed minutes. Seconds.

"No!" Beardsley bellowed from the front seat.

"Wake up, man!" Beardsley shook Thomas by the shoulder. "Come on, wake up!"

The airbag had exploded straight into Thomas's face. His body swayed like a rag doll as Beardsley continued to shake him. His panic filled the car like smoke—thick, choking, frantic. Good. Let him panic. After what they put me through—I wished he was dead. One less monster in the world.

Beardsley's distraction with Thomas opened up a chance for me to get away. The zip ties had been so tight, they bit into my flesh, sending a white-hot sting up my arms. My skin rubbed raw from trying to wrench my hands free. Blood slicked my palms enough to make my fingers slippery. Slippery could work. I twisted again, harder this time. The plastic cut deeper, biting into exposed skin.

"Come on," I whispered through clenched teeth. "Come on, come on—"

The zip-tie didn't budge. Lucian's body flashed in my mind. The way he flew backward. His body made a sickening sound when he landed on the concrete. My heart cracked open, but I wasn't giving up. Not when he might still be alive. Not when everything in me screamed to fight.

I looked around for something sharp enough to break plastic. There. On the track that adjusted the seat from front to back was a sharp piece of metal. I pressed my wrists against the sharp edge and yanked downward. Pain exploded across my arms, but the tie scraped, frayed. I did it again, jerking harder this time, and bit my lip so I wouldn't scream.

The plastic stretched. My skin tore. Blood spilled. "Break—" I gasped. "Fucking—break!"

A sharp crack snapped through the car. I froze and stared down at the broken zip-tie. I'd done it. My hands fell apart, free. I almost sobbed from the shock of relief.

Beardsley didn't hear me as he pounded on Thomas's chest like some deranged medic. "Wake up, you stupid son of a bitch!"

I curled my raw, bleeding fingers toward me, ignoring the agony as feeling rushed back into them like knives. I swallowed a cry. No noise. Not yet.

It would be near impossible to slide my feet on either side of that sharp edge and cut the plastic around my ankles. I was so close to freedom, I could taste it. As long as Beardsley kept pounding on Thomas, I had time. I picked up my feet and tried to bring them down on the sharp piece of metal, but I kept hitting the bottom of my feet instead of the plastic.

Dammit, maybe I could hop to safety. Anything was better than sitting in this car. I scooted toward the door and reached for the door handle.

Something hard pressed up against the back of my head. I froze, breath locking in my throat as Beardsley swung the gun in my face.

"Don't you dare open that door," he growled.

My fingers slipped off the handle, hands folded tight into my lap. Every muscle in my body trembled.

"You are not leaving this car without me."

With the cold steel of the gun against my temple, he climbed over the seat and sat beside me. Then he lifted his arm, aiming past me at the window. I didn't see anyone outside, but I still slapped my hands over my ears a second before he fired.

The explosion of sound tore through my skull. My whole body jolted, and my ears rang. My hands weren't enough of a buffer for such a loud bang at close range.

I spun toward him. "Are you insane?" My voice sounded distant, like I was underwater.

His mouth moved, sharp and fast. I caught a word here and there. Something about glass?

"What?" I shouted.

He grabbed my wrists and yanked my hands away from my ears.

"I said it's good you got your hands free. Now break the glass out so I can talk to the cops."

Although the ringing in my ears muffled his voice, I made out some words.

"I am not putting my hand through glass," I snapped.

"If you don't use your hand, I'll use your head."

That shut me up. I'd always heard people say someone had "dead eyes." I never understood it... not really—until now.

"Have you lost your mind?" My whisper shook.

"What do you think?" He pressed the muzzle of the gun against my cheek, cold and unyielding.

"Please... let me go." I begged. I'd never been so scared before in my life. "They'll go easy on you if you surrender."

"Now you're the crazy one." He huffed a laugh, sharp and humorless. "I'm not going back to jail. Now—" he jabbed the gun harder into my skin, "—push the damn glass out. If you're so worried about your delicate hands, cover them with the bag on the floor."

"Can you get it for me? My ankles are still bound?"

"Figure it out. I'm not releasing your legs. Kicking is your favorite form of attack," he huffed. "Do you think I'm stupid?"

"That's debatable," I muttered, reached down, and flipped the bag upside down. Warm ketchup packets, wilted lettuce, and stale chunks of bread spilled onto the floorboard. My stomach churned.

"What the hell are you doing?" he snapped.

"What does it look like I'm doing?" I shot him a glare over my shoulder.

"You are so fucking mouthy," he muttered. "I told Thomas we should've picked someone else."

"Oh, woe is you," I muttered back.

His glare could've cut steel. Good. Let him rage—I needed any edge I could get.

Hand inside the bag, I punched outward, driving my fist into the shattered frame. Shards sliced through the thin material and into my skin. White-hot pain shot up my arm. I winced—but kept going.

Piece by piece, I pushed the broken window out, clearing the glass. The more open space available, the better chance the officers had of seeing inside. Of seeing me. Of ending this.

Chapter 45

Judge... My New Bestie

Josie

"I want to talk to someone with authority!" Beardsley yelled out the window.

"I'm Captain Jay Carmichael of the Jones County Sheriff's Department." His voice crackled through a speaker, calm but edged with authority. "Who am I talking to?"

"Garrett Stein!" Beardsley bellowed. 'And I have demands!"

So his name wasn't Aubrey Beardsley after all. Great. Another alias to add to the list of nightmares.

"You shot one of our officers," Captain Jay replied. "What makes you think you're in any position to make demands?"

My heart clenched, and I closed my eyes. *Please, Lucian... please be alive.*

"You shot my friend," Beardsley laughed—a wild, manic sound. "I'd say we're even except I've got a pretty little hostage. And... I'm not going back to jail."

"Let her go, and we'll talk," Captain Jay said evenly. "We can work something out."

"Not a fucking chance in hell am I letting her go."

"Fine," Captain Jay conceded. "Then tell me what you want."

Garrett tapped the gun against my head. "What do I want? What do I *want...*"
He stared at Thomas, whose head lolled lifeless against the deflated airbag.
"Thomas, what would you ask for?" Silence. Then he snapped his fingers. "Got
it. Thanks, buddy."

Okay, he wasn't just dangerous—he was unraveling.

"I want a cop car and ten grand. You got one hour." Garrett looked at his
wristwatch. "Then I'm gone."

"You can have mine!" A woman's voice shouted.

Was that Charlotte? She was giving up her car for me?

"Officer Charlotte is offering her unit," Captain Jay said carefully. "But ten
grand in an hour—that'll be difficult."

"Then get ready to send Josie to the morgue!" Beardsley roared, laughing
under his breath before leaning in so close I could smell his sweat. "Guess
you're not coming with me to Tennessee after all."

"I'd rather die." I stiffened.

"You might just get your wish...after I have some fun." His smile twisted. "We
have an hour to kill. Whatever will we do?"

Before I could brace myself, he dragged his tongue from my chin up to
my temple. Revulsion rolled through me. His hand slid around my torso and
clamped around my breast—hard. Pain shot through me. No. No. No.

I shoved him—gun be damned. I was not letting him violate me in front of
Lucian's colleagues, not letting him take anything else from me.

He snarled and lunged again, shoving his hand under my shirt, fingers
fumbling with the clasp of my bra. Panic tore through me. I grabbed the door
handle and yanked—

"HELP! He's trying to rape me!" I screamed, voice cracking, praying the
officers heard every word.

"Garrett Stein!" Captain Jay barked. "STOP! We're getting the money. Leave
her alone. You harm her, we're done negotiating!"

Beardsley froze. Slowly—finally—he pulled his hand back.

Relief washed through me so fast my vision blurred.

"Fine!" he shouted toward the shattered window. "Let me know when you've
got the cash. Time's ticking!"

"Sit back." He turned a cold, shark-eyed glare on me. "Don't move a muscle."

I nodded and leaned against the seat, my body trembling in fear. But in my
head, I planned. Searching for my next chance. I wasn't dying in this car. Not
today. Not for him.

The next hour crawled by in a haze of terror and strategy. Captain Jay kept
trying to talk Garrett down, but he ignored him—lost in his one-sided chat with
the corpse in the front driver's seat. *Did he even realize Thomas was dead?*

His mind had cracked straight down the middle, but even in that mess, one thing was obvious. Thomas had been the mastermind. Garrett was the tech nerd turned muscle. A dangerous combination... and an unstable one.

I remained silent. Let him talk. Gathered every scrap of intel I could in case I survived long enough to tell the cops. If he let me live.

I kept scanning the area outside the shattered window, searching for escape routes. Trees. Sand. A cluster of police cars, but no ambulance. *Had they taken Lucian to the hospital? God, I hoped so.*

I needed distance and a blind spot—just one—but Garrett wasn't giving anyone a clean shot. He kept himself half-hidden beside me, slouched low so the officers couldn't risk firing without hitting me too. If they'd had a clear shot, I knew he'd be dead already.

Minute after minute ticked by. The nerves wound tighter than a drawn bowstring. *What were the officers doing? Why weren't they rushing us? Why weren't they charging in?*

Garrett checked his watch again. His breathing sharpened. Then—

"Time's up!" he screamed, voice cracking.

"Okay," Captain Jay responded without hesitation. "We have your money. Step out slowly and walk toward my voice. Officer Charlotte will drive her unit forward. Let Josie go."

My hand shot for the door.

"Oh, hell no." Garrett's snarl was instantaneous. "You're coming with me." His eyes cut to me, unhinged and glittering. "Open the fucking door."

"It's locked," I said, hoping—praying—he'd have to put the gun down to open it himself.

Instead, his fist closed around a chunk of my hair, wrenching my head back so hard my eyes watered. He dug into his pocket, keys jangling, and thumbed the unlock button.

Click.

"Open it," he hissed. "Slowly. Or I'll shoot you in a place that'll make you beg for death."

"I can't," I snapped through clenched teeth. "My ankles are still tied."

He placed the gun on the seat behind him—close enough for him to grab, nowhere near close enough for me. Then he reached into his pocket and pulled out a switchblade. The metallic *snick* of the blade startled me.

"Don't move a muscle," he hissed, eyes locked on mine. "If you do, my knife might slip and slice your feet off."

I gave a stiff, jerky nod. Terror scraped down my throat. He was unstable—wild-eyed and vibrating with adrenaline. No telling what he'd decide to do next.

He crouched, blade gleaming, and dragged it toward the zip-tie around my ankles. The first pass skimmed the surface. The second dug too close. The third sliced through the plastic and my skin in one brutal swipe.

Pain shot up my leg. "Ahh—" I gasped, reaching instinctively for my ankle.

He yanked my hair so hard my vision blurred. "I said. Don't. Move."

I went still, lungs quivering, every nerve begging to react but afraid to. He tossed the knife onto the front seat and snatched up the gun.

"Now," he growled, his lips brushing my ear, breath sour and hot on my skin, "we're getting out. Nice and slow."

I slid toward the door, every inch deliberate, until fingers curled around the handle.

He moved with me—pressed to my back, his grip tangled in my hair, the muzzle of the gun shoved into the soft spot between my shoulder blades.

"Open it."

I pushed. The door didn't budge.

"Kick it," he snarled. "You're good at that."

I swallowed hard, braced myself, and kicked the door with both feet several times before it flew open, sunlight flooding the car, snapping across my face like a slap.

My feet hit the ground first. His followed, his legs bracketing mine, keeping me caged.

Shouts erupted from every direction—officers, multiple units, a wall of voices.

Garrett jerked me closer, his arm cinching around my shoulders until it hurt to breathe.

"DON'T SHOOT OR I'LL SHOOT HER!" he roared, voice cracking under the strain. "BACK UP!"

He shoved the gun harder into my spine. I squeezed my eyes shut against the terror swelling in my chest.

Please. God. Not like this. Not here. Not now. Not while Lucian might die because of me.

We climbed out of the car one inch at a time. Each attempt to hurry earned a hard yank on my hair, pain flaring across my scalp. He kept me moving in short, shuffling steps, my legs shaking beneath me, threatening to give out with every move I made.

We cleared the door, and he pivoted, planting his back against the car and trapping my body against his—using me as a shield.

Police lights strobed across the trees and pavement—red, blue, red, blue—painting everything in emergency colors. It wasn't just the Haven Island

PD anymore. Jones County patrol cars were everywhere. Lucian must've called in every ounce of backup he had.

Lucian.

I scanned the scene, pulse rioting, desperate for even a glimpse of him. No familiar stance. No tall outline. No sparkling blue eyes locked on mine. He had to be okay, and I had to get to the hospital.

Charlotte drove her car forward, stopping with the front end facing us, and stepped out of the car, leaving the driver's side door open.

"Turn the lights and sirens on." Garrett motioned to her with his head. "Then, put the keys on the hood. Don't try anything stupid."

Charlotte did as she was told and stepped back away from her car.

We inched toward her car. My feet dragged. My wrists throbbed. The world shimmered with tears I refused to let fall. *Where were Ry and Judge?* They had to know what was happening. They had to be here—somewhere.

We reached the front bumper of Charlotte's car. She looked at me—no, past me—her gaze flicking to the right.

A heartbeat later, a deep, feral growl ripped through the air. Beardsley's grip loosened in my hair.

"What the—!" Beardsley snapped.

The pressure of the gun vanished from my back. I twisted just enough to see Judge. Pure muscle. Pure rage. Pure justice. Charging straight at Beardsley like a missile.

I didn't think. I bolted toward Charlotte. She grabbed me and we dove behind her open car door. An explosion of gunfire erupted behind us, echoing off the pavement, the cars, the trees. I curled into myself, arms shielding my head, heart trying to climb out of my throat. Charlotte covered me with her body.

Then—Silence.

"It's over." Charlotte's voice whispered in my ear, steadying me with an arm around my back. "You're safe now."

My breathing hitched as I forced myself to look where I'd stood seconds ago with Beardsley. He lay sprawled on the asphalt, blood blooming beneath him, multiple bullet wounds across his chest.

"Attempting to shoot one of our K9 officers," Charlotte murmured, "is the same as shooting one of us."

"Judge!" I gasped, stumbling forward.

He trotted toward me—tail high, tongue out, eyes bright and proud—and pressed his powerful paws onto my shoulders. I collapsed into him, sobbing into his fur, clinging to the dog who'd just saved my life.

"I'm so glad you're okay, Judge. Thank you. Thank you." My voice cracked as I wrapped my arms around his big furry neck.

"Hey," a familiar voice drawled, "I sent him to save you. Don't I get a thank you?"

I whipped around. Ry stood a few feet away, hands on his hips, trying to look cocky—but the worry in his eyes gave him away. A sob tore out of me as I rushed him and threw my arms around his waist.

"Thank you for being here," I whispered, words thick and shaky.

"You're welcome, Jo." He rubbed my back, grounding me. "We've got you. You're safe."

"How's Lucian?" I pulled back and grabbed his arms, gripping hard. "Don't lie to me. Please."

Ry's expression tightened enough to send panic ripping through me.

"He's with the doctors now," he mumbled. "Come on—I'll drive you to the hospital."

"Is he going to be okay?" The question scraped out of me like it hurt to speak.

"I think so." His jaw clenched. "But I'm not sure yet."

"Where was he hit?"

Silence.

"Ry—where?"

He exhaled as if the words weighed a thousand pounds. "The shoulder... and the chest."

A broken sound tore from my throat. "Oh, God." I slapped my hand over my mouth, fighting the scream clawing up my throat.

"Come on," he murmured, guiding me toward his patrol car with a steady arm. "Let's go. We'll get there fast."

I slid into the passenger seat, hands shaking as I fumbled with the seat belt. Ry didn't wait—he hit the gas, tires throwing up dust.

"Hurry," I begged, my voice cracking. "Please. I need to be there."

He nodded once, jaw set.

As the world blurred outside the window, my thoughts spun louder than the engine.

A bullet to the chest. *Did he have his vest on? Was he conscious? Could someone survive that?* No. No. I wouldn't go there.

Please, Lucian. Hold on. I'm coming.

Chapter 46

Waiting

Josie

"**W**as he wearing a vest?" I asked Ry while he drove like Speed Racer to the hospital. My throat felt tight and dry.

"Everything happened so fast. One minute he was rushing toward me and the next...," my voice cracked, "he fell back out of my sight."

Lucian drove me insane—infuriating, charming, impossible. The kind of madness that made life burn brighter. The thought of never seeing him again carved a hollow in my chest, a space only he could fill with his sharp gaze, filthy mouth, soft heart, and undeniable sexy swagger.

"He was," Ryker said quietly as he tore down the road toward the hospital. "Vest caught the chest shot. Probably knocked the wind clean out of him."

I exhaled a shaky breath. Relief and fear tangled together in my lungs.

"How are you holding up?" he asked.

"I'm fine," I lied. "My face, wrists, ankles... they hurt, but I'll live."

"I'm having the doctors check you out when we get there."

"Ry, seriously, I'm fine. Nothing a shower and ice packs—"

"Nope." He shook his head, eyes glued to the road. "Lucian will kick my ass if I don't make sure you're okay."

That earned the tiniest smile from me. "You're impossible."

"And you're stuck with me." He winked as he swung into the hospital's emergency vehicle lane.

"You can park in an actual spot, you know," I muttered, glancing at the parking lot.

"No need. I'm an emergency vehicle," he said smugly. "And you, sweetheart, are definitely an emergency."

"Fine." I rolled my eyes.

A full, dramatic, Josie Hale signature eye roll. Lucian hated when I did that—Ry, of course, just laughed. He'd known me too long to take offense. Lucian would learn soon enough... eventually.

I rushed to the check-in desk. "Where's Detective Lucian Warrick?"

"She needs a doctor," Ryker said simultaneously.

The woman behind the desk looked between us... then down at Judge, who placed his paws on her desk and whimpered.

"You," she pointed at me, "fill out this form. Are any of you related to Detective Lucian Warrick?" she asked, already typing.

"No," Ryker said. "But we work with him. And she's with me."

"Alright." The woman nodded. "He's in surgery on the third floor. There's a waiting room where you can wait for updates."

"What about this?" I lifted the clipboard with shaking fingers.

"You can turn it in at the nurses' station on three. They'll bring it to me."

"Thank you so much."

We hurried upstairs. The waiting room was too bright, too quiet, too cold. I filled out the forms with hands that wouldn't stop trembling. The nurses listened to my story with wide eyes and gentle voices before telling me to sit tight. A doctor would examine me soon.

When I returned, Ry was sitting with his elbows on his knees, hands clasped, staring at the floor. Judge lay curled at his feet, chin resting on his paws, ears flicking at every distant hospital sound. The sight of them—my best friend and the dog who had saved my life—made my chest twist.

"Anything?" I whispered.

"Not yet." Ry raised his head. "Is the doctor coming for you?"

"As soon as they are available. She told me to wait here."

"Good." Ry nodded and patted the chair next to him. "Sit."

I sat beside him, close enough that our shoulders brushed. Close enough that neither of us felt alone.

Ry leaned back, his head against the wall, exhaustion written in every line of his body. I slipped closer and rested my head against his shoulder. He didn't say a word—just let me lean—his steady warmth grounding me for a moment.

Dear God... please let Lucian be okay. He was only trying to save me. He always tried to save me.

My head throbbed harder than before, each pulse a hammer behind my eyes. Pain meds would help, but if I said a single word, Ryker would tear down half the hospital until someone gave me an IV drip and a full neurological workup. I didn't have the energy for that.

I glanced at the clock. Twenty minutes. *Had it really only been twenty minutes?*

It felt like hours—years—even though the rational part of my brain knew surgeries took time, bullet wounds took time, survival took time. But my heart didn't care about time. My heart wanted Lucian. Breathing. Awake. Smiling that arrogant, reckless smile. I squeezed my hands together before I pulled my hair out.

"Josie Hale."

A voice cut through the room. A doctor stood in the doorway holding a clipboard. My spine snapped straight.

"I'm Josie." My voice scraped out.

"Come with me," he said, his voice low.

Ry stood to follow, but I pressed my hand to his chest. "Stay. In case they come out with something about Lucian."

His jaw tightened, but he nodded and sank back into the chair. "Call me if you need anything."

I followed the doctor down the hall.

"I'm Dr. Barnes," he said, shaking my hand. "Let's take a look."

In the exam room, I walked him through everything—being grabbed, the crash, the hits, the zip-ties, the panic. Saying it out loud made my chest tight all over again. He checked my pupils, my balance, the bruising along my face and wrists. His touch was clinical but careful.

"After the morning you've had, you're surprisingly okay," he said at last. "A concussion is unlikely, but you will be very sore for several days. Are you in pain?"

"Yes." Physically, emotionally—everywhere.

"I'll write you a prescription. A nurse will be in shortly to clean and wrap your wounds."

"Thank you."

He paused at the door. "If you notice any changes in your vision, call immediately. Eyesight isn't something to gamble with."

"Okay."

He finished jotting notes on my chart and stepped out.

White walls closed in, bare and unforgiving. I dropped my gaze to the floor tiles, counting the lines between them while my pulse hammered and my thoughts skidded. Please, please, please let Lucian be okay. Several minutes later, a nurse entered.

"Hi, I'm Olivia." The nurse's smile was soft; her voice gentle. She placed a bottle and several gauze pads at the end of the exam table. "This might sting a little, but we need to clean you up. I'll start with your face, then your wrists and ankles."

She reached into her pocket and pulled out a small plastic cup with two pills, then handed me a mini water bottle.

"These are the same meds Dr. Barnes prescribed—something for pain and swelling. They'll make you drowsy." Her eyes flicked over my cuts with a touch of sympathy. "Do you have a ride home?"

"Yes. My friend Ry can drive me. He's in the surgery waiting room." I nodded and swallowed the pills.

Olivia dabbed my face with the damp gauze—light touches, but every one burned.

"You mean Officer Forrester with K9 Judge?" she asked.

"Yes."

"Are you two dating?" She grinned at me as if she already knew the answer.

"No." A thin laugh slipped out. "We're just friends. We grew up on the island together."

"Gotcha." She stepped back to study my face. "All right, this is as good as it's going to get for now. Let me grab some more supplies for your wrists and ankles."

She left, and for the first time since the crash, silence pressed in around me. My pulse thudded in my ears. Lucian was somewhere near me, cut open, fighting. The thought made my stomach twist until breathing hurt.

Olivia returned with a plastic bedpan filled with water, an ice pack, and towels.

"Hold this against your face." She handed me the ice pack and sat on her rolling stool, dipping gauze into the water. "I'll clean your ankles next."

The first swipe across my torn skin made me hiss.

"You fought hard," she said. "Zip-ties?"

"Yes. You see these a lot?"

"Unfortunately." Her expression darkened. "Some cases I wish I could forget."

"I don't think I want to know."

"You really don't." She steadied my ankle, movements sure and precise. "Your wrists must hurt like hell."

"They do." My voice wavered. "I just... I wanted to get out of that car and find Detective Lucian. Do you know how he is?"

Her hands paused. "He's still in surgery," she whispered. "Is he your boyfriend?"

"Yes." My throat tightened.

"I've seen him around. Nice guy. Quiet,"she smirked. "Not sure how you cracked that shell, but I'm glad someone did. The nurses already mourn that another hot officer is off the market."

A startled laugh burst out of me. "Does he come here often?"

"That's a line I haven't heard in a while," she teased. "Definitely not to visit someone else."

"Sorry," I sighed. "I was fishing."

"I figured." She winked. "But to put your mind at ease. No, your handsome detective hasn't dated anyone here. When he comes in—he's all business. No flirting, no lingering. He does what he needs to do and leaves. Though," she added, "plenty of nurses have tried."

"That doesn't sound like my Lucian," I muttered.

"Oh, really?" Olivia arched a brow as she finished wrapping my ankle. "Do tell."

God, it felt good to talk to someone who wasn't panicking or bleeding or yelling orders. Someone who didn't know the mess of everything but just listened.

"He used to be grumpy and overbearing. But now he's caring, sweet, and funny."

"Wow," she laughed. "He likes you."

"You think? Because I'm..." I swallowed hard. "In love with him. But you can't tell him."

"My lips are sealed." She taped the last bandage into place. "All right, you're all set. Keep these dry for 24 hours. After that, use this ointment." She dropped a small tube into a bag. "In the bag is Dr. Barnes's card. If your vision gets hazy or glassy, call immediately."

"Thank you," I whispered. "Can I go to the waiting room now?"

"Yes." She handed me the bag. "You also have a prescription in the bag for the pain. You can fill it downstairs or anywhere you prefer."

"Thank you."

"Take care, Josie."

She held the door open for me.

I walked straight back to the waiting room, each step making my heart beat faster. Ry stood the second he saw me, eyes searching my face. "Are you okay?"

"On the outside. Any news?" I asked, breath shaky.

He shook his head once, jaw tight. "Not yet."

I sank into the chair beside him, ice pack still pressed to my cheek, and whispered, "Please let him be okay."

Chapter 47

I Love You

Lucian

Every inch of my upper body ached, as if a Mack truck had rolled over me, reversed, and finished the job. Every breath scraped fire through my ribs, and my shoulder throbbed in a slow, brutal pulse that synced with my heartbeat. But I was alive.

Thank God for my vest. If I hadn't been wearing it, I wouldn't be in a warm hospital bed. I'd be downstairs in the morgue on a slab colder than a witch's tit in a brass bra.

Not that I'd care—I'd be dead. But Josie... Jesus. Thinking of her having to see me like that? It gutted me worse than the bullets.

The doctor came in and rattled off my injuries—shoulder wound, bruising that looked like I'd lost a bar fight with a sledgehammer, and the path of the round that had sailed through my shoulder missing my jugular by inches.

Fucking miracle.

But none of that hit me as hard as the memory of Josie's face. Her eyes were wide as her mouth screamed my name. Pure, raw terror on a woman who should never have had to look that terrified in her whole damn life. Begging the universe not to take me away from her.

No—if she was going to scream my name, I wanted it breathless, desperate and shaking, while she clung to me in that bed of mine. And it looked like—thank every star in the sky—I might get another shot at making that happen.

What was I thinking? Was Josie okay? Had they saved her?

I tuned back in to the doctor's voice.

"...sealed both entry and exit wounds, and I'll prescribe pain medication. You'll need physical therapy for the shoulder."

"Okay." My throat was dry as sandpaper. "When can I leave?" I had to find Josie and make sure she was safe.

"I'd like to keep you here for twenty-four hours to monitor for any signs of infection. After that, you're free to head home."

"What? No. I have to go. I need to make sure Josie is okay."

"Is the girl you're talking about Josie Hale?" He arched an eyebrow.

"Yes, do you know her? Is she here?" I planted my palms on the mattress to stand, but a bolt of pain tore down my right arm. "Fuck!"

"Easy there, Detective. One of our nurses cleaned her up. She's going to be fine."

I sagged back into bed. Josie was okay.

The doctor checked something off on his chart. "Are you up for visitors? Because you've got a waiting room full of officers—" he paused, lips twitching "—and one very impatient young lady named Josie Hale."

Josie. My chest ached, and it had nothing to do with bruised ribs.

"Yeah," I said, voice rougher than I meant it to be. "Yeah, I want to see her and them." I swallowed. "Can you let them in?"

The doctor smiled as if he had guessed right and won the lottery.

"I'll let the nurses know to send her in first." The doctor sighed and shook his head. "There are some seriously broken hearts and a cloud of disappointment at the nurses' station now that you're taken."

"How do you know I'm taken?" I tilted my head and frowned. *Had Josie said something?*

"Uh, by the behavior of the woman in the waiting room. I'd say you're taken." He smirked.

"You spoke to Josie?"

"When you came out of surgery, yes. She wasn't happy she couldn't see you." He scribbled something on his clipboard, then headed to the door. "I'm going out to give them an update—and to let her know I didn't mess with you too much."

"Thanks, Doc."

So, my Josie was worried sick about me. Well, now we're even because I was worried as hell about her. I knew my brothers in blue would get her out of that damn car, but I hated I wasn't the one to save her. I'd wanted it to be me.

The door swung open, and a brown and black furry missile planted his paws on my bed, assaulting my face with wet, sloppy kisses.

"Hey, Judge," I laughed, holding his muzzle so I could plant a kiss on his snout. "Good to see you too, boy."

"Judge, no!" Josie scolded breathlessly from the doorway.

"He's fine." The words rushed out. "He's not hurting me." I patted the bed beside me. Judge climbed up at once and sprawled across it, his head settling heavy in my lap.

"But," I added with a grin, "I would like to kiss my girl."

Her steps faltered as she drew closer, and my gaze cataloged every injury. Swollen face with black and blue marks. Wrists and ankles bandaged. Each bruise on her skin struck me like a fresh wound of my own, heat and fury rising fast and sharp.

Josie's eyes filled the moment she reached my bedside. She launched herself into my arms, pressing against my chest as if touch alone could prove I existed. I closed my arms around her, ignoring my pain, and held on. Then I lifted my gaze to Ryker, standing just behind her.

"Tell me you got them," I growled.

"Yep," Ryker said. "Both dead. One from the accident. The other from several bullets."

"Good," I exhaled, pressing my face into Josie's hair.

She smelled of antiseptic and fear and still somehow like the woman I loved more than my own damn breath. If Thomas and Beardsley weren't already dead, I would've dragged myself out of that bed—with tubes, stitches, and all—and finished the job myself.

"I'm so sorry I didn't get to you at the resort," I murmured into her ear.

Josie pressed a shaking kiss to my neck. "And I'm sorry I didn't run to you."

"You helped that older lady. I can't fault you for that," I whispered. "That's who you are. And I wouldn't change a damn thing about you."

Her head lifted, lips swollen, but her smile... her smile cracked something open in my chest.

"Really?"

"Yup." I brushed a piece of hair behind her ear. "Not even your smart mouth."

She grinned. "Not even that?"

"Nope." I smirked. "I love your smart mouth. The words that come out of it... and what it can do."

"Okay, stop, please stop. Eww," Ryker groaned and covered his ears. "I do not need to hear those words about my best friend and one of my brothers. That's traumatic. Come on, Judge, let's wait outside until these two are ready to act like responsible adults. Let us know when you're done with the mushy shit."

Her cheeks flushed. "You are so naughty."

"Only with you," my voice deepened, softened. "I love you."

Josie blinked in surprise—then her eyes filled. "I love you, too."

I cupped her jaw, leaned in, and brushed my mouth against her bruised lips, careful not to hurt her.

Josie moved to pull away, but I laid my hand over my chest. "Come up here with me."

"We're not allowed," she whispered.

"Don't care." My voice cracked—the truth bleeding through. "I need to hold you and make sure you're okay."

"That's my line," she murmured, but she climbed into the bed and laid her head on my chest, right where the vest bruise throbbed.

Not that I cared. I had everything I ever wanted in my arms.

"Are you done yet? Cause we're coming in." Ryker announced before he swung the door open and all the people I loved filed in.

I ran my hand over her hair and looked up at my work family standing shoulder to shoulder next to my actual family. Every single one of them crammed into the doorway or against the walls, smiling at Josie and me like they'd been holding their breath since the moment the ambulance pulled away.

Hudson. Charlotte. Sawyer. Roman. Ryker with Judge at his side. My mom, dad, Aunt Ruby, and Uncle Charles. A couple of officers from patrol. Even Corey and Kyle had shown up still in their tech gear, like they'd sprinted here straight from the station.

Exhaustion lined their faces. Worry. Relief. Pride. Every emotion fixed on us—on her. On the woman I almost lost before I could say the words that mattered most—I love you.

My throat tightened. I wasn't the emotional type—not openly—but hell if that moment didn't crack something in me.

"These people," I murmured into Josie's hair, "they'd go to war for you."

She lifted her head, eyes still soft and glassy, following my gaze around the room.

"And they'd go to war for you too," she whispered back.

Ryker grinned. "We already did."

A few of the others chuckled under their breath, the tension in the room finally—finally—loosening.

I tightened my arm around Josie, careful of my stitches, and said, "Thank you. All of you."

A chorus of "anytime," "of course," and "don't scare us like that again" filled the room. Judge barked once, adding his own two cents. I stroked Josie's back as her head settled over my heart again.

I kept my arm around Josie, fingers threading through her hair, anchoring myself to the warmth and weight of her breathing against my chest. I could touch her. She was here.

My gaze drifted to everyone gathered in the room. My brothers in blue. My family. Each face carried some mixture of fury, relief, and—God help me—love.

"All right," I exhaled. "Tell me everything."

"So Thomas Kincaid—the man who attacked Josie at the house on Leonard Street—aka Cade Gaines—was in cahoots with Garrett Stein?" I asked, my voice low, dangerous. I already knew the answer, but I needed to hear it out loud. Needed the confirmation so I could justify every dark thought rattling around in my skull.

Corey nodded. "Yep. Stein had several aliases. Vincent Van Gogh, Aubrey Beardsley... a bunch of artist names. Probably thought it made him clever." He snorted. "Gaines—Kincaid—whatever the hell name he used that day—met Stein while they were serving time on aggravated assault charges. They bonded. Real gems, those two. They raped and killed several women across multiple states. They were always on the move, always slipping through cracks in the system."

A cold, heavy silence dropped into the room.

Josie shivered beside me. I tightened my hold on her. My body moved before my mind even caught up. Instinct. Protection. Possession.

"That's enough," I blurted. "It's upsetting Josie. I'll get the rest of the details later."

"No." Josie lifted her head and held my gaze. "Let them finish. Then we end this—together."

Every person in the room felt the shift—Sawyer, Roman, Ryker, Judge—they all quieted, their gazes turning toward Josie with a mix of sympathy, simmering rage, and pride.

My jaw clenched so tight it was a miracle my teeth didn't crack. "So they were hunting together," I said, barely above a growl. "Watching her. Planning."

"Yeah." Corey nodded once. "From what we can tell, Josie wasn't random. She was targeted."

Josie sucked in a sharp breath.

I looked down at her. Her eyes were glassy, wide, trying to process the level of evil that had zeroed in on her like she was prey. It made something ancient and feral flare inside me—like I could kill those men all over again and still not be satisfied.

"Hey," I murmured, tipping her chin up gently with my fingers. "Look at me."

She did.

"They're gone," I hissed, but with a steel edge. "Both of them. They will never touch you again. They will never breathe near you again. You're safe."

She blinked, a tear slipped out and trailed down her bruised cheek. My thumb brushed it away. Fuck, I hated seeing her cry. Hated that anyone had put that fear in her. Hated how close I came to losing her.

"There may still be investigation work ahead, but, Josie..." Corey cleared his throat, glancing between us. "They can't hurt anyone else anymore. You survived them."

Her lower lip trembled. "I shouldn't have survived," she whispered. "Other girls didn't. Girls who did nothing wrong."

My grip tightened around her waist. "You listen to me." My voice dropped, sharper, harder. "You didn't survive because of luck. You survived because you fought. You screamed. You bought us time. You are alive because you're strong. Do you understand? Because you're goddamn unstoppable."

She looked at me like she wanted to believe me—but wasn't sure she could yet.

I leaned my forehead against hers, careful of her bruises. "And because I love you," I added softly. "And I would've torn apart the entire state to find you."

Her breath hitched.

Ryker exhaled in the corner. "Well... shit," he muttered.

Sawyer blinked. "He finally said it out loud."

Roman elbowed him. "Shut up, Sawyer."

Josie gave a tiny laugh—broken, tired, but real. She looked at them. "He told me before you guys came in."

"About damn time." Ryker blurted.

She curled into me, her arms slipping around my waist, face pressing to my chest.

Silence settled over the room, no longer pressing down but standing guard. No one spoke. No one moved. They gave us space, as if words might break something fragile. We stood in the wreckage of what almost took us apart. My hand stroked her back, anchoring us both.

"Stein and Gaines didn't win," I murmured into her hair. "You did."

"I know," she whispered. "Because of all of you."

I looked back at the crowd of people who'd refused to give up until they brought her home—to me.

"We don't leave our own behind," Ryker murmured.

"No," I agreed. "We don't."

I held her as the room filled with stories, teasing, relief, and the soft hum of people who cared. Her body softened against mine, no longer bracing for the next blow. She let herself rest in my arms, and the doubt finally loosened its grip.

For the first time since that fire alarm went off... I could breathe. I felt whole. Loved.

Chapter 49

Epilogue

Lucian

The doctor cleared me the next morning after I endured twenty-four hours of machines, needles, and nurses poking at me at all hours of the night. Josie came with me. Of course, she did.

She insisted on being my "personal nurse" in and out of the bedroom since she healed quicker than I did. Best damn medical care I've ever received.

Between the bandages, the bruises, and the god-awful stiffness in my shoulder, she made recovery something I looked forward to. Every night, she curled up with me, careful with the injured shoulder. Every morning, she woke me up with a smile that made every shitty part of my therapy day's worth it.

After two weeks, I finally convinced her to move in with me. Correction—I begged. She said yes. I won.

Now, I see her every fucking day. Her clothes in my closet, her hair in my shower drain, her voice echoing through my house—our house. Everything in my world finally clicked into place.

Her smile warmed me on the days when work went to hell or physical therapy turned into medieval torture. *Shoulder therapy sucked.* Getting shot in the right shoulder meant no writing, shitty aim, and taking an eternity to type a damn report. Every misplaced keystroke made me want to throw the keyboard out a window.

Josie never complained once. She drove me to every appointment, sat through every grimace and curse, kissed me when I wanted to break something, and climbed into my lap when she wanted to distract me from the pain.

She was my peace. My comfort. My fire. My everything.

That first night back home, when she curled against my chest and finally slept without jolting awake, I realized something with the same clarity as a gunshot. I never wanted to spend another day of my life without her. Ever.

So I did what any man who almost lost the best damn thing he ever had would do—I bought a ring.

I just needed to figure out how the hell to ask a woman who survived two psychopaths, a kidnapping, a high-speed chase, and a shootout... to spend the rest of her life with a stubborn, overprotective detective who can't type for shit.

Lucky for me—she already loves me. And I don't plan on ever giving her a reason to stop.

We were having a cookout today to celebrate my last day of therapy. I was ecstatic—not just because I could finally return to work, but because life finally felt right again. My shoulder was healed. My badge was waiting. And Josie... Josie was home.

After several rounds of the best sex of my life, we dressed and headed to Ryker's house. He'd offered to host, and we agreed because holding a party at someone else's house meant we could leave the second we wanted to drag each other back to bed.

With my health at one hundred percent, I wanted Josie *all the damn time.* Morning, noon, middle of the afternoon... no surface or location was safe. We'd christened every room in our house.

Our last session had been in the shower, and, yeah, we were doing our part to conserve water. After I gave her a couple of O's that echoed off the tiles, I forced myself to leave her in there to finish getting ready. If I'd stayed, she wouldn't have made it out of the bathroom for another hour—or two.

Her screaming my name was music to my ears. The kind of music I never wanted turned off. The blow-dryer finally clicked off. Josie was almost done. I sat in the living room, nerves and anticipation fighting for space in my chest.

Life was good. Better than good. My job was secure. My family strong. Friends who would bleed for me. And I lived with a woman who made the world brighter just by existing.

I reached into my jacket pocket and pulled out the small velvet box. The ring inside glinted in the sunlight spilling across the couch. Tonight, I wanted to make her my fiancée. To put the promise in stone—hers and mine.

She'd better say yes. Hell, I knew she would. But the ring still felt heavy with meaning in my palm.

Footsteps padded down the hallway toward me. Soft. Familiar. Capable of unraveling me. I stood and slipped the box back into my pocket, tugging my jacket closed to hide the outline. My pulse kicked up.

Josie appeared, beautiful as always, hair shining, cheeks flushed from the hot shower—and probably from remembering the way I'd had her pressed against the tile minutes ago.

She smiled. God, that smile. It hit me straight in the chest every damn time. "I'm ready."

I swear, I almost dropped to one knee right then. Not yet. Tonight. Somewhere perfect.

"Yeah," I murmured, stepping toward her and brushing a strand of hair behind her ear. "So am I."

Josie's hair was down—long, soft waves brushing her shoulders. She knew I liked it that way. I loved using it as my anchor when I made love to her, easier to feel her arch into me when I tugged just right. Her lips were pink and shiny, coated in that strawberry lip gloss I was addicted to tasting. And that dress—a strapless pink sundress scattered with tiny daisies—showed off the smooth line of her shoulders, her curves, and those strappy sandals revealing her cute pink-painted toes.

She looked perfect. Sweet and sexy. Sunshine wrapped in temptation. She caught me staring.

"Stop looking at me like that, or we'll never leave." She brushed past me, grabbing her purse with a little sway of her hips that she knew would kill me.

She wasn't wrong. After seeing her in that cute ensemble, I wanted to take it off piece by piece with my mouth. But we'd promised Ryker and the boys we'd show up—at least for an hour or so.

"Okay," I relented, though my voice came out rough. "But we're not staying long."

"Long enough to eat." She threw me a look over her shoulder, lips tilted in a teasing smile. "I'm starving."

"Fine. But you're my dessert," I murmured, stalking toward her, "and I want you spread naked on my bed while I eat you."

"Stop!" She smacked my shoulder, but her eyes were blazing with heat.

Her mouth said, stop. Yet her eyes screamed Don't you dare. But I behaved. Barely. I'd feed her, play nice with my friends, and then devour her later. Slowly. Thoroughly.

I opened the door for her, led her to the car, and we drove to Ryker's on the other end of the island. Several cars lined his driveway. Ryker opened the door before we even reached the steps.

"What took you so long?" he barked, looking at his wristwatch. "You were supposed to be here thirty minutes ago."

"We were busy." I smiled, and Josie blushed enough to make my entire damn day.

"Hey, there's Sammie!" Josie blurted, hugged Ryker, and made a beeline for her friend.

"Nice." Ryker punched my arm. "Way to embarrass her."

"You're just mad I beat you to it." I shoved him back and stepped inside. "Where's the beer?"

"Aren't you supposed to be the best detective in town? Where do you think?"

"You are such a pain in my ass." I headed to the fridge and grabbed two bottles—one for me, one for Josie.

I walked back to her and kissed her cheek as I handed it over. "Here you go, beautiful."

Her smile damn near stole the breath from my lungs. "Thanks."

She lifted it toward me like a toast, still glowing as she stood surrounded by Sammie, Charlotte, Cassie, and Rosie—all greeting me with warm hugs.

"Have fun, ladies," I said, brushing my hand down Josie's back. "I'll be with the boys."

"Okay." She rose on her toes and gave me a quick peck on the lips.

I winked before heading outside.

"Hey! There's our favorite detective—and cousin!" Sawyer shouted, clapping me hard on the back as Judge bounded over for a head scratch.

"'Bout time you got here," Chief grumbled, one brow raised before taking a swig of his beer.

"Aww, Chief..." Roman jumped in, elbowing me. "Give him a break. He was just playing doctor with his pretty nurse."

"Shut up," I muttered—no bite behind it—glancing around at the mix of my fellow officers and cousins. It hit me all over again how damn grateful I was to still be standing here, breathing, surrounded by the people I loved. "Anyone seen my parents?"

"They're on their way. They agreed to carpool with Caroline, and she's not there yet. Shocker." Sawyer rolled his eyes. "Stupid move on their part."

That tracked. Caroline ran on her own version of island time—slow and scenic.

"Burgers and dogs ready in twenty!" Ryker hollered from the grill. Hudson hovered beside him, trying to offer tips he had no business giving. Ryker waved him off as if he were shooing a fly.

"I saw there's been a lot of activity at the marina," I said, leaning back in my chair. Working the desk while recovering meant I read more reports than any sane person should.

"Yeah." Sawyer rubbed the back of his neck. "I need to do some recon. Something fishy is going on over there, and I don't think Silver's caught wind of it yet."

"Enough shop talk," Chief cut in. "Let's chill and talk about actual fishing instead of something fishy. Who's up for a Saturday fishing trip?"

"Yeah, do it now," I agreed, "because in a few weeks we'll be knee-deep in holiday tourists. They love the boat parade and lights show." I gave Hudson a look. "You ready for some serious foot patrol?"

"You know it." Hudson lifted his beer proudly. "I'm always ready!"

"That's not what she said," Ryker muttered.

"Hey!" Hudson snapped. "What kind of wingman are you supposed to be?"

"I'm not your wingman." Ryker pointed his spatula at Roman. "That's his job."

"Facts," Roman said, fist-bumping Hudson. "Right, bro?"

"Never leaving you hanging, dude." Hudson confirmed.

"You young uns..." Ryker muttered, pulling the burgers off the grill.

"Hey, you're only two years older than me," Roman shot back.

"Feels like more," Ryker grumbled. "Food's done!"

"Perfect timing!" my dad said from the sliding glass door.

"Uncle Luc!"

Sophie barreled into my arms. I caught her mid-jump as she wrapped herself around me.

"Hey, Soph." I kissed her cheek. "You look beautiful. What took you so long?"

Sophie cupped her hands around her mouth and stage-whispered, "It was Mommy, not me."

"Traitor," Caroline muttered, stepping up behind her and ruffling her hair. She kissed my cheek, and I nodded toward the house.

"Josie's inside."

"We said hello," she said. "But we're going back in, but Sophie wanted to say hi to her favorite uncle."

"Her only uncle," I reminded her with a grin.

"Hey, man," Stephen said, clapping my back. "Glad you're doing better."

"Thanks."

Caroline carried Sophie back inside to tell the ladies the food was ready.

We all ate out on the patio—some in chairs, others on the sand. The sun began its slow descent over the waves, painting everything gold and pink. And as I watched Josie laughing with my mom, her hand resting on Sophie's back, something inside my chest damn near burst.

Tonight. I was doing it tonight. I set down my empty plate and brushed sand off my jeans before standing.

"Josie... can you come with me a sec?" I held my hand out to her.

She paused, frowning a little as she handed her plate to Sammie, but she put her hand in mine. "Sure."

I led her toward the shoreline. The surf rolled in and out beside us. She faced me, brows knitting in concern.

"Lucian? What's—"

I dropped to one knee.

Her breath hitched. Her hands flew to her mouth.

The whole damn world narrowed to just her, me, and the sound of waves crashing next to us.

"Josie Hale," I began, my voice rougher than I intended. "You burst into my life with your sassy mouth and take-no-prisoners attitude. You broke through walls I didn't even know I had—and landed right in my heart."

Her eyes shimmered.

"I didn't think love existed for me. Not really. But loving you... is the best thing that's ever happened to me. I treasure your smile every damn day, and I want to see it for the rest of my life."

My hand shook as I reached into my pocket for the ring box.

"You're everything I didn't know I was missing. Everything I want. Everything I need. I love you, Josie. I want to spend the rest of my life with you."

I opened the box. The ring caught the last light of the setting sun.

"Will you marry me?"

Josie dropped to her knees so fast that sand sprayed up around us. She grabbed my face with both hands and kissed me breathless.

"Is that a yes?" I laughed against her lips.

"Yes. Yes," she whispered, crying and laughing at the same time. "Absolutely yes."

I slid the ring onto her finger.

"I love you, Josie Hale—soon to be a part of this crazy Warrick family."

"I love your crazy Warrick family," she said. "But not as much as I love you."

And then our families and friends erupted behind us—cheering, hooting, hollering—and sprinted toward us like a stampede.

I kissed her again, the weight of what we survived passing between us, the certainty settling in that she belonged in every tomorrow I had left.

She wasn't just the love of my life. She was the last piece of my puzzle.

My everything.

My forever.

Turn the page for part of Chapter 1 of Book 4: Officer Hudson.

Chapter 50

Sneak Peak

Book 4: Officer Hudson

C hapter 1 – Blast From the Past – Hudson

Officer Charlotte and I were patrolling Main Street on foot—again. Break-ins at shops and rental properties had everyone on edge, so the chief wanted extra visibility. We'd just grabbed coffee from Hi Grill and were heading north toward the station when Charlotte slapped a hand across my chest.

"Hud, stop."

I walked straight into her palm. "What now?"

"I need to run in and say hi to Sammie." She said it with a casual shrug, but her eyes drifted toward the Siren Boutique's display window.

"Yeah, right?" I snorted. "This wouldn't have anything to do with the dress in that window we passed on the way to Hi Café, would it?"

Charlotte had been my partner going on four years. I knew her tells better than I knew my own. Clothes were her kryptonite—and Siren Boutique was her personal church.

"Caught me," she sighed. "I'll be right back. Two minutes."

"I'm sure I could walk all the way to the station, turn around, come back, and you'd still be—" I made air quotes,"—talking to Sammie."

"Nope." She shot me a don't mess with me look. "Swear. I'm just asking her to put it aside for me."

"Fine." I nodded. "I'll walk slow."

Charlotte darted into the store while I continued toward Book Haven. Rowan, the owner, always had the newest bestsellers displayed out front. A couple caught my eye, but before I could get closer, movement from inside the store stopped me.

A small waif-like blonde woman—familiar somehow—had stopped dead in her tracks. Her mouth parted as she stared straight at me.

Did I know her? She was gorgeous. *Should I know her?*

And yet... my mind came up empty. Oh hell. She was walking toward me. And something in my chest kicked hard—like I should remember her. Like I *needed* to.

"Hudson Shaw?"

The blonde woman stepped out of Book Haven, clutching a paperback to her chest as if it might leap away. Relief flooded her features the second our eyes met.

"Thank God I found you."

"Uh..." I crossed my arms as best as I could with my coffee cup in one hand, giving her my best friendly-cop smile. "You have me at a disadvantage. Do we know each other?"

She was beautiful—too beautiful for me to forget. And yet, I couldn't place her. Over the years, I'd dated my fair share of one-night stands with tourists, but I'd remember *her*.

"Verie Tate."

Nothing. Not even a flicker of recognition.

"I'm sorry," I admitted. "Your name isn't ringing a bell."

"I'm from Jones County. Our football teams were rivals. You babysat my brother, Pike, and sister, Stacci."

I blinked. Then it hit.

"Holy shit—Pike and Stacci Tate? That was like seven years ago."

"Yep," she said with a small smile. "I'd just gone off to college, and my mom finally let you take over as the stand-in babysitter."

"Well, uh... wow. I babysat them only a handful of times." I held out my hand. "It's nice to finally meet you without Barbies being thrown at my head."

She grinned and slipped her hand into mine. A zing shot all the way up my arm.

I cleared my throat. "How is the little dude and your sister?"

Her expression dimmed. Shadows gathered in her eyes.

"My sister is fine. But Pike... Pike ran away. We think he's here on Haven Island. That's why I came looking for you. Your mom told my mom you're an officer here now. I—I need your help."

Chapter 51

Special Thanks

Thank you to all my readers. You are the BEST! I am beyond grateful for your continued support.

Heartfelt thanks to **Michelle K.** and **Michelle Z.**, who always take time out of their busy lives to read my manuscript, edit my copies, offer honest feedback, and make every story better.

Without the assistance of many individuals, this book would never have been written. Any mistakes or imaginative liberties taken are entirely my fault. Thanks to their insightful feedback and extensive knowledge, my story was transformed into something much more captivating.

I'm not an expert in real estate, but I'm fortunate to have my dear friend **Pam Lockwood** as my trusted source. Pam has spent the past eleven years as a realtor. She is currently with Round Table Realty. Her knowledge, professionalism, and generosity made all the difference while I wrote this book. Her insight gave authenticity to every scene, and I'm deeply grateful for her time, patience, and friendship.

I'm beyond grateful to know these amazing first responders. Every time I send a late-night text, email, or call with a "quick question," they answer with the same dedication they bring to their jobs. **Sgt. TJ Williams, Sgt. Stacci Sastre, K9 Deputy Bryan Wright, and Corrections Deputy Nathan Lebon**—the finest in blue. Thank you for your time, your insight, and your patience. You're truly the best support team a writer could have.

As always, to all the first responders out there—the ones I'm blessed to call my friends and those I haven't met, please stay safe out there. It can be a little crazy. Thank you, thank you, thank you, for what you do for all of us in your community daily.

The tide brings new stories to Haven Island, but sometimes they get lost in the waves.

Follow me on Amazon so you'll never miss a new release—or a steamy night with my favorite island couples.

Reviews help others find their way here, but I know your time is precious. So, whether you drop a few stars or just keep reading under the covers, thank you for coming back to the island with me.

Happy Reading and Thank You!

Neri

Chapter 52

About the Author

Neri Lopez

Neri is a two-time Global Book Awards winner, celebrated for her Romance–Action & Adventure novel *Red Path* and her Romance–Suspense novel *Deputy Sean*.

Her stories blend emotional depth, high-stakes suspense, and heartfelt romance, often rooted in cultural history (the Path Series) and character-driven drama.

A lifelong creative, she has been a stay-at-home mom to triplets, a graphic designer, and a high school teacher of Spanish, 2D Art, and Digital Design. She now writes from her home in Florida, where her two rescued cats—Salem and Sabrina—dutifully assist by walking across her keyboard at crucial moments.

Neri loves to hear from her readers. You can email her at: nerilopezauthor@gmail.com or join her mailing list by going to her website: nerilopez.com

When you sign up for her newsletter, you will receive a FREE downloadable bookmark of Red Path.

If Neri's books made you laugh, swoon, or stay up a little too late reading, she would be grateful if you left a review on Amazon or Goodreads. Reviews help her stories reach new readers.

Or follow her on:
Facebook: Neri Lopez - Author

instagram: Neri_Lopez_Author
(She is most active on Facebook.)

Reading Order:

Haven Island PD: Protecting Paradise
    Book 1: Deputy Sean (Sean and Cassie)

The Path Series (entire series is available on Amazon)
    Book 1: Red Path (Thunder and Isa)
    Book 2: Unconquered Path (Alex and Tori)
    Book 3: Wagering Path (Holt and Freya)
    Book 4: Unexpected Path (Mark and Maggie)
    Wedding Novella Book 4.5: Double Trouble Path
    (Tori/Alex and Freya/Holt weddings)
    Book 5: Twisted Path (Barrett and Angel)
    Book 6: Blue Path (George and Lizzy)